So Buck Rawlings didn't count her among his friends....

Fine, Caitlin thought. She didn't want to be his *anything*—anything except an employee able to handle this assignment.

Anyway, it was her policy not to mix business with pleasure. And Buck Rawlings was one pleasure she couldn't afford. The very sight of the man destroyed her concentration and made her mouth turn to cotton. For God's sake, she'd climbed mountains, hiked the wilderness, battled rapids. She was strong, successful, resourceful. So how could the sight of Buck Rawlings make her feel like she was standing on the edge of a precipice with a high wind at her back?

No. She didn't want to have anything to do with Buck and his lone-wolf ways. Ever. There were far easier ways to go crazy in this world....

Dear Reader,

Welcome to Silhouette Special Edition... welcome to romance. We've got six wonderful books for you this month—a true bouquet of spring flowers!

Just Hold On Tight! by Andrea Edwards is our THAT SPECIAL WOMAN! selection for this month. This warm, poignant story features a heroine who longs for love—and the wonderful man who convinces her to take what she needs!

And that's not all! *Dangerous Alliance,* the next installment in Lindsay McKenna's thrilling new series MEN OF COURAGE, is available this month, as well as Christine Rimmer's *Man of the Mountain,* the first story in the family-oriented series THE JONES GANG. Sherryl Woods keeps us up-to-date on the Halloran clan in *A Vow To Love,* and *Wild Is the Wind,* by Laurie Paige, brings us back to "Wild River" territory for an exciting new tale of love.

May also welcomes Noreen Brownlie to Silhouette Special Edition with her book, *That Outlaw Attitude.*

I hope that you enjoy this book and all of the stories to come.

Happy Spring!

Sincerely,

Tara Gavin
Senior Editor

Please address questions and book requests to:
Reader Service
U.S.: P.O. Box 1325, Buffalo, NY 14269
Canadian: P.O. Box 1050, Niagara Falls, Ont. L2E 7G7

NOREEN BROWNLIE
THAT OUTLAW ATTITUDE

Silhouette®

SPECIAL EDITION®

Published by Silhouette Books
America's Publisher of Contemporary Romance

Dedicated with love and gratitude to Jerry Chan,
my husband, my best friend, my own personal Rainman.
Thanks for the rainbow—here's to the gold.

And with warm thanks to Irene Goodman, my agent and friend,
who never stopped believing.

And finally, to Wendy Morgan,
black-belt voluptuary and forever friend
who understands the lure of tribal fire.

 SILHOUETTE BOOKS

ISBN 0-373-09888-X

THAT OUTLAW ATTITUDE

Copyright © 1994 by Noreen Brownlie

Books by Noreen Brownlie

Silhouette Special Edition

That Outlaw Attitude #888

Silhouette Desire

Savannah Lee #436
'Tis the Season #468
Race the Wind #513

NOREEN BROWNLIE

grew up in a large family on the Oregon coast, surrounded by Victorian houses, fishing boats and romantic sunsets. She met her husband while she was
working inland as a television writer/producer, and
the couple recently resettled in Seattle, where he con-
tinues to work in broadcasting and Noreen lives her
dream of writing fiction full-time. There are always
close family ties in her romances—a subject that is
dear to her heart. Noreen has also written as Jamisan
Whitney.

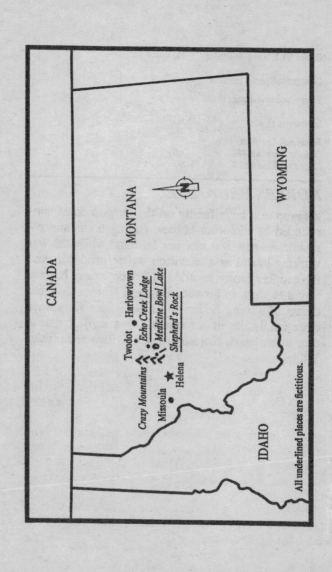

CANADA

MONTANA

WYOMING

IDAHO

Crazy Mountains

Twodot • Harlowtown
Echo Creek Lodge
Medicine Bowl Lake
Shepherd's Rock

Missoula
★ Helena

All underlined places are fictitious.

Chapter One

It was Caitlin O'Malley's habit to put old hurts and losses in orderly boxes in some far corner of her mind and to focus on the future. Yet, with every twist and turn of her Jeep on the remote mountain road, Caitlin drew closer to a past she'd been unable to package neatly or jettison into the void. Her memories of Buck Rawlings and that final summer at the Echo Creek Lodge rebelled against closure. If she were smart, she'd turn around the next time the narrow ribbon of gravel widened. She'd avoid new hurts, avoid the one man capable of shattering her calm.

A clearing yawned before her and Caitlin inhaled sharply as the majestic Rawlings lodge came into view. When she eased onto the dirt drive, Burrito and Fajita, her two Border collies, whined and shook with nervous frenzy on the seat beside her.

"Now, now, it's all right, girls." She soothed her dogs with familiar words and the caress of her hand. "I'm the one who should be shaking."

Suddenly, Farley, Buck's golden Lab, scrambled down the massive porch steps, barking and bounding the short distance to the Jeep. Her collies responded with bared teeth, forming a protective barrier between Caitlin and the strange dog.

Before she could open her mouth to stay her pets, the door of the lodge swung in a wide arc and Buck Rawlings appeared on the porch, giving his dog a single sharp command. Immediately, each animal fell quiet. Caitlin found the silence that followed more unnerving than the barking of three fiercely protective canines.

She stared at Buck. When they'd first met almost fifteen years ago, the man had seemed a god to her. Nothing had prepared her for such a powerful male presence. He'd clearly been in charge, overseeing the first catalog shoot with a firm hand, exuding power with his every command. For a sixteen-year-old on the verge of discovering her sexuality, she'd found Buck set apart from all other men at the lodge by his striking good looks and air of authority. He exhibited a mastery of the outdoors that rivaled her father's and brought out her own competitive streak.

She hadn't had a prayer that summer—or years later during her twenty-third summer when their mutual attraction spiraled out of control and they'd acted on their passion. Inhaling sharply, she studied the man who'd remained half saint, half sinner in her memory.

With her photographer's keen eye for detail, Caitlin noted even from a distance that Buck Rawlings had not lost his taste for finely made things. His trademark black Stetson gave him a lethal air of raw-edged confidence and danger. As he stepped into the dappled sunlight on the porch stairs, the silver conchos on his headband glinted like a beacon of warning, sending a frisson of cool fear skittering through her veins. Her attention was drawn to his black boots, handcrafted no doubt, and she recalled her girlhood fantasy of awakening to find those boots beside her bed, their owner's body next to hers, his breath hot upon her neck.

With a shudder, Caitlin shut out memories of the morning seven years ago when that girlish fantasy became reality.

The man who approached her now had the same haunting green eyes touched with sorrow, flecked with gold. He was thirty-five but the raven-black hair at his temples was still untouched by gray. On his tall, well-muscled body, the bad-boy uniform of faded denim jacket, white T-shirt and snug jeans gave him a commanding virility that tempted her to start the ignition and turn tail.

She shooshed her dogs out the passenger's side then slid out of the driver's seat and hit the ground with wobbly knees.

"Buck . . ." She smiled and held out her hand. "It's been too long."

"O'Malley." His tone was as cool as moonlight on silver. He touched the rim of his hat, then slipped his hands into the back pockets of his jeans and looked at her with flat, unspeaking eyes. "What the hell are you doing up here? Where's your father?"

"Chase didn't call you? I talked to him yesterday from the hospital."

"I haven't heard from my brother since I left Missoula."

"But we have an agreement."

"What agreement?" He widened his confrontive stance. "Why don't you just start at the beginning, O'Malley. And make it short."

How dare he? Caitlin straightened. She'd waited for this meeting far too long to hurry anything.

"My father broke his leg in a fall two days ago. Multiple fracture. He asked me to step in and shoot the catalog for him and Chase agreed to the substitution. You were in transit, Buck."

As his gaze raked down her body, then traveled slowly back up, she felt a rush of warmth. His eyes met hers and her chest tightened. Already, he was toying with her. Buck had always been a master at manipulating her with his long, lingering outlaw looks.

"We got a big problem here," he muttered sullenly. "I don't find you suitable for the job."

"It's probably a matter of not being aware of my credentials. I've been selling my work since I was seventeen. My scenics have appeared in numerous magazines and my portraits are—"

"If you get back in your Jeep now, O'Malley, you'll make it to Twodot before dark." The shadow of his beard emphasized his firm jaw and the soft fullness of his lower lip. "I'll reimburse all expenses for travel and lodging."

"Wait a minute. My father believes I'm more than qualified. Since he owns a considerable share of your company, he has a vested interest in the success of this catalog. He wouldn't do anything to jeopardize—"

"Look, I'll be blunt. This is a men-only thing that goes on up here every year. Poker games, cigars, cussing. The guys change wardrobe outdoors. No one wants some nosy female watching him strip down to his shorts or—"

"I spent two summers helping my father shoot for your catalog, Rawlings," she interrupted, stepping toward him until the shaft of sunlight warmed her cheek, "and I managed to respect the privacy of others. No one objected then. You certainly didn't."

A wave of unmistakable pain passed over his features and she felt it echo in her heart. Was he thinking of the nights Caitlin had spent in his arms seven summers ago? Or was he thinking of Sarah Rawlings? In all these years, had he finally shifted blame for his sister's death away from her?

For long moments, she waited for some sign, some gesture that might indicate where she stood in his memory.

"It's different now." He took a step forward, casting a shadow in the shaft of sunlight that separated them. "I think it's best you gather your critters and head to Twodot, O'Malley. My tailor's sister is a teacher there and I'm sure Bess will take you in for the night. Then I'll call my brother and have him hire another photographer."

The finality in his voice angered her, making her even more determined not to bow to his intimidation. Caitlin remembered how her father was depending on her and vowed not to leave the Crazy Mountains and Echo Creek until she completed Sean O'Malley's assignment. It was obvious she had to appeal to Buck's business sense.

"Forget your smug little plan, Rawlings. I'm not going anywhere. I have some ideas of my own, like how your company might appeal to the female customer."

Buck looked at her and wondered how long it had been since she'd picked up an Echo Creek catalog. "We don't make clothing for women and we never will!" he snapped back, turning to stalk toward the lodge. This conversation had lasted long enough. There was no place left in his solitary life for Cat O'Malley.

"But women buy clothing and gear for the men in their lives." Caitlin raised her voice as she followed him the short distance to the porch stairs. "I can duplicate my father's style of photography if that's your preference, but I also know what appeals to a woman."

"Appeals to a woman?" Buck turned back toward her, his boot resting on the bottom step, and caught her bold gaze sweeping the length of his body. "I know what appeals to a woman, O'Malley. I certainly don't need your advice on my area of expertise."

She was wearing Echo Creek clothing, obviously tailored to fit her curvaceous female frame, topped off with a silk scarf and earrings. It was blasphemy. Women's catalogs far outnumbered those produced for men and O'Malley's daughter chose to bastardize his company's designs. Her glossy chestnut hair was pulled back into a French braid, her perfect skin tanned naturally from her work outdoors. Wisps of hair escaped her braid and curled about her high cheekbones. Late-afternoon sun filtered through the pines, giving an unearthly radiance to her large golden eyes.

He had reason to hate her. Good reason. He'd vowed years ago that Caitlin would never step foot on his mountain again. Did he have to force her back into her Jeep and ride shotgun until she was off his family's land and out of his thoughts forever?

Perhaps honesty was best. The straightforward approach would cut a swath through the emotional landscape that bound them together as former lovers. If he stood here another minute inhaling the clean floral scent of her hair and studying the hills and valleys her breasts created in his best tartan plaid, that landscape would envelop him like quicksand.

"I simply don't want you here, Caitlin." His tone was far more blunt than he'd intended. "Can we just leave it at that?"

"I don't think so." Her voice was equally cold. "I'm a businesswoman representing my father's interests and income. Furthermore, I have an agreement with Chase Rawlings. I'll start unloading my gear now."

"Like hell you will. I'm the senior partner at Echo Creek Outfitters." He took three strides to the spot where she stood with defiant rigidity. "On top of that, I pride myself on my business instincts, and right now they tell me you're trouble."

"You pulled this authoritative crap on me years ago, Rawlings. I'm thirty now, and a recognized professional." Buck watched her yank the scarf from her neck and ball it up in her fist. "It's obvious the only one around here who knows the value of a good woman is your brother."

"My brother knows nothing about the real Cat O'Malley. That's my department. You and I have a history, lady. The worst kind of history. I choose to ignore it."

"Ignore it?" She repeated his words in a stunned whisper that tore at his heart. "And you dare to call me Cat?"

"A clear mistake. The only thing we share is a fondness for Sean O'Malley and stock in the same company."

"A company that's had major losses this past year."

"I'm not in the mood to stand here and exchange insults, O'Malley."

"It was just an honest observation. When does Chase arrive?"

"He'll be here in four days, maybe five."

"I won't leave unless Chase personally fires me. I don't want your expense money or directions to Twodot. I want this job. So step aside, Mr. Rawlings. I have to unpack."

She turned from him, walked to the Jeep, reached inside and pulled out a camera bag. "Where do I bunk?"

The woman was exasperating! Buck stepped toward Caitlin, peeled the camera strap from her shoulder, set the bag back in the vehicle and spun her around to face him.

"You haven't changed a bit, O'Malley. You're still as mouthy and spoiled as ever. Your father should have turned you over his knee when you were five."

"I see you haven't changed, either, Rawlings. You still have a caveman mentality. And if I recall correctly, you turned me over your knee last time we met. Now let go of me. I'm tired and hungry and I'm not in the mood for your macho games."

"I'm not playing games. I'm running a business." Buck held her firmly in his grasp. "Look at me, Caitlin." He tipped her proud chin upward and searched her defiant eyes. "I may have pulled you over my knee in anger that last summer but I never laid a finger on you. Remember that. You were reckless and headstrong, risking your life and mine that day. I had to find a way to get your attention."

"How do you get the attention of women these days, Buck?" she demanded. "Hold a gun to their head?"

He released her. He knew O'Malley's daughter would bring havoc, mayhem and heartache if he allowed her to stay. No other woman could make him this crazy, this hot, this filled with regret.

The murmur of male voices pierced the fog surrounding him. By now the porch was most likely lined with members of his crew, watching this public display. Damn. He had a position of authority to uphold. He also had a reputation for fairness and compassion. He would have to let her stay until Chase arrived.

Caitlin reached back into the Jeep and hoisted two camera bags onto her shoulders. "I assume we start shooting first thing tomorrow?"

"No, you and I meet to discuss ground rules before breakfast. And don't lift another thing. My crew will help you unload." With that comment, Buck turned on his heel and stalked back to the lodge.

Caitlin was left beside her Jeep, openmouthed and dumbstruck, her hands clutched tightly around the straps of her camera bags. Just then Burrito and Fajita streaked past her, followed by Farley. The pattern reversed without warning and the female dogs chased the lone male back across the clearing. Had she and Buck just played a similar game?

How had it gotten so twisted? Their fathers had been the closest of friends. Sarah Rawlings had been the sister Caitlin never had. Over half a dozen years ago, Buck had sworn his love for her on the porch just yards from where she stood at this moment. She'd spent the years since staring at images of Buck in the Echo Creek catalog and waiting for a chance to set things straight, to share her secret and unburden her soul. Would the opportunity ever arise?

Devotion to Sean O'Malley had prompted her to sacrifice her long-planned Alaskan wilderness trek to pinch-hit on his annual catalog shoot. Would she spend her time here struggling between devotion to her father and mentor, and her desire to reconcile with Buck?

First, Caitlin had to prove herself as a photographer. If she could pass that hurdle, there'd be time in the next few weeks to make amends. Tomorrow morning and Buck's listing of ground rules couldn't come fast enough. She intended to make a few demands of her own.

Caitlin felt for the pocket of her shirt and smiled as she touched the outline of the small notebook her father had prepared for her. His advice ranged from which model to use for certain styles of clothing, how to handle personalities and individual sensibilities, and technical expertise learned by trial and error.

What she really needed at the moment was advice on how to handle a lone wolf like Buck Rawlings. But she doubted such wisdom would fit into her pocket.

After making another futile attempt to reach Chase in Missoula, Buck pushed the antenna down with the palm of his hand and set the portable phone on one of the dozens of boxes of clothing being stacked on the porch by his crew of men. Caitlin's belongings had been unloaded an hour ago and she'd retreated to the room of her choosing on the lodge's isolated third floor. Buck pulled the worn Stetson off his head and slapped it against his thigh.

"Have we got a photographer or not?" Lester Owen asked abruptly, his small frame half-hidden behind the tall crate holding his sewing machine and the tools of his trade. The balding tailor narrowed his gaze at Buck. His everpresent toothpick stopped bobbing in the corner of his mouth. "'Cuz I won't be unpackin' this crate and hand steamin' all those shirts and pants 'til I know."

"I suppose we owe it to Sean to give her a chance." Buck threw a loose piece of firewood into the wood bin in the corner.

"She's a damn pretty package. Better'n average proportions. Good height. I'd say she's got a thirty-four-inch inseam on her now."

Buck didn't want to think about Caitlin's inseam or any other part of her delectable anatomy. The memory of every silken inch of her still haunted him after all these years.

"Bustline looks like a presentable C cup, boss." The tailor's eyes had a faraway look.

"Damn, Lester, for a guy who tailors only men's clothing, you sure seem to know a lot about women's sizes and such."

"I may have settled in Montana, but you're forgettin' I got my start in a lingerie factory in Chicago." Lester took the toothpick from his mouth and tossed it. "Truth is, Buck, I'm gettin' a little tired of compensatin' for these over-the-hill models you insist on bringing up here every year. I think we need some new blood—with less alcohol content."

Buck glanced out into the clearing where Joe, Pete, Klyde, Carlos and Rusty stood beside one of the trucks, taking yet another break from unloading supplies and clothing. Each gripped a can of beer in his hand.

Fifteen years ago, when Buck had talked his father into producing a larger, slicker catalog, August Rawlings hand-picked these men and they'd posed in exchange for a couple of new shirts. The years had taken their toll on the models. How could he tell old friends of the family they were too old or out of shape to represent the company?

Buck slipped his hat back on, hoisted an armload of firewood and carried it into the massive three-story log cabin his grandfather and great-uncles had built more than sixty years ago. Outside, the pine logs had silvered with age, but the interior had taken on a soft golden glow offering a sense of safety, comfort, home. He dumped the wood in the bin next to the immense stone fireplace and shoved his hat back on his head with the tip of his thumb.

He should never have left Chase in charge back in Missoula. Differences in their management styles had become increasingly apparent over the years but in the past six months, the warmth and rapport between the brothers had begun to erode. A tense peace remained. Buck had hoped the catalog shoot would provide a chance to discuss the future of Echo Creek Outfitters with Chase and to reconcile their differences. If O'Malley's daughter stayed, those opportunities would be limited.

Damn. He liked his women to look gentle, feminine, refined. Caitlin's masculine mode of dress only served to remind him of her risk-taking adventure years ago.

And the ultimate cost of her carelessness.

Some part of him wanted to welcome Caitlin back to Echo Creek but he just wasn't ready to open the door to forgiveness. If Sarah's accident had never happened, if his sister were still alive, he might have married Caitlin and shared the bright future they'd planned so innocently.

But Sarah was dead. Nothing could resurrect his beloved sister or the dreams of a life with Caitlin that had died with her.

Caitlin looked up from her father's notebook to stare at the whimsical willow bed that dominated her third-floor room. Sarah's old room. Standing up, she walked to the bed and reached out to touch one of the four posts that rose almost to the ceiling. She followed the overlapping pattern of high arches with the tips of her fingers. It was an odd blend of rustic and romantic, as was every room at the Echo Creek Lodge.

The next few weeks would give her a chance to confront Buck on old issues but it would also be an opportunity to finally say goodbye to her beloved friend. How many nights had she sat on this bed with Sarah, secretly wishing they'd been real-life sisters? Back in Missoula, their lives entwined frequently throughout their high school years and they'd attended college together in Seattle. They'd shared secrets, dreams, fears and in that final year, a fierce competition for Buck's attention.

Caitlin looked away from the willow arches and concentrated on unpacking. She took a handful of books and pamphlets out of the bottom of her suitcase and thumbed through the titles. At the hospital in Missoula, she'd learned her diabetic father had developed retinopathy and could soon be blind. Suddenly the health insurance Sean O'Malley earned shooting the Echo Creek catalogs took on more importance. She had to complete this shoot for him no matter what obstacles Buck Rawlings threw in her path.

While the men unloaded trucks outside, Caitlin had taken a short tour of the lodge. Sepia-toned photos matted with birch bark and laced with rawhide straps lined the log walls throughout the massive structure. Contemporary leather sofas, ladder-back rockers, wicker chests, and twig and craftsman-style furniture added to the cocoonlike warmth and comfort of the mountain home. Tin lamps with parchment shades gave a soft glow to the vast living room where handcrafted depression-era rugs added a homespun flavor.

During her last stay, there'd been little time to notice these details. Her every moment had been devoted to impressing Buck with her skills as a photographer's assistant and her willingness to please him as a woman.

Hearing the first call to supper, Caitlin glanced in the cheval mirror, then followed the tantalizing smells to the kitchen and took a seat at the end of a long table.

She was aghast at the motley crew of men waiting to be served. Caitlin remembered the five models from her previous visits, but some of them had aged considerably in seven years. She recalled the notes she'd read in her father's notebook.

Joe believed he had a great butt and liked to rattle off baseball stats while sitting on his asset. Pete, a proud descendant of a Buffalo soldier, fancied himself an African-American Hemingway and sulked if someone else was assigned a fishing vest or waders. Easygoing Klyde liked to model as many items at once as possible—but was too overweight for the layered look. Carlos favored hats and was a closet magician. Red-haired Rusty brought his own props including musical instruments and was the resident entertainer.

Caitlin had purposely taken the end of the table, avoiding Buck who sat in the midst of his men. Lester strolled in late, sat down opposite her and immediately ingratiated himself by complimenting her expert tailoring. Caitlin couldn't help smiling back and asking Lester about his work at Echo Creek Outfitters.

Louie the irascible cook set a large cast-iron pot on the table, lifted the lid and proudly displayed a fragrant stew. When he returned with plates of hot biscuits moments later, Caitlin thrust her hand into the chaotic scramble of male fists, but found the plate nearest her empty.

"Hey!" Buck hollered. "Either you guys develop some manners fast or I'll give the lady first crack at the food and make you watch while she eats." He tossed his biscuit down the table to her. "Next time, sit in the center so you get a fighting chance, O'Malley."

Caitlin held the warm biscuit between her palms and watched Buck dish up a bowl of stew. He passed it in her direction without making eye contact, but the eyes of seven other men followed the passage of the bowl with extreme interest.

"Thank you for your concern, Mr. Rawlings." She broke open the biscuit and inhaled the delectable aroma. "But I prefer to sit at the edge of the group where I can keep an eye on my dogs."

"They need constant supervision, do they?" Buck looked up, his dark brows arched in mock surprise. "Are they working dogs or simply pets?"

"Burrito and Fajita are rugged outdoor—"

"I don't cook Mexican!" Louie slammed a kettle of green beans on the table and stood over her, glaring angrily.

"I—I wasn't asking you to cook Mexican—" Caitlin stammered. "Burrito and Fajita are my dogs."

"Louie, you gotta turn that hearin' aid up," Lester admonished. "She was talkin' 'bout her dogs. No one's complainin' 'bout your food, man."

As everyone mumbled their agreement, Caitlin stood and stretched to spoon up a serving of green beans before Buck Rawlings could do it for her.

He gave a low rumbling chuckle. "You do that very professionally, O'Malley. If you don't work out as our photographer, who knows...?" He looked down at his stew for a moment then glanced up at her, with just a hint of a smile.

Caitlin recalled long years of fantasizing about this meeting with Buck Rawlings. Biscuits, string beans and flirtatious tailors had never figured into the scenario. But the man's devastating smile and wicked humor had been a key element in her daydreams. She held on to the hope that the old Buck hadn't disappeared forever.

Chapter Two

Buck placed the last of the catalog layouts on the gaming table and watched intently as Caitlin moved slowly in and out of the circle of overhead light, studying the preliminary designs. She'd chosen to wear another custom-tailored Echo Creek design this morning, accessorized with pearl earrings and a silk scarf, and topped off with a red baseball cap. A long chestnut braid snaked out the hole in the back of her cap and down her back. She looked sexy and fresh.

Last night's supper had been hell. With every bite, he'd been tempted to send her packing. With every reflective sip of Louie's coffee, he'd been tempted to find some excuse to get her alone and explain as best he could what happened between them so long ago and how it had haunted him. Watching her clean her cameras and talk to the men last evening had been pure torment.

Now that they were alone to discuss layouts and set ground rules, Buck just wanted to be somewhere on his mountain, far from Caitlin O'Malley and complicated explanations. He liked things simple. He'd once told Chase, if his life were a book, he'd want large type, small words and few mysteries.

"You seem to prefer Echo Creek clothing, O'Malley. All those alterations must set you back quite a bit."

"If something suits my taste, any expense is worth it." She looked up at him, her face shadowed by the brim of her cap. The overhead light spotlighted her exquisitely shaped mouth. She tipped her hat back slightly and smiled. "I like your designs and the quality of your materials. I also find the workmanship superb, and frankly, I love your grommets." She tugged her hat back down on her forehead and concentrated on the layout in front of her.

Grommets. What kind of female was impressed by the quality of metal eyelets? Buck moved back into the shadows of the large gaming room. It was impossible to read the woman. There was no single label that suited her, and in today's ever-changing Montana, he found labels a near necessity for keeping things simple.

"You need more action scenes," she announced suddenly.

"There's plenty of action." Buck felt a ripple of irritation. Why did he feel so protective of a business he wanted to be rid of?

"More action. Wake people up, Rawlings. If you're selling clothes for kayaking, show us kayaks. Maybe a couple of your models can't handle it but I assume you and your brother can. Chase is the perfect age to appeal to that female audience you may want to go after. He's about twenty-seven now, isn't he?" she asked without looking up.

Buck felt a surge of possessiveness. Caitlin had been hired by his brother but she'd had little contact with his charismatic sibling. Seven years ago, during that fateful final summer, Chase had been away at college, earning his degree in business and interning on Wall Street. When the younger Rawlings male arrived in four days, Buck was certain he would attempt to charm O'Malley's daughter. Few women could resist Chase's earthy humor or model-perfect good looks.

"Chase turns twenty-eight next week."

"Wonderful. We'll have to have a party." She leaned a shapely hip against the table and folded her arms. "Now about the catalog—what if we shoot some scenes around a campfire? Or a home fire? Outdoor clothing isn't just for outdoor wear anymore."

"Go on. I'm listening," he told her.

"With the lodge, the lake, the creek and these foothills and mountains, you could vary your shots without traveling a hundred miles to do it."

Moving from panel to panel, they discussed the existing shots and possible changes. Buck was impressed with her keen grasp of design and knowledge of his inventory.

"Your ideas have merit," he said, somewhat begrudgingly. "I'll give them some thought. I do, however, want to maintain the masculine tone and traditions of the catalog."

"What traditions?"

"The trout centerfold."

"Trout centerfold? I've never noticed. Is it a . . . single trout?"

"As opposed to a married trout? Of course not." Buck laughed and grabbed last year's catalog from the edge of the table and flipped it open. "It's a montage of happy customers wearing Echo Creek clothing and displaying their prize trout."

"Does it really sell the product?"

"We sell fishing gear. The trout centerfold stays."

"That's odd." She pointed to a photo of a smiling couple. "Look, this woman's wearing Echo Creek clothing head to toe—and aren't those your boots? And this woman in the lower left corner—that's your top-of-the-line parka."

"Blasphemy," Buck muttered. He took the catalog from her and studied the photos. When he looked up, Caitlin was standing next to the pool table on the far side of the gaming room, staring pensively as she tested the weight of the cue ball in her palm.

Seven years ago, an innocent game of billiards had led to a playful night of passion. Yesterday, he'd vowed to ignore the history they shared, but how could he ignore the memory of Caitlin's ivory skin and chestnut hair splayed against the lush green felt? The image haunted him every time he picked up a pool cue.

Caitlin curled her fingers around the cool, smooth surface of the ball and sought some vestige of control over her pain. The lodge was an obstacle course of old memories. Had Buck chosen this room on purpose—to stir up the most painful images and throw her off guard? She set the cue ball down, then propelled it across the sea of green felt, but it never reached the side pocket. She looked up to find Buck standing opposite her, the white ball captured in his hand.

"So—" she ran her fingertips along the wooden edge "—how's your game, Rawlings?"

"I don't play much anymore. And you?"

"It's been years. I pretty much lost my taste for it."

He leaned into the rectangle of light. "Cat—"

"That name belongs to someone you chose to forget, Buck. Please don't use it in my presence again. Only my father has the right to use it."

"I think we should—"

The sound of a boot kicking the door of the game room and the gruff announcement of "room service" interrupted their conversation.

Buck set the cue ball down. "That's got to be Louie with our breakfast. I asked him to serve us in private so we could discuss ground rules, O'Malley."

The massive wooden door opened and Louie entered, carrying a tray of rattling dishes and clinking silverware, and swearing beneath his breath. Lester followed with a coffee-pot and two mugs. The wizened wild-haired cook elbowed past Buck and Caitlin and set the tray on a counter near the wet bar. He exited without acknowledging anyone.

"Louie's in fine form this mornin', boss," Lester warned. Then turning to Caitlin, he smiled, toothpick abobble, and bowed his head slightly. "How do you like your java, Miss O'Malley? We call Louie's mornin' brew the Fogcutter."

"Actually, Lester, I brought my Italian espresso machine along and set it up in the kitchen last night. Enjoying good coffee is my one vice."

"Great!" Buck put his hands on his hips. "That explains Louie's mood. The kitchen is his shrine. No one messes with anything."

Caitlin shrugged and smiled apologetically at Buck. "I'll just run out and make myself a latte and make amends with Louie."

"Like hell you will, O'Malley." Buck cut her short. "We're in the middle of a business meeting. Your fancy coffee can wait. Pour the lady a cup of Fogcutter, Lester."

"Well, isn't that somethin'. I got myself an Eye-talian machine at home, too." Lester poured the coffee as directed and handed the mug to Buck without a glance in his direction. "I'd be happy to rustle up a double tall with no fat, Miss O'Malley. Now, you look like you'd love Amaretto—"

"Lester—" Buck cleared his throat "—doesn't your sewing machine need oiling or something?"

Lester straightened to his full height, took the toothpick from his mouth and studied it intently. "I guess we'll continue this culinary discussion later, Miss O'Malley. *Bon appétit.*" With the tip of an imaginary hat, he left the room, closing the door behind him.

Caitlin stared at the carved wooden door for a moment, trying to understand Buck's sudden anger. "The man was just being polite."

"Are you blind? He's an outrageous flirt, O'Malley. Don't encourage him."

She heard the clink of cutlery and turned to find Buck setting their breakfast dishes on a table nestled in front of two leather chairs. He opened the drapes, sending soft muted light onto the blue stoneware plates and illuminating the vast room. His mouth was a rigid line as he poured a mug of black coffee and set it beside the plate intended for her.

Caitlin approached the cozy setting hesitantly, certain that she didn't want more light shed on the high-calorie meal awaiting her. Eggs and sausage were piled next to biscuits and gravy on the plate, leaving little space for a slice of cantaloupe, an island of health in a sea of cholesterol. A heavily buttered cinnamon roll congealed nearby. It was evident Louie had little regard for the human heart.

She glanced up at Buck, and this view of him made her forget Louie's heavy-handed slinging of animal fats. The dim light over the pool table had cheated her out of the full impact of Buck Rawlings in the morning. He'd showered but he had not shaved. The dark shadow of his beard gave him a hungry, haunted look. She knew there was a whisper of Shoshone blood in his veins, a legacy from his mother. This light emphasized his high cheekbones and compelling eyes, turning the whisper into a soft shout. Some feminine part of her twisted. His tweed mountaineer's sweater emphasized the broad expanse of his shoulders and highlighted the green of his eyes. Intense eyes. Focused on her. He gestured for her to sit.

Eyes on one another, they both lowered themselves into the chairs with the wariness of gunslingers sharing a breakfast nook just before their scheduled shoot-out.

"So, how does this work?" she asked, opening her white napkin and noting its similarity to a flag of surrender. "You list the ground rules and I listen?"

"No. I list the ground rules and you agree to obey every one of 'em." He took a sip of coffee, gave her a teasing smile that disappeared so quickly, she wondered if she'd imagined it, then lowered his mug. "The rules are simple,

O'Malley. First, I want respect for privacy during wardrobe changes. Secondly, we'll have daily conferences to check our progress and to hash out any problems that might come up." He looked at her expectantly.

"Is that it? We're having breakfast in here so you can list two ground rules?"

"There's one more." He ate a forkful of eggs and tore off a piece of his cinnamon roll and pointed it at her. "Third and last, I won't tolerate reckless behavior of any kind."

"I see. And just who gets to define 'reckless'?" She sliced her cantaloupe into neat, bite-size pieces and speared one with her fork.

"You know exactly what I'm talking about, O'Malley. I don't want you taking chances. Remember the boulder incident? You're impulsive. Period."

"I was sixteen when I climbed that boulder."

"You were twenty-three when you went windsurfing on the lake with a storm approaching. A person's basic nature seldom changes."

Caitlin quickly ate the square of cantaloupe on her fork, letting the icy fruit sit on her tongue, hoping the cold would magically dispel the heat that had enveloped her at the blanket accusation. When Buck grew silent and began eating again, Caitlin refolded her napkin and set it on the table. She pushed her plate away.

Buck pushed it back. "You can't be finished. You haven't touched a thing." He leaned toward her. "You'll be getting a man-size workout today, O'Malley. I insist you eat something substantial."

"Another ground rule? Are you going to be adding to the list every day?"

"Eat your eggs and maybe a biscuit. Try the coffee. I know it isn't up to your standards—"

"This is ridiculous. I know what my body needs."

"Oh, yeah?" He picked up her fork. "Eat! You're underweight. A stick. You're all cheekbones and eyes. You've got no butt, O'Malley."

"Dammit, I've got a butt!" She stood up, bumping his outstretched hand and sent the fork clattering to the table. "But you're missing something—you haven't got a heart, Rawlings!"

"Whatever you don't eat, I'll bring along on the shoot."

The image of Buck packing a sack lunch filled with cold eggs, sausage, biscuits and gravy made her sit back down in the chair.

Buck wiped his mouth, sat back and stared at her. He wanted to bar the door and spend the day hashing out their past, to be done with it.

"We're regressing," he said quietly after regaining control. "The two of us argued like this seven years ago."

"I remember. But then, we argued like this when I was a teenager. We've always locked horns." She rose to her feet. "You know, I have a few demands I haven't mentioned."

Buck stood up and waited, sensing yet another confrontation.

"In the free time that I have, I plan to hike up the mountain by myself, Rawlings, to shoot some marketable nature photographs. Having to sub for my father cuts into my own income and—"

"By yourself?" Buck raised his voice. "Shouldn't you have a guide?"

"I'm a cautious, resourceful and expertly qualified outdoorsperson, Rawlings."

"There's no such thing as an *outdoorsperson*. There are outdoorsmen and there are women. You are a woman. You need a guide." He moved toward the door. "And that's final."

"If you'll let me finish..." Caitlin added, following him. "I simply ask that you respect my right to do what I please when I complete the daily shoots. And I have a second request. Please do not arrange for us to meet in this room again. Last night you said we had history, the worst kind of history. Let's just say this room and that pool table are two historical sites I don't care to revisit."

"All right, but I've got a request of my own," he blurted out, wrenching one of the ornately carved doors open. "The subject of our former relationship and my sister's death are off-limits for the next two weeks."

By noon, Buck had spent three hours watching Caitlin take charge of the catalog shoot with the same good-natured professionalism he'd come to expect of Sean O'Malley. And like her father, she charmed the crew with her warmhearted cajoling and expert suggestions. When Klyde discovered he'd gained a shirt size over the winter, she'd halted Lester's grumblings with a single glance and smoothed over the potentially embarrassing and disruptive situation.

Buck studied her slender silhouette as she adjusted a tripod. He needed to be away from the woman for a while, away from other people. Setting a handful of catalog layouts on the portable table behind her, Buck secured them with a large stone and set off to view the lake. Farley barked excitedly and loped off ahead, followed by Burrito and Fajita.

From a productivity standpoint, selecting Medicine Bowl Lake as the site for the first day of shooting had been a wise choice. There were numerous settings—grassy knolls, cliffs, tree-spotted hillsides, a shack and corral—which allowed the crew to vary the shots. But the setting triggered old memories. His eyes followed the jagged shoreline to a finger of land jutting out to a rocky point strewn with boulders. These oddly shaped stone sentinels had been witness to a bitter fight he'd had with Caitlin when she was sixteen and assisting her father for the first time. He'd caught her atop the highest boulder, camera in hand. In a rage, he'd driven her to Harlowtown and put her on a bus bound for home. The next morning, she'd appeared at breakfast, and the mystery of her journey back to the lodge was never revealed.

Farley approached with a stick and Buck chuckled at the Lab's wild-eyed eagerness. Caitlin's dogs quickly followed, and giving in to their natural herding instinct, herded Farley away from Buck before the three broke into a playful game of tag.

Buck returned his attention to the vividly blue waters of Medicine Bowl Lake. Besides his angry encounter with Caitlin, the beautiful and mysterious lake held other painful secrets. There in the distance, in a sheltered inlet marked by a grouping of black cottonwood, he'd scattered his sister's ashes seven years ago.

A number of long-buried recollections of Sarah had been unearthed since Caitlin's arrival last evening. Was it Caitlin's coltish gait or her impetuous, risk-taking nature that brought fond memories of his little sister to life? O'Malley's daughter had chosen to sleep in Sarah's quarters on the third floor. Buck hadn't stepped inside the room since his sister's tragic death. Before leaving Missoula two days ago, he'd vowed to sit on Sarah's willow bed, surrounded by her possessions, and force himself to bring his grieving to an end.

Buck had no wish to spend time in Sarah's room while Caitlin was in residence. The woman planned to hike up the mountains alone. Already, she was showing signs of her foolhardy nature. He could not afford to get emotionally involved again with Caitlin. He had no desire to watch another woman die.

With a sigh, Buck sat on a nearby stump and looked up at the sky, studying the clouds on the distant horizon, scanning over to the snow-topped mountains that beckoned to him at every glance. The foothills and forests, rocky cliffs and summits held images of childhood and later years spent exploring with his wildflower sister.

He was highly disciplined in mind and body. He'd find a way to shut out these painful recollections of that final summer with Cat O'Malley.

"Hey, can you hear me? We need you, Rawlings."

He turned from his reverie at the sound of Caitlin's voice. With her red baseball cap and matching silk scarf, she was easy to spot against a backdrop of scrub pine and bear grass.

"What's up?" he asked.

"Louie's setting up for lunch. After we eat, we're moving the camera equipment and necessary props to the north shore for the next series of shots. I just wanted to show you the scenes I shot while you were walking with the dogs."

"Let's eat first, then show me the Polaroids."

After nodding in her direction, he scrambled up the incline to help Louie who was already grumbling and clanging metal plates. Fifteen minutes later, as the crew sat on boulders and camp stools, biting into roast beef sandwiches, Buck watched Caitlin slip much of the beef from her sandwich to her dogs.

The last to be served, he walked to the stump where she was seated and sat down beside her. "I believe you've rallied the men to new levels of enthusiasm."

"Oh, thanks." She gave him a nervous smile and fidgeted with her sandwich. "The crew's been great about wardrobe changes and props. They're terrific. We're steaming right along." She took a stack of shots from her shirt pocket and passed them to Buck.

Like her father, Caitlin took a Polaroid before committing each scene to film. As a result, the crew had instant feedback and everyone felt a sense of accomplishment at the end of the day. The photos also made it easier to avoid duplicate poses. Buck studied each picture intently, pleased with the angles, lighting and poses, but concerned about the speed with which she worked. The shoot was already ahead of schedule.

"These all look fine," he said, handing the photos back.

"Do you miss working with my father?" she asked softly, slipping the pictures back into her pocket.

"Of course, working with Sean is different. He's a friend." After he'd spoken, Buck realized his choice of words was a bit insensitive. Well, she wasn't a friend in the true sense. O'Malley's daughter was a . . . working acquaintance. No, she was more than that but he was hard-pressed to find the correct word. He doubted he and Caitlin could ever be good friends. They lapsed into silence. It was then that Buck looked around the circle and realized every man had his eyes riveted on the two of them.

Damn, he did miss the old companionship he shared with Sean O'Malley. The older man was like a father to him in many ways. They shared a mutual love of the outdoors and enjoyed trading stories of each year's adventures. Sean was an excellent storyteller and an even better listener. The Irishman also understood Buck's need for solitude and never questioned the younger man's absences during the shoots.

Caitlin's father shared Buck's concern for Montana's vanishing ways: old ways that didn't include movie stars buying ranches, the rapid growth of tourism or designer coffee. Buck missed his Irish friend and decided to give Sean a call that evening after supper.

The men were in various stages of wardrobe changes. Obeying the first of the ground rules, Caitlin had her back to the crew, allowing them privacy and giving her a moment to gaze at the blue reflective waters of the lake. So, Buck Rawlings didn't count her among his friends. Fine. She didn't want to be his anything—except an employee able to last the full two weeks that came with the assignment.

Unlike her father, it was her policy not to mix business with pleasure. Every friendly remark, every good-natured ribbing and humorous aside was meant to maintain the momentum of the shoot. For years, she'd watched her father tell stories and listen as others shared their tales. He'd wasted valuable time in a profession where daylight and good weather were essential.

Buck Rawlings was one pleasure she couldn't afford. The very sight of the man destroyed her concentration and made her mouth turn to cotton. For God's sake, she'd climbed mountains, hiked the wilderness, battled grade-five rapids. She was strong, successful and resourceful. How could the sight of Buck Rawlings make her feel as if she were standing on the edge of a precipice with a high wind at her back?

No. She didn't want to have anything to do with Buck and his lone-wolf ways. Ever. There were far easier ways to go crazy in this world. She wished her father knew how much of a hardship this was for her.

"Miss O'Malley, your subjects await." Lester tapped her on the shoulder and she smiled at the sight of his gap-toothed grin lined with straight pins. He handed her the shot list. "Accordin' to this here plan, Buck'll be wearin' the sexy new Winchester vest and Maverick hat—yup, that's it—followed by Pete showin' his bountiful self in the Olympic fishin' vest and demonstratin' assorted gear right by the water."

She had to suppress a smile every time Lester announced the next scene, sounding like a twangy announcer for a fashion show. More than anything, she appreciated the tailor's organizational skills and flair for props.

Caitlin looked up from the rumpled piece of paper to find Buck already in place, slouched indifferently against the weathered shack that bordered the corral, one boot resting against a rail. She picked up her tripod and camera and approached him, feeling as though she were stepping back more than a century. His unshaven jaw, black hat and leather vest gave him the air of an outlaw, circa 1880. A story line came to mind. A misunderstood man wronged by women and by life, falsely charged and nearly executed. A man with secrets to reveal and a posse on his behind. If he stood there a moment longer with that outlaw attitude written all over him, she'd rally to his defense.

Instead, Caitlin calmly set up her reflectors and stood back to dispassionately block the shot. Buck took off the black hat and studied the braided leather band with an air of intense interest before he glanced in her direction.

"Tell me what you want from me, O'Malley."

"I want you to think dusty, hungry, wanton thoughts, Rawlings."

"I'm way ahead of you."

"Why don't you keep your foot on the rail—it shows off the lines of the jeans."

"Not just any jeans, O'Malley." Buck spoke in a husky, teasing tone. "I'm wearing Echo Creek's Sundance jeans."

"Miss O'Malley," Lester interrupted, "these new Sundance jeans are s'posed to fit like the caress of a very inquisitive woman."

"Oh, really?" She adjusted one of the reflectors to avoid eye contact with Buck. "Will the catalog put that unique design feature into print, Mr. Rawlings?"

"Heck, no," Buck countered. "It's just production line talk. Sew a few dozen yards of denim a day and you'd be talking trash, too."

Caitlin suspected the remark had nothing to do with factory fatigue but everything to do with the way the man turned jeans into a statement with that rebel walk of his.

Seven years ago, she'd been a very inquisitive female, blatantly revealing her interest in Buck Rawlings. At thirty, she planned to keep her hands in her pockets and ignore all temptation. After all, in his eyes, she didn't even fit into the category of friend.

Caitlin completed the scene, squeezing off the last shot with fingers trembling on the remote shutter release. She needed to speak to someone about this swirling hurricane of emotions and the pull of the past. She'd call her father after supper to see how he was doing. Maybe she could sneak the subject of Buck Rawlings into the conversation.

That evening, Caitlin waited for the men to amble off to other areas of the lodge, leaving her alone in the kitchen with one of the few phones in the three-story building. After preparing a latte, she held the number of her father's hospital room in her hand for a moment, recalling the sight of her handsome, robust father confined to an impossibly small white bed.

Despite his insulin-dependent diabetes, he'd lived life to the fullest, hiking the most rugged wilderness areas of America to capture his world-renowned photographs. He was her only parent, her trusted friend, her wise and patient mentor. It was impossible to imagine Sean O'Malley hampered by poor vision, or worse, total blindness. She hadn't liked the finality in Dr. Leahy's tone when he'd discussed the prognosis. There was little hope for the left eye and his doctor said it was impossible to predict, in months or years, the probability of hemorrhage in the right. Laser surgery would be risky if not impossible in her father's case.

Caitlin felt her throat constrict. Photography was as much her passion as it was her father's. She knew the challenge of finding the perfect vantage point, the near-spiritual high of framing nature's glory and the proud moment when her work sold and was appreciated outside of Montana's borders. It was so unfair. Her father was meant to soar, to climb, to tackle life, not to be limited by the loss of vision.

She dialed the hospital's number and envisioned the sharp contrast between her Irish father's rich auburn hair and the white of his pillow.

"Dad, it's Caitlin. How are you feeling? Are you still in much pain?"

"A bit. I'm not used to sitting on my duff doing nothing. I had these fine people move me to a room with a view of the mountains. Now I can lie here, look out the window and imagine myself climbing." Her father's slight brogue enlivened his words. "But enough about me. How are things at Echo Creek?"

"The first day of shooting went well. We're ahead of schedule." She sprinkled cinnamon atop her latte and took a sip. "We return to Medicine Bowl Lake in the morning."

"Details, I want details, daughter."

Caitlin quickly covered the more technical aspects of some scenes, described her room on the third floor and related news of Buck's crew. "Lester's been a great help."

"Aye, the man can talk the teeth out of a saw, but he always means well. Make good use of him. You haven't mentioned Buck. Is everything all right, darlin'?"

Caitlin pulled a chair up to the window and looked out at the slices of twilight hidden between the trees as she sipped her latte from the colorful designer mug she'd brought from home. She pondered her reply. For seven years, her father had asked about the trouble between Buck Rawlings and herself, and had seemed deeply saddened by the rift. In all this time, she'd danced around the issue. How could she explain Buck's sudden abandonment or why her letters had been returned unopened? Caitlin didn't understand it fully herself.

"Well." She hesitated, knowing her father would attempt to delve deeper no matter what response she gave him. "When I first got here, Buck didn't believe I was qualified to take your place. So I'm on a ridiculous four-day trial until Chase arrives and the brothers make a decision as to whether I'll stay on."

"What nonsense! The Buck Rawlings I know would never doubt my judgment."

"You've worked with Buck for fifteen years, Dad, and he's like a son to you. I haven't seen him for more than half a dozen years. Things are strained between us, and I have the feeling nothing I do during the next two weeks will change that. He's stubborn and arrogant and bossy."

"Buck still has feelings for you, Cat. I'm sure of it."

"I'm here to shoot your catalog, Dad and I intend to do the best I can. When I drove up here, I had hopes of finally saying goodbye to Sarah and clearing up whatever misunderstanding Buck had about me but now—it's not worth the effort."

"Cat O'Malley, you once loved the man. I want you to be happy again, as happy as you were that last summer you were at the lodge. Please, please try to break down those old walls, daughter. Don't build new ones.'' The pleading tone in her father's voice brought moisture to her eyes. Caitlin would do anything to please this man, anything but face the pain of the past.

She suspected her father had an additional reason for insisting she substitute for him and that would be his desire to reunite her with his best friend's son. Nothing was simple or as it seemed. Most likely it was best to be honest with Sean O'Malley and dash his hopes of such a healing.

"I'm here to look out for your financial interests, Dad. The truth is, I just want to get the job done quickly and get away from Buck Rawlings as soon as possible."

"Lord, you're as stubborn as he is and twice as foolish. Ach, there's a nurse looking in on me, Cat, and she's a door full of woman. I best say goodbye. Next time we talk, I pray I hear good things about you and Buck."

Had he listened to anything she'd said? Caitlin wondered as she hung up the phone. She put her feet on the windowsill, leaned her chair back on two legs, closed her eyes and thought of the Alaskan trek she'd sacrificed. Most likely, Buck Rawlings would have objected to her hiking the wilderness with three women.

Burrito was suddenly at her side, resting her head on Caitlin's lap. "Good puppy," she crooned, smiling at the dog's forlorn expression that mirrored so closely her own melancholy mood. She wove her fingers through the thick fur on Burrito's neck and sighed.

How could she feel so attracted to a man she thoroughly despised? She was a strong, independent woman with myriad interests and friends and a full calendar. Why did Buck Rawlings make her feel as though there were spaces in her life she needed to fill? Tomorrow, while working with him, she intended to fight her attraction all the more.

Buck stood transfixed near the kitchen door, watching Caitlin tilted back in a chair, stroking one of her dogs. He'd gone to the kitchen to call Sean O'Malley, only to discover she'd been one step ahead of him. Trying to make sense of one side of her conversation with her father was tough, but he'd heard enough to know she was unhappy with him and arrangements at Echo Creek. He put his hand on the door-jamb.

The woman despised him. And she'd made it clear she was doing nothing more than taking care of her father's business interests. Her heart wasn't truly in the job. He couldn't afford to sacrifice quality on this year's catalog. Fall and Christmas sales were a substantial part of their annual earnings. Profits had dipped this past year, further delaying his plan to exit Echo Creek Outfitters and start his own wilderness guide service.

Was Caitlin's desire to hurry the project a threat to his company and his lifelong goal? He'd watch her more closely in the morning. If he suspected compromise, tomorrow would be a day of reckoning for O'Malley's daughter.

Chapter Three

Early the following morning, Buck found Caitlin in the library studying a topographical map on the wall. Her still-damp chestnut hair hung in a tumble of waves over her shoulders and back. She leaned closer to the map, tracing a ridge with her fingertip. A faint rose flush dusted her high cheekbones. He'd yet to figure out whether she wore a layer of makeup like most women. Instead, he chose to believe her heightened color and glow resulted from her intensity for life. Did that intensity include all things financial? She'd sounded somewhat ruthless on the phone last night.

Or was that his distorted judgment, which tended to be harsh?

Buck had always felt distanced from other people. It wasn't until he was in his teens that he realized his need for solitude was the exception, not the rule. Rather than attempt to conform, he proudly labeled himself a loner and continued to spend time alone in the mountains or hiking in the foothills.

His sister, Sarah, had always known how to coax a smile and infrequent laughter from him, but she'd been intimidated by his dark moods. It was Caitlin who'd broken through his carefully erected barriers with amazing precision and speed. The walls were higher and stronger now, but still, Cat O'Malley threatened to find the hidden passage back to his heart.

As Buck murmured a polite "Good morning" and stepped closer, he was struck by the strength in her profile and in her determined stance. Caitlin had never been one to show her vulnerability, to show him that she truly needed him beyond the realm of lover. He wanted a woman who allowed him to be her protector, who reached out to him and sought his strength.

"Almost time for breakfast," he told her from the doorway, keeping his voice devoid of warmth.

"I just wanted to have some sites in mind for my own shooting." She glanced at him then pointed at the map. "If I position myself here, will I have a clear view of the lake or will it be obscured by timber?"

"That's a long climb, O'Malley." He kept his distance, only guessing at the location she'd indicated.

"It's not that steep a terrain. I figure an hour at most if I leave right after we finish shooting this afternoon." She divided her hair into strands as she spoke and began to braid them with quick, sure movements, taming the wild tresses into a smooth plait.

"An hour? Yeah, I guess that should do it." He remembered braiding Sarah's hair for the first time. Had she been in the third or fourth grade? He also recalled the last time. His sister had asked for his inexpert help the day of her death. He turned away before his eyes could make that painful journey on the map, tracing their doomed route.

"I'm just a little surprised," she murmured a moment later, "that you're not insisting on acting as my guide."

"You're off the clock." He answered too quickly. "Whatever you want to do is your business. Just carry a whistle—a very big whistle—in case you need help."

When she gave him an odd look, as if to question his brusque manner, Buck eyed her coolly and said nothing. He wasn't in the mood for a confrontation, not with images of his sister swirling through his head. Buck looked down at the Oriental carpet, attempting to lose the remnants of his grief in the intricate pattern.

He heard Caitlin's measured steps, saw the tips of her boots and heard her hands digging into the pockets of her moss-colored jeans. Echo Creek's signature jeans. How was he going to render himself immune to her presence? The wily woman could assault his senses and non-senses from ten yards away.

"We better get into the kitchen, O'Malley." Buck decided to keep it strictly business. "I talked to Louie about his meals and suggested he offer lighter fare for those who want it."

"Thank you," she murmured. "That was a thoughtful gesture."

"I would have done it for anyone. Keeping employees content is my job," he said tersely. In the next three days, he prayed he'd find some easy excuse to let O'Malley's daughter go.

"I smell rain," Caitlin announced just before lunch. Instinctively, she made a quick visual check of the location of all of her gear. She glanced overhead at the bright blue Montana sky, then scanned the horizon. Cirrostratus clouds appeared between south and northwest, a sure indicator of an approaching storm.

"I felt it in my hip this mornin', Miss O'Malley," Lester drawled. "Had a dickens of a time pullin' on my red briefs. No sir, not a good way for a man to start the day layin' on his back across the bed cussin' at some invisible force. Well, now I know what that force is."

"Yeah, it's called elastic, you fool!" Carlos laughed heartily.

"You're hardly one to talk, Carlos." Rusty tossed a belt buckle from the wardrobe box. "Lester could blow away in a high wind. With your big butt, you crack a smile every time you bend over."

Caitlin ignored the friendly barbs being exchanged by the crew. Her attention was focused on Buck. Yesterday, he had been almost good-natured at times. What had happened to change him so abruptly overnight? He'd barely said a word to her in the library. The breakfast fare was a vast improvement, but he didn't even glance in her direction to see if his intervention with Louie pleased her, or to check her caloric intake.

He removed the white hat he'd been modeling and scanned the ridge above the lake, his head cocked to one side, as if tuned to some invisible voice. At last, Buck glanced in her direction.

"We might have an hour if we're lucky," he said, clapping his hands before cupping a palm to his mouth. "Fellas, let's get cracking. Make your wardrobe changes now. We've got that four shot coming up. Lester, bring the shot sheet over here and help us get this pile of shirts on the right men."

Before Caitlin had time to turn her back, Buck began to work the button fly of his jeans, seemingly oblivious to her presence. A fluttering warmth clutched her midriff and emanated downward like the awakening of some hibernating need. Rather than turn around and risk drawing more attention, she picked a black Stetson off the table and shielded her face from the sight.

Her nostrils were immediately filled with a mixture of woodsy pine and dark spice and she realized too late that the hat belonged to Buck. Instantly memories of past intimacies played over each of her senses. Closing her eyes against a swirling crazy quilt of impressions, Caitlin was shocked to hear Buck's name torn from her lips. Had she really spoken it?

Suddenly the hat was taken from her hands and the shock of glaring sunlight made her start and open her eyes.

"You're holding my hat, O'Malley!" Buck's lean, rugged face was inches from her own. "If you wanna give the crew privacy, turn your back." He frowned deeply as he inspected the crease along the top.

"I hope I haven't damaged it, Rawlings. I thought it was just another prop. I'll replace it if you like."

"You don't get it, do you?" He set it back on his head and glared at her. "This hat has history."

"The word *history* seems to be coming up frequently in our conversations, Mr. Rawlings. Perhaps if you lifted your moratorium on discussing the past, we wouldn't have to tiptoe around each other."

"Talking about it would probably make it worse, O'Malley. Let's just bury it and get back to work. You're getting paid to shoot a catalog, lady, not unearth the skeleton of some infatuation."

"Infatuation? Is that honestly how you saw it?" Caitlin stepped up to Buck, grabbed the black Stetson off his head and shook it at him. "Damn you, Rawlings. You show more emotion about ten ounces of felt than you do about what we had!"

"Cat, this isn't the time or the place."

"Then, name a time and place and I'll be there, Buck. I have questions only you can answer and I have information about Sarah I feel you need to know. I tried to tell you years ago but—"

"Who in hell said we were discussing my sister?" Buck held his hand out. "Give me that hat. We've got work to do, O'Malley. There's a storm coming."

Caitlin handed the hat back to Buck then looked up into his strained features. "I'm just asking you to be reasonable, Rawlings. This is our second day of shooting. Things will go faster and smoother if you and I aren't dodging all this crap from the past."

He folded his arms and bent his head for a moment. "All right," he said gruffly, looking out toward the lake. "We'll talk. Not today or tonight. Maybe tomorrow. Until then, just bury it."

Buck sat in his father's old ladder-back rocker, his boots resting on a porch rail, and stared out at the rain. He'd expected the squall to end quickly like many of the storms that hit the area in late spring and early summer. After two hours of heavy drizzle, he called the weather service and discovered showers and high winds were predicted for the next few days. So what was he going to do with O'Malley's daughter?

He took his Stetson off and stared at it blankly as if the answer dwelled within. Quickly he brought it to his nose. Something was different. The sweatband that lined the interior must have absorbed her perfume.

"Sorry to interrupt, Rawlings—" She was standing a few yards away, leaning against one of the porch supports. The rain formed a gunmetal-gray backdrop, giving her flawless skin an ivory glow.

"You're not interrupting anything," he responded. Yeah, sure. He was just smelling the interior of his hat. Had she seen him? He slipped the Stetson back on his head, feeling the heat in his face.

"Look, I'm sorry about the hat. I thought it was from Wardrobe. I had no idea."

"Most women don't understand about a man and his hat."

"Is it badly damaged?"

"Too soon to tell." He lifted his hand to the crown protectively. "Too soon."

"Well, do keep me informed." She seemed to dismiss the issue of his hat with a wave of her hand. "I have an idea for the shoot."

"Okay, let's hear it."

"I think we can catch a few more scenes today if we use the interior of the lodge and possibly the porch."

When she looked at him expectantly, he said nothing, enjoying the sight of Caitlin's large tawny eyes. The woman had become more than a physical presence. She was invading the private recesses of his mind, overturning his orderly thoughts and leaving the scent of her haunting perfume in the vacant, empty spaces no woman had invaded before. No woman but a sixteen-year-old tomboy with a rebel heart. His fascination with Caitlin was older than any hat he owned. And far more important.

He wanted to capture her and carry her down the stairs, to stand in the downpour and watch her high-and-mighty facade melt, to feel her slide down the front of his hard male body, those same golden eyes dark with desire.

"Right now," she continued in her confident tone, "the men are gathered around the fireplace drinking coffee. And the light out here on the porch, with the rain in the background... Well, I thought—"

"You thought what?"

"We don't need to waste time because of a little rain."

"I happen to like the rain." He walked to the post opposite her and leaned back against the aged and polished wood. In their remarkably similar Echo Creek clothing, they looked like bookends. "What were you going to say about the porch?"

"It's hard to put into words." She shook her head and frowned. "I like standing here and looking beyond the clearing to the tops of the trees and down to the lake. Reminds me of being a kid in a tree house. Safe and secluded and almost secretive. It's—"

"Romantic?"

"I guess you could say that." Her look was one of surprise. "Although I'd prefer to think in more productive terms."

Productive? Buck almost choked. The shrewd business-woman probably thought she could wrap up the shoot early and grab another assignment. Damn. Was she also willing to compromise quality?

"Well, what do you say, Rawlings?" she urged.

"Why do you want to rush everything?" he asked out-right. "We've run into weather delays before and the cata-log always got done."

"Two, maybe three days of stormy weather is more than a delay. When I commit myself to completing a project in two weeks, I like to keep on some kind of schedule—no matter what." She pushed herself away from the wood pil-lar and stood with her back to the rain, arms folded across her chest. She gave Buck a sidelong glance. "Just humor my idea, okay?"

Buck felt her stance was far more confrontive than her words. The woman knew how to use her body language to full advantage. He suddenly wished he'd been given the chance to become fluent in that language.

"All right, O'Malley, I'll come inside in a minute to help you revise the shot sheet."

He watched her close the door behind her before he looked beyond the porch to the rain. When he inhaled, an-ticipating the clean fresh scent of Montana rain, Caitlin's elusive perfume predominated. It still emanated from his hat, reminding him of an alpine meadow dusted with wild-flowers and sunshine.

Caitlin O'Malley would probably scoff at such an image, labeling it unproductive.

Buck looked down at the weathered porch. He'd often visualized making love here on these planks with the rain falling at a slant so it drenched his skin, turning it slick be-neath a woman's fingertips. He doubted if O'Malley's daughter would care to hear about that particular fantasy when they discussed possible scenes on the porch.

How did she really feel about him? Was Caitlin pursuing a discussion of their past because she wanted to rekindle old feelings or put them to rest once and for all? And if that was her purpose, did she expect the same from him?

While the wind gusted against the bank of kitchen windows, Caitlin brushed errant tendrils back from her forehead and put her eye to the viewfinder, pleased with the scene that filled the frame. Joe, Klyde and Pete stood around the kitchen's wood stove staging a scene she could have titled "men cooking breakfast in long johns." Louie stood nearby ranting about the use of his cookware and antique stove.

"Watch your wrist, Klyde. That ain't no way to hold a spatula," Louie instructed with all the patience of a drill sergeant. "Damn fool. Use a light touch with the handle of my skillet."

"Sorry if I get my fingerprints on it, Louie." Klyde was uncharacteristically sharp in his retort. "Echo Creek hasn't started makin' oven mitts yet!"

Five minutes later, the scene was completed. Caitlin was delighted once again with the results of the interior shoot. She lined the Polaroid pictures up on the tabletop to gloat. There were men in front of the stone fireplace, men with dogs, men tying fishing flies.

Suddenly Buck was at her side, studying the photos.

"These are good. I like the humor and the warmth."

She thanked him for his compliments and gathered the pictures together. "You're next," she said crisply, dreading the next scene. *Single male alone in his bedroom modeling Buckhorn Special.* "If you're busy, Rawlings, I could use Rusty."

"I've always modeled the Buckhorn. My father named the shirt after me, O'Malley." He slipped a faded work shirt off one of the clearly marked hangers in the kitchen's apron closet and threw the garment over his shoulder.

As she gathered her gear together for the trek up to the second floor, she recalled how adamant he'd been about tradition. Add the Buckhorn Special to the likes of the trout centerfold. He picked up most of her equipment and followed close behind her on the stairs.

She stopped on the landing and looked down at him. "Should we ask Lester to come along?"

"Why? You think I've gained a shirt size since this afternoon?"

"No, not at all."

"Give him a rest, O'Malley. We can handle this one alone."

Alone. He gave the word special emphasis.

"Lester's good with props," she argued, resuming the climb up the wide staircase.

Buck ignored her. When they reached the second floor, he hefted the tripod to his shoulder and walked ahead to open the door.

Caitlin tried to enter Buck's room with the objective attitude of a professional photographer, anxious to size up the situation and get to work. Two steps onto the woven rug, her attempts at objectivity were abandoned. Every unpretentious detail demanded her immediate and complete attention.

"Your bed—" She stood, bathed in remembrance at the sight of the immense oak structure, a stark masculine contrast to the flowing arches of Sarah's willow bed. She glanced at Buck and kept her features expressionless, unwilling to reveal the impact this room had on her. "I remember you saying it was a family heirloom."

He curled his large hand around one of the massive posts. "My grandfather built it as a birthday present for my grandma. See how he used buckskin to lash the timbers together?"

"You don't need to explain, Buck. I've, uh, seen this bed a number of times."

"I hadn't forgotten," he answered moments later, his voice thick and low.

How could she remain strictly professional in this sensual setting filled with intensely personal memories? She had to concentrate. Her father was depending on her. Sean O'Malley was in a hospital bed made not of heirloom oak or whimsical willow, but of ungiving metal. For a moment, she stared at the Native American design of Buck's goose-down comforter, then pulled back from her reverie, intent on completing the job at hand. A gust of wind hammered against the side of the building, rattling the windows facing the lake.

She turned to judge Buck's reaction to the disturbance but he was standing in the center of the room, his chest bared. With deft movements, he pulled on a pale gray Buckhorn Special, one of America's best-known shirts. As she set up her tripod, Caitlin watched him fasten the horn bone buttons she'd felt so often beneath her own fingertips. She fumbled with the lens on her Hasselblad camera when he unzipped his jeans and, with neat efficient strokes, tucked in the tails of the legendary work shirt.

"What about whittling by candlelight?" She broke the long silence.

"I'm not the whittling type."

"Reading?"

"The Buckhorn is a rugged work shirt."

"I see. You probably want to polish your gun."

"We don't sell hunting gear, but I like the idea of polishing. How about belt buckles?" He opened a dresser drawer and brought out a carved wooden box, a can of cleaner and a polishing cloth. He set these on the table next to the bed and opened the lid of the box. With near reverence, Buck selected a number of buckles, including the one she'd given him that last summer.

"Props-R-Us," he said with a half smile.

As rain lashed at the windows, they placed lamps with parchment shades strategically around the room, then lit candles. She tested light levels with her meter and judged the scene with the unforgiving eye of an artist. They worked in a companionable silence. Buck sat on the bed polishing, a fistful of buckles on the table, gleaming in the candlelight.

Caitlin positioned reflectors, making certain the reflected light didn't detract from the rustic atmosphere they'd created.

Satisfied at last, she picked up her Polaroid camera and stood back to give the scene her final scrutiny. The colors were cinnamon and smoke. The mood was vintage Montana. A bed designed for Big Sky dreams. A man to fulfill them.

Her eyes were riveted on Buck. She imagined herself wrapped tenderly in his powerful arms, and a portion of her heart began to bend, give, bow to this man. Caitlin snapped a Polaroid.

"Let's have a look." Buck motioned her over.

She stood in front of him, holding the print in her palm as the image came up and sharpened. Even from her topsy-turvy viewpoint, she could see the beauty and warmth. Cinnamon and smoke. Candlelight and silver.

Buck lifted his eyes to her. "Hurry," he whispered hoarsely.

Hurry? Was she working too slowly or did Buck have other things on his mind? She carried the promise of his whisper back to her Hasselblad. With trembling fingers, she squeezed the bulb activating the shutter. How could he unnerve her with a single word? How could two people determined to keep their distance from one another turn their every encounter into an emotional tempest?

She vowed to concentrate on the technical elements of her work. Hadn't she photographed far more attractive men, men of fortune, fame and power, without such strong feelings of distraction?

"We're done," she said long minutes later.

Buck set the last belt buckle and the polishing cloth down on the oak table beside the bed.

"Come here." He stood up and motioned to the bed. "Let's trade places."

"I don't understand?"

"I want to take your picture, Caitlin." He took her arm and directed her toward the bed before stepping behind the camera. "Is everything set?"

"Yes, you just need to focus, but this is silly." Feeling suddenly self-conscious, she smoothed a hand over her hair. Wispy curls had escaped the confines of her braid. "If you want to play photographer, Rawlings, you have a house full of men and three dogs willing to pose."

He smiled stiffly at her comment. "I've watched your father photograph those men for fifteen years. There aren't many surprises left."

"You expect me to sit on your bed and do something surprising?" Stepping away from the oak structure as if it were afire, she walked over to one of the reflectors. "Sounds like you have the makings of a paparazzi, Mr. Rawlings. Since my work here is done, I'll pack up my gear." Caitlin reached for a wing nut on the stand.

Buck stayed her hand, then let go and looked into her eyes. "Your dad always complained about never having any photographs of himself."

"I don't have that complaint."

"Indulge me for a moment, Caitlin." Still looking into her eyes, Buck reached around her shoulder and lifted her long braid. Slowly he took off the elastic band that restrained it and unfurled her hair, moving behind her to rake his fingers through the long cascade of waves.

Caitlin found his nearness almost unbearable. She fought the desire to flee to some remote corner of the lodge. The growing intensity of the storm made his rustic bedroom appear tranquil and safe. When she felt his fingers stroke the hair near her neck, the image of sanctuary faded. She was in an outlaw's lair.

As much as Caitlin wanted to confront the past, she wasn't eager to confront her rekindled attraction for Buck and the pain that attraction could bring.

She sat down on the comforter to escape his touch.

"You look frightened. Is it the storm?"

"I'm never afraid," she lied. Nothing in this world could bring her to her knees faster than thunder and lightning or howling winds. Tonight, nature was giving the Echo Creek area a complete show.

"Then it must be me." Buck picked up the Polaroid camera and stepped closer. "Is there something about me that frightens you?"

"Not a thing," she lied again. "You're nothing more than an employer."

He snapped a Polaroid and set it atop the bureau. "It's obvious something is upsetting you, lady."

"I'm capable of taking care of myself, Rawlings. Traveling with my father from the time I was a child taught me independence." She rose from the bed and began disassembling the nearest reflector. "No matter what the situation, I've seen it all."

"What about your work? Can you say your heart's in this job?"

The wind buffeted the lodge with a series of intense gusts. Caitlin held the folded reflector in her hands, positioning it protectively across her chest, wishing it would shield her from Buck's senseless questioning.

"What are you getting at, Buck?"

She detoured around him and set the reflector by the door.

"I want to know if I can trust you, O'Malley. I'll come right out and say it. I overheard you talking to your father last night. You seemed anxious to finish this job and get away from Echo Creek."

"Isn't that what *you* want?" When she attempted to detach the Hasselblad from the tripod, Buck caught her by the shoulder and turned her to face him.

"I just want to be assured that you won't cut corners or sacrifice quality, Caitlin."

"Trust me, I'm a professional." Caitlin swore and shrugged out of his grip. "Right now I think it's time I explained my fences, Mr. Rawlings. There's a fence around my body you have no right to touch, to sit on, to climb over or climb under.'' With the tip of her boot, she drew an imaginary line on the rug. "This is where the fence starts. Understood?"

"You haven't lost your ruthless streak, O'Malley."

"It's necessary around you. If I recall, Buck, you love nothing more than a challenge."

"And climbing fences," he added coolly.

"I am able to add an electrical charge when needed, cowboy."

High winds slashed hail against the window and howled with new ferocity. A tree creaked incessantly beyond the window. Suddenly a giant cracking noise split the air, followed by a tremendous crash that shook the lodge. What few electric lamps were in the room flickered, then went out, leaving them bathed in candlelight.

"What the hell!" Buck touched her sleeve as if to reassure her, then rushed past the bedroom door to the hall. Shouting from the first floor made Caitlin follow.

After a few chaotic moments, Joe led a group of men up the first flight of steps, their flashlight beams darting over the darkened log walls. "We think a branch came through one of the third-floor windows."

"Go down to the kitchen and stay away from the windows," Buck ordered Caitlin, his hand on the railing as the men raced past him up to the third story. Someone passed him a flashlight.

"I want to see if my room's damaged." Caitlin tried to press past Buck. "I have expensive equipment up there."

"Lester, take this woman in hand, would you?" Buck commandeered the tailor. "Don't let her near the third floor. And blow out the candles in my room before we have another disaster. Then take O'Malley down to the kitchen!"

Lightning flashed, illuminating Buck's anxious expression. He took off up the stairs as another peal of thunder ripped through the lodge.

"Of all the arrogant—" Caitlin muttered, fists clenched. She stormed down the hall to his room, Lester trailing behind her.

"Now, would you look at the buckaroo's boudoir!" he exclaimed. "I can't imagine the boss sittin' still for all this candlelight and atmosphere, Miss O'Malley."

Caitlin blew out a candle with such force the hot wax spilled onto the oak nightstand. "Lester, I don't want to discuss that insufferable—"

"Young lady, you watch your talk when it comes to Buck Rawlings." Lester stood right behind her as if he expected her to bolt to the third floor any moment. "Don't you recognize a protective male animal when you see one? Buck and me—we're made from the same cloth. Good quality cloth, you understand? If you were my woman, I wouldn't allow you near no danger, neither. Lord knows if another tree branch—"

"I am certainly *not* his woman, Lester." She blew out the remainder of the candles save one, which she handed to Lester. Quickly Caitlin stored her equipment safely in a corner of the room. "I have every right to go upstairs and check my belongings for damage."

Holding the candle, Lester guarded the doorway with the fervor of a newly deputized fanatic. "Miss O'Malley, I don't like the way you're talkin'. I'm takin' off the kid gloves right now and we're going to have ourselves a walk to the kitchen. I do believe Buck knows what's best for you."

"Okay, all right!" Caitlin gritted her teeth and allowed the normally affable Lester to guide her down the darkened stairway.

Buck felt a cold dread envelop his body as he followed the sound of male voices to Sarah's old room. He placed his palm flat against the door casing and stared at the carpet, unwilling to look inside and tear open old wounds.

"Hey, Buck, there's a lotta rain coming in here."

"What about O'Malley's cameras?" Buck asked from the hallway.

"The camera bags are safe and dry over here in the corner."

"Good. A couple of you run down to the basement and grab plywood and nails." He looked up, shone his flashlight into the room, and swallowed hard at the sight of Sarah's pencil drawing of him on the wall. His chest tightened to an ache. "Make sure of all Caitlin's things are away from the window."

He paused on the threshold, moving the beacon of light through the room. The delicate willow bed with its fanciful arches was in the same spot it had been seven years ago. He recalled his father's order that nothing be changed. Nothing except a father's relationship with his oldest son. That had changed overnight. The blame was laid and never forgotten, never lifted. The shroud of his sister's death extended over the fabric of the entire family.

The frantic actions of his crew and sporadic light prevented Buck from studying the room in detail. He'd seen enough. Reaching out, he gathered a small white rock from the top of Sarah's bookcase and grasped it tightly in his hand. The wrenching enormity of his loss overpowered him. He had to get away before he was completely overpowered. His men had the situation in hand. Buck stepped out into the hall then ran briskly down two flights of stairs and slipped out to the back porch. Lightning illuminated the heavy rain drenching the fir trees behind the lodge.

With his back braced against the heavy wooden door, Buck inhaled great gasping breaths in an effort to prevent the images, memories of that day from playing out in their tragic entirety. Slowly he allowed himself to slide downward until he sat on his haunches. A single sob escaped, lost in the roar of the wind, but he would not allow the tears that filled his eyes to spill over. Frantically he blinked them back.

At last, feeling in control, he opened his hand and stared at the small white rock in his palm. Sarah had always claimed the piece of quartz to be magic. A wishing stone. A talisman against bad weather and their father's fury. Buck slipped the rock into his shirt pocket, ran his fingers through his hair and exhaled deeply. Sarah was gone. Forever. He had to stop expecting her to lope up the stairs of the front porch, laughing, teasing, trying to grab his hat.

Hats. Sarah loved to mug with his hats. Suddenly he understood the source of the anger he'd directed at Caitlin earlier that day when she'd put his Stetson over her face. How many times in the next two weeks would the woman dredge up unwanted memories?

Was he being fair to Caitlin? Tonight in his bedroom, he'd glimpsed the Polaroid of himself. Her camera brought out the best in him. But a photograph was his image frozen in time. Buck was flesh and blood, and in real life, O'Malley's daughter was bringing out the worst in him.

Chapter Four

Under Louie the cook's watchful eye, Caitlin put another pot of coffee on the wood stove and lined mugs up for the crew. When lightning played across the bank of latticed windows that formed one wall of the large room, she shuddered and steeled herself for the boom of thunder that followed.

"Do you have oil lamps or lanterns, Lester?" she turned to ask the wiry tailor who stood in the doorway attempting to calm three fidgety dogs and keep them away from the windows. "We need more than a couple of candles to light up these cavernous rooms on the first floor."

"Buck keeps hurricane lamps and bottles of oil in the storeroom in the hall, Miss O'Malley. I'll start pullin' 'em out." Lester scurried to the hallway, followed by the dogs. Caitlin soon heard the creak of cupboard doors opening and grabbed a box of matches from atop the stove. The best way to fight her fear was to keep busy.

An hour later, the main room was cast in the soft romantic glow of lamplight and two of the older men milled around the fireplace, grasping mugs of steaming coffee and trading stories of stormy nights.

"Miss O'Malley, I'm takin' some lamps up to the second floor so the men won't be washin' up in the dark when they finish their repairs." Lester paused on the bottom step of the wide staircase. "You keep an eye on those wily dogs and stay put. If Buck catches you runnin' upstairs to look at the damage, I'm likely to be sleepin' in a crate tonight."

"Lester, don't worry. You can trust me." Caitlin motioned him up the steps. Inside the kitchen, she counted the remaining lamps on the table. She might as well make herself useful. There were some pretty dark spots on the first floor she could light up.

"Now don't be sissies," she admonished her collies, commanding them to stay in the kitchen. Taking a lamp from the table, Caitlin walked down a long hallway to place it in the larger first-floor bathroom. She glanced up at the mirror. Even in this dim light, her pinched features clearly reflected the strain of her first full day at Echo Creek Lodge. She had the feeling the night would prove to be just as challenging.

Why did Buck have to be so distrustful of her? Sure, he'd overheard her callous remark on the phone, but certainly he knew her well enough to realize she'd never compromise the quality of her work. It wasn't fair to compare her to her father. Her working style was simply more efficient, her training more technical, her equipment more state-of-the-art. These factors could only benefit Echo Creek Outfitters.

Did Buck expect her to duplicate her father's constant cajoling and storytelling? It wasn't her way. She hadn't kissed the Blarney stone. She'd kissed Buck Rawlings, had loved this man intensely, and memories of their intimacy made her efficiency all the more necessary. No, she wasn't about to ingratiate herself to a cynical loner like Buck just to prove her ability as a photographer. The proof was in the photos.

The howling wind continued to lash rain and tree branches against the massive log building. The storm formed a tunnel of focused sounds and brushed its fingers of dread across Caitlin's soul, stirring up memories of a tempestuous night in an Irish castle long ago. Staring at her image in the mirror, Caitlin recognized the panicked expression of a frightened ten-year-old child called Cat. Normally her father left her in convent schools while he was on overseas assignments, but that year he'd chosen to take her to Ireland while he photographed haunted castles for a major magazine. Her childish dread gathered momentum with each location. Then close to the end of their trip, she'd gotten lost and encountered unspeakable horrors in the most notorious of all the castles at the height of a violent squall— a squall quite similar to the one howling outside the lodge.

Caitlin prayed for an end to tonight's thunderstorm, and more important, an end to her senseless terror of storms. In his bedroom, Buck had been quick to see past her bravado and attempted to confront her fear. It was the only hole in her tightly woven armor, and she usually patched it well with brave smiles, busy work or a retreat to privacy. But there was no retreat from the terror that had shadowed her for twenty long years. Being in the presence of a virile, overprotective male like Buck only made her feel more vulnerable, and that was an emotion she had little time for. She couldn't allow him to see her in this agitated state.

Lightning arced and blossomed against the paned window reflected behind her in the mirror that stretched the length of the counter. A second bolt of light revealed the chilling silhouette of a wolfen creature against the bottom of the shower curtain. Thunder battered her senses and seemed to shake the room. Caitlin stared in terror as the animal image reflected in the mirror turned and impaled her with wild otherworldly eyes. Dumbstruck, she whirled to face it and backed against the cold tiled wall. The savage eyes remained unblinking, twin fires eerily reflecting the light of the hurricane lamp on the counter. The creature rose up on its haunches. Her splayed fingers brushed a towel hanging from the rack beside her. Grabbing it, she held it over her mouth and edged toward the open door.

"Cat, what the hell—"

A large hand touched her shoulder while another tore the towel from her mouth, unleashing her anguished scream. The sound seemed to rush upward from every cell in her body, knotting each muscle with icy fists of fear.

"What happened?" Buck demanded in the stark silence that followed. He moved her swiftly down the darkened hallway then held her at arm's length. "O'Malley, you're shaking. Are you hurt?"

"Eyes...glowing...by the shower," Caitlin stammered. She tried to pull away, longed to hide in the safest corner of the lodge, but Buck brought her up against his solid chest.

"Boss, I just left her for half a heartbeat." Lester's strangled voice broke through her fog. The small-framed man held a lamp in his hand that cast frightening shadows against the pine walls and gave his weathered face a monstrous quality.

"Something in the bathroom gave her a scare, Lester." Buck's hand made a lazy comforting circle on her back. "I just want to get Caitlin calmed down. You take a look, buddy."

"Oh, lucky me," Lester muttered, switching his toothpick from left to right before he moved furtively toward the bathroom door.

"I'll calm myself down, Rawlings, once I know what's in there." Caitlin pressed her hands against the Buckhorn Special work shirt she'd photographed so lovingly an hour earlier.

"I'm not letting go of you until you stop shaking, O'Malley." Buck relaxed his hold, but his voice had a ring of finality that made her feel twice as captive. "What happened in there?"

"A wolf—" As soon as she'd spoken the words, she felt foolish and struggled to gain control over her hammering heart.

"Miss O'Malley, the only critter in here is Farley." Lester shooshed the golden Lab down the hall. "Darn dog loves to get into the linens and tear things up a bit when he's spooked."

Buck released Caitlin and took the lamp from Lester's hand. She felt his watchful stare.

"His eyes—his eyes were g-glowing," she explained, watching Farley retreating down the darkened hallway and realizing the dog truly had little in common with his wolf cousins.

"Well, now, a canine critter's eyes can get to glowin', Miss O'Malley." Lester rubbed the stubble on his chin. "I remember a time, sittin' 'round a campfire when Buck was pretty young, and the boy thought he saw—"

"Lester, thank you for your help," Buck murmured, dismissing the older man with a nod of his head.

Caitlin caught a deep breath, leaned back against the wall and considered following the tailor to the kitchen.

"Why didn't you admit you were terrified of storms when I asked you earlier, O'Malley? I'd never have left you alone, if I'd known." Buck stood opposite her, holding the lamp, one hand on his hip. His rugged features were softened in the faint light. She realized he hadn't laughed, or spoken with contempt or ridicule. His gold-flecked eyes held a tenderness she hadn't seen for seven years.

His show of concern opened a new floodgate of vulnerability. Caitlin straightened and folded her arms across her chest.

"You put Lester in charge of my welfare, if I recall." She had the sudden urge for a cup of strong coffee and a room full of people discussing nothing more personal than the weather. "I don't need anyone's protection, Rawlings," she added with a toss of her head, and dropping her arms, began walking down the long corridor.

Even in lamplight, Buck could easily see her sashay her shapely behind as if to announce her annoyance with him. He caught up in three strides. "Maybe that's your problem, O'Malley. You won't let me or anyone else offer a little comfort. You don't have a fence around your body, lady. You have a wall six feet thick and twice as tall."

"Oh, yeah? What about you, Rawlings?" She hurried her pace, annoying him further. "You have to admit you have some pretty thick barriers of your own. When Sarah died—"

"We're not discussing my sister."

"Exactly what are we discussing, Buck?"

"Your fear of storms. I've seen you in situations that would have frightened the hell out of anyone. This doesn't make sense."

"I'm surprised my father didn't tell you the whole sordid story. He's a good man, Buck, a regular father of the year, but in this instance, your good buddy Sean O'Malley is to blame."

At the entrance to the kitchen, Buck stepped in front of her, grabbed the frame above the door and blocked her way. "What happened, Cat?"

"What difference does it make to you?" She ducked under his arm and headed for the wood stove. "You can't change the past. It happened twenty years ago."

Fine. If Cat O'Malley wanted to make this a public forum, he'd discuss it with her in front of the crew scattered around the kitchen. Buck put the lamp down, grabbed two mugs from the table and followed her to the stove. She looked up at him in surprise then poured coffee into each mug.

"Outlaws like you take their coffee black, am I right?"

The challenge in her tone irritated him. Would the woman ever realize he was trying to have a serious discussion?

"Nothing, not even sugar, changes the taste of Fogcutter."

"And I'm not in the mood to discuss an innocent case of mistaken identity. Farley looked very wolfish and—"

"The way I see it, Caitlin, I've got a right to know how big a problem this fear is for you. We've got four days of stormy weather left. If you're going to be seeing wolves in every darkened corner, you're bound to disturb the peace around here. And what about your work? Are you going to be able to concentrate on your work when you're all spooked and skittery?"

"Skittery? Listen, Rawlings, I am not your dog. I don't make a habit of getting into the linens and tearing things up when lightning strikes!" She picked up a mug, gave him a look of scorn and stalked into the Big Room. Buck scowled at the bemused faces of the men in the kitchen and followed her.

The fool woman retreated to a remote corner on the padded soffit that lined the perimeter of the room. Her dogs gathered faithfully at her feet while Farley squeezed between them and lay his chin on her knee like a lovesick suitor.

"Are you following me, Buck?" she accused, glancing up.

"Why don't we sit by the fire where it's warmer, O'Malley?"

"I don't like the way the flames reflect in your eyes, Rawlings. Gives them an unnatural glow."

Buck smiled at her remark. He sat down a short space away, took a sip of coffee and studied her for a moment. He'd loosened her braid in his bedroom before the chaos erupted, and Caitlin had left her hair loose, flowing in riotous chestnut waves around her breasts. Her ivory Aran knit sweater glowed in the soft golden light of the lamp at her elbow, giving her a look of innocence and need, making him want to reach out to protect and comfort her all the more. He moved closer, opened the wicker trunk that sat only a few feet away, pulled out a flannel quilt and offered it to Caitlin.

"I'm told my grandmother designed this specifically for the worst of storms."

After giving him a wary glance, Caitlin opened the coverlet and draped it over her lap. "Thank you," she said simply as she traced a square with her fingertip.

Over by the fireplace, Rusty put his battered fiddle to his shoulder and laughed as other crew members listed a series of musical requests.

"Somethin' sweet and low," Lester called out, "to calm this storm."

Buck smiled as Rusty played an old family favorite.

Caitlin spoke when Rusty began a second tune. "Klyde said the tree hit the window, but my cameras and belongings are fine. How soon can I sleep in my room again?"

"We'll have to get a carpenter from town out here in the next few days to do repairs. The crew put plywood up but the damage is extensive to a few of the rooms."

"Then I'll grab a sleeping bag and find a spot next to the fire tonight."

"Actually, I'm going to insist you sleep in my bed, O'Malley. You'll be warmer and safer—"

As he spoke, a gust of wind slammed against the windows in the front of the lodge and swept down the chimney, sending a flurry of sparks flying. The wrenching sound of a tree snapping and hitting the side of the lodge followed. Rusty's fiddle grew still. Crew members stepped back from the fireplace and exchanged anxious glances. A second tree split and crashed onto the porch yards from where they sat. Buck stood up.

He heard her sharp intake of breath, but by the time he'd turned to check her reaction, Cat O'Malley had pulled her mask of stoicism on.

"Here we go again, guys. Grab some flashlights and let's get a look at the damage," he shouted. "We better get some plywood up over these front windows before we lose 'em."

"This time I won't be relegated to the kitchen, Rawlings," Caitlin announced as she stepped past him. "I'm helping out."

"Don't feel like you have to prove how fearless you can be." He caught her arm.

"No, you got it wrong." Caitlin held her chin at a defiant tilt. "I simply want to show you how capable I can be, Buck."

With a grunt, Caitlin helped two men lift a panel of plywood in place over the kitchen window. Grabbing a hammer out of her belt, she began to nail the board in place. Swirling debris, a mix of mud-soaked leaves and small branches, whisked across the porch and stung her back and thighs. She swallowed hard, lowered her head and continued hammering.

Buck had handed out hard hats before assessing the damage. He'd placed one on Caitlin's head first and made a teasing comment about hardheaded women. He was referring, no doubt, to her refusal to let him comfort her during the storm.

Perhaps she was being stubborn, but she couldn't afford to give in to her attraction to the man. Mixing business with pleasure was against her work code. She'd created that code after her last summer at Echo Creek. Even though she'd acted only as her father's assistant, her emotional involvement with Buck had impacted her judgment and slowed the production until it stretched into a costly third week. Of course, concern about being overbudget had been the last thing on her mind that year. Buck Rawlings had become an obsession, the center of her world, the cornerstone of the castle of dreams she envisioned in her bright future.

A few weeks after Caitlin's return to Missoula, Sarah had died in a mysterious accident. When Buck returned home, escorting his sister's body, he asked Caitlin not to attend the funeral. In a space of days, she'd lost her precious best friend and Buck had cut himself out of her life without an explanation or a glance backward. Caitlin's castle had crumbled. Her future had paled.

Grief was too weak a word to describe the devastation that overwhelmed her the final week of that summer.

Caitlin hammered another nail into the side of the lodge with more force than necessary. Many mornings, she'd stood at this very window with Sarah when they were sixteen, looking out over the lake and planning another adventure together. At twenty-three, her focus had shifted to Buck and every spare minute before breakfast was spent locked in his arms or sharing a long sensual shower. Would she ever be able to banish the memories of their intimacy? After the hurt and pain of his abandonment, wasn't it insane for her to pick up his brand of soap in department stores and to inhale his tangy wood scent?

Caitlin dropped a handful of nails onto the rain-soaked porch, then frantically blinked back tears as she searched the planks with numbed fingers. No man would hurt her in that way again.

She'd moved two thousand miles away to New York, a city of concrete canyons and cold stares. When her assignments began to include portraits of celebrities, every male subject was measured against the template emblazoned on her mind by a summer of smoothing her palms over the hard masculine planes of Buck Rawlings's powerful body.

How many years would this torment continue? When the pain grew sharper, she'd found new ways to cut memories of Buck out of her life. But the temptation to thumb through her father's catalogs for Echo Creek Outfitters was too great. After a few years, she'd realized nothing could stop the images from fleeting across the landscape of her mind. Distancing herself from the land and people she loved would not purge Buck's memory. She'd stopped accepting East Coast and European assignments, gave up her New York apartment and moved back to Missoula to be close to her father and her beloved Big Sky country.

Feeling blindly in the dark, she recovered a half-dozen nails and immediately resumed hammering the plywood panel over the window. Caitlin wished it were as easy to board up old memories. Tiny plywood panels for the mind. The thought was silly, but nothing else had worked. If she could board up her memories, she'd be able to look at Buck Rawlings without pain and regret, and perhaps she'd be able to weather a storm without terror.

Buck had urged everyone to hurry inside as soon as the boards were in place. After completing her duties, Caitlin slipped past the others and continued on to the huge store-room where the Echo Creek equipment was sorted and tagged for use in specific photo shoots. The beam of her flashlight crisscrossed over a sea of backpacks and sleeping bags. She chose a premium goose-down bag, grabbed a set of colorful thermal wear and slipped into a first-floor bath-room to shower and change.

An hour earlier, Buck had ordered her to sleep in his bed. After the little conversation she'd had with herself on the porch, her path was clear. Only a monumental fool would choose to sleep in the bedroom of a former lover. The storm be damned. Caitlin walked boldly back to the Big Room, planning to unfurl her sleeping bag and bed down alone for the night.

Buck was standing in front of the hearth, staring into the dying embers. The soft firelight heightened the slant of his high cheekbones and the thrust of his chiseled jaw. The waves in his freshly washed hair glistened blue-black in the faint glow of an oil lamp on the mantle. While photo-graphing him in the Buckhorn Special, she thought him ruggedly handsome but attributed much of his appeal to the sensual setting she'd created. But here, silhouetted against a stark backdrop of stone on stone and crimson embers, he was magically compelling.

The three dogs rolled on their backs as she approached, inviting her gentle touch. The massive room was empty, the lamps extinguished save the one on the mantel. Caitlin heard showers running and the voices of men talking good-naturedly on the second floor. She didn't want a confrontation with Buck. On the other hand, she didn't want a cozy scene. Caitlin simply wanted the man to leave her alone, with the dogs left behind to comfort her, of course. Perhaps boldness and honesty were the best approach.

"Buck, why don't you stick some long-burning logs on that fire?" she drawled casually as she untied the sleeping bag, hazarding a look in his direction. The man did not look pleased. "I'll need the extra warmth tonight."

Nature chose that moment to begin a new onslaught of lightning, thunder and howling winds. Caitlin swore softly beneath her breath. The impact of her statement was lost, unable to compete with the cacophony of thunder. Her fingers fumbled with the zipper on the sleeping bag.

"If I remember," she muttered, attempting to keep the conversation away from discussion of sleeping arrangements, "the catalog says these are no-stick zippers. Do you stand by your guarantee?"

Buck watched her struggle for a moment. She had the nerve to strut around the lodge in Echo Creek thermal underwear. The teal blue top was designed to double as stylish outerwear. That was fine for a man, but on Caitlin, underwear was underwear. The woman hadn't inherited her father's common sense. He made no move to help her with the sleeping bag's zipper.

"It'd be smarter to start a new fire in my room, O'Malley," Buck countered, picking up a poker and scattering the embers. Is this what he wanted to do with the dying embers of their past love? he asked himself. Scatter the old memories and rekindle a new flame?

"You're sleeping in my bed, lady. Safe, warm and secure. I'll just curl up on the floor across the room. C'mon, Farley." He took the oil lamp from the mantel, crossed the room, took the sleeping bag from her hand and stuck it under his arm. "Call your dogs and we can head upstairs."

Wordlessly, she took the sleeping bag from the crook of his arm and tossed it onto the mission-style sofa facing the dark fireplace.

She rested her hands on her hips, her stance defiant as she faced him. Her still-damp hair was a tangle of waves, softening her stern expression.

"Buck, you can dictate the catalog shoot and menu selections and anything that pertains to the work at hand. But when it comes to where I sleep and anything personal, I'll decide what's best."

"I don't think so." He stalked across the room and grabbed the down sleeping bag off the sofa. "You're afraid to admit your fears. You want to put on this big brave front, O'Malley. You'd probably toss and turn down here in the cold and the dark, unwilling to climb the stairs and admit I was right."

There was a visible battle of emotions in her features as she glanced at the darkened room and scattered embers. Her collies jumped up and followed Farley to the landing.

"Smart dogs, foolish choices," she chided, stepping toward him. "You know, there's no need for both of us to spend a sleepless night, Buck. I can find some spare room on the first floor."

"We're not playing musical rooms." Buck touched her elbow and edged her forward. "The way I see it, O'Malley, any night I sleep under the same roof with you is going to be a little bit sleepless."

"What are you saying?"

"You bring out the worst in me."

She stopped on the landing and gave him a look of surprise. "If this is your worst, Rawlings, you've mellowed."

"*Mellow* isn't in my vocabulary." Buck shook his head. "For one thing, you make my overprotective streak go on full alert."

"I wondered if you were this concerned about your entire crew."

"Very funny." He opened his bedroom door and motioned her inside. Three wiggling dog bodies squeezed past her. "Hey, you mutts, have some manners," he growled at the dogs. All three jumped on the bed and jostled for space at the foot.

Buck closed the door and set the lamp on the table beside the large four-poster bed. Immediately an uncomfortable silence stretched between them. He watched her stare at the comforter then touch it hesitantly, as if to test for snakes or wolves. He busied himself with stacking wood on the grate and starting a fire. Minutes later, when the flame was growing steadily, he turned and found Caitlin tucked inside the covers, her gleaming chestnut waves rippling over his pillow.

Buck recalled the fit of her body against his and the soft sounds she made while she slept. No woman had filled his arms so completely. When had she stopped being his? Had he ever really let go?

"There's nothing wrong with this zipper, O'Malley." He spread the sleeping bag in front of the fireplace. She didn't respond to his comment. Buck let the silence stand a minute longer before walking to the bed and bending to scratch Farley's head.

"Warm enough?" he asked gruffly.

She tossed back the comforter, leaving a blanket and flannel sheets covering her. "These thermals are cooking me."

Buck reached out to touch the fabric on her sleeve. "No wonder. You chose our expedition weight. I usually reserve those for hiking in the snow."

"It was dark in the storeroom."

"And you were shaken by the storm, right?"

She glared at him and moved away from the edge of the bed. "I should go up to the third floor and get my own nightshirt."

"It's freezing up there. Wait until morning, O'Malley. Relax. Let's just pretend we're a couple of teenagers on a church camping trip."

"Okay, we're on a camping trip. Where are the chaperones?"

"They're at the foot of the bed. Three of them. We could also pretend we're friends."

"Pretend? We used to be *good* friends, Rawlings. About a century ago."

"Two centuries." Buck nodded and smiled at the memory. He sat on the edge of the bed, resisting the urge to touch and caress her hair, to cup her cheek in his hand. "You were such a cocky kid, O'Malley, when you and your dad first arrived in Missoula."

"I thought I was a fairly mature sixteen-year-old." She remained resting on her side but raised up on her elbow and smiled softly.

"You were a paradox. Half sophisticate, half tomboy with a touch of bobcat. As young women go, you don't find many who can lasso a hood ornament in a strapless prom dress and four-inch heels."

"That story's been embellished over the years. I was wearing three-inch heels."

Buck reached over to the bedside table and picked up one of the belt buckles he'd been polishing earlier. He studied the design thoughtfully. "With all your fancy manners, O'Malley, and our age difference, whatever attracted you to me?"

With a chuckle, she rolled onto her back and stared up at the ceiling. "There was always something about you, Buck, something wild and untamed and tempting. You'd walk into the Black Bear Café and within ten minutes, there'd be trouble. Your car was too fast, your music too loud and your women were always a little too willing."

"*Women?* Why the plural?"

"I was sixteen. You were twenty-one and unattainable. One woman was too many in my imagination. I remember how they looked at you."

"Lord, you make me sound like some street hood."

"Stop trying to sound innocent." She threw the spare pillow at him. "I was always partial to bad boys. Remember *Bonanza* on TV? I thought the Cartwright boys were much too nice."

"Even Little Joe?"

"*Especially* Little Joe. Those guys had it too easy. I was more taken with the men in black passing through Virginia City, the kind with trouble on their tails. I always had a soft spot for those lonesome strays, the restless edgy ones who made James Dean look tame."

"So you're putting me in the same class as a bunch of rowdy, no-good drifters?" He moved closer, then reached out to touch her cheek with the tips of his fingers.

"No one's all bad." She surprised him by leaning her cheek into the curve of his palm. "Sometimes those men played hero parts. But they never settled. Ever notice that? They always seemed to move on. Tumbleweeds."

Buck wove his fingers into the hair at her temple. Lamplight glittered in her large tawny eyes and changed the high color in her cheeks to a golden pink. She'd lassoed his heart years ago but he'd chosen to cut the rope.

"Some men are simply designed to spend solitary lives," he said quietly.

"And some are designed to break promises." She spoke in a husky whisper.

The teasing had ended. Buck heard the pain in her voice, saw the sadness in her large shimmering eyes. The wick on the oil lamp flickered, deepening the shadows. With her hair fanned out over the pillow and the flannel sheet drawn demurely over her breasts, she looked like a bride from another century. He took her hand, brought it to his mouth and kissed her fingertips.

Seven years ago, she'd given herself to him completely in this very bed, trusted him to initiate her in the ways of loving. The memory of that sweet moment of surrender washed over him, followed by a flood of guilt.

"I didn't do right by you, Cat, but I had my reasons."

"I wish you would have explained." She pulled her hand away and looked down at it. "You hurt me, Buck. I can't forget your coldness—"

"There was no easy way to end it." He stood and pulled the comforter up to her shoulders. Anger surged through him. "You knew what kind of man I was before you got involved with me."

"I never tried to change you, Buck."

"Oh, you changed me all right, O'Malley—you and your risk taking."

It was time to pull out the stops and tell her the truth. Buck stepped back from the bed, set his hands on his hips and faced her.

"Because of you, my sister lost her life. If you don't think death changes a man, you're more insensitive than I thought."

Chapter Five

"**D**amn you!" Caitlin tossed the covers aside and rose up on her knees on the mattress. "How dare you! Seven years, Buck, seven years, and you wouldn't talk about it. When I went to the funeral home you made it clear you blamed me...then nothing. No chance to clear myself." She choked on the words and felt the fire of unshed tears scorch her throat. "Tell me now, once and forever, what makes you think I'm to blame?"

"You know damn well why! How many times had I warned you about involving my sister in your hare-brained adventures? You had a big influence on Sarah, O'Malley."

Through tear-filled eyes, Caitlin watched Buck cross the narrow space of carpet and stand next to the bed, his stance confrontive. "You were like twins. She idolized you, even left her family and followed you to the University of Washington rather than stay in Montana."

"Sarah encouraged *me* to go the UW." Caitlin sat back on her heels and quickly wiped away her tears. Searching for words, she looked down at her hands and found herself nervously pleating the blanket in her lap. "When I met your sister, she was as adventurous as I was, Buck. And she got more adventurous with time. Are you blind to the truth? Sarah was just like *you!* Wild and impulsive."

"That's bull!" Buck slapped his hand against the oak post not far from her head, causing the whole bed to shake.

Her collies growled protectively and moved to her side followed by Farley. Caitlin reached out to assure them but sensing her distress, they drew even closer. She took a deep breath.

"We both loved her, Buck, and she loved us. What difference does it make who influenced her more?" Caitlin hesitated. Was it best to tell him about the letters she'd brought and the truth about Sarah? No. This was not the time. "It's over and done with," she proclaimed. "We can't bring her back by placing blame."

The sweet sad refrain of Rusty's fiddle tugged at the edge of her awareness. Lester was singing a mournful Patsy Cline tune. Caitlin bit her lip and felt a part of herself fall to pieces just like the words in the song. She watched Buck tilt his head and guessed that the lyrics were having the same effect on him.

"I vowed never to have anything to do with you, O'Malley, to keep you off my mountain, and never to speak my sister's name again. But now that I have, let me finish, dammit!" Buck's hand remained clasped on the bedpost, his head bent, tucked against his shoulder. He sighed and looked at her with eyes filled with pain. "I *don't* want to blame you. I can't forget we had something between us years ago—"

"You referred to it as an *infatuation* this afternoon."

"Let me talk, Caitlin. You've been wanting to dig up old history and put it on the table since you arrived. That's exactly what I'm doing, lady."

"Then finish digging, Rawlings," Caitlin said curtly.

"Don't be flip about it, O'Malley. I've been haunted by my sister's death for seven long years. It's torn my family apart. Remember how close I was with my dad? That's all changed. He blames *me*."

"Looks like the need to place blame is a family trait." Caitlin couldn't resist the pointed remark. Buck's words were slicing into the core of her with deadly accuracy. Anger and sarcasm were her only defense against a tearful reaction. Tears were a rare phenomenon for her, better left for a private moment or held in check.

She couldn't forget he was her employer, that she needed to present a confident, professional front at all times. Her father was depending on her for the income and insurance. What was she letting herself in for? In a matter of hours, Buck Rawlings had seen her frightened senseless and driven to tears. Caitlin tried to garner her strength and steel herself against any further hurt.

She looked back up at Buck's anguished features. "Go on," she urged, keeping her voice cold and flat.

"I can't let go of your last visit to the lodge, Caitlin. You set a new record for recklessness." His words lashed out at her. "Sarah would never have pulled that stunt on Shepherd's Rock if she hadn't seen you risking your neck weeks earlier."

"Shepherd's Rock? Above the south trail?" Caitlin felt a cold fist envelop her heart. Please—anywhere but there. She hadn't known. All this time she'd assumed the accident had occurred on a higher slope. She rose up on her knees again at the shock of her discovery. A month before Sarah's death, Caitlin had teasingly challenged her friend at Shepherd's Rock.

"Oh, God, Zorro." She sobbed the nickname she alone used for Sarah Rawlings. "I didn't know...I n-need to be by myself." She slipped off the edge of the bed and stepped blindly in the direction of the bedroom door. The one person who could comfort her at this moment had died seven years ago. The realization of her loss hit her fully. The box she'd tucked into a corner of her mind opened and her secret guilt unraveled.

Buck stepped in front of her and wrapped his hands around her upper arms. "I—I thought you *knew* the location."

"No one told me. I doubt they told my father. You Rawlings men—you and your father and brother—" she shook her head and covered her tear-streaked face with her hands "—you were all like a wall of ice." The dogs nudged her thighs and whined. Caitlin murmured assurance to them, then struggled to free herself of Buck's grasp. She didn't want him or anyone else to see her like this. "Let me go, Rawlings."

"No, I won't let go. Not just yet."

Caitlin closed her eyes. She would not allow herself to seek his strength. He'd caused her this pain tonight. She'd be a fool to feel comforted by his touch. Her mind was too muddled to sort out what was wise or foolish. For long minutes, he held her against him, simply rocking her. Yet she felt the anger in him, the straining tension of his muscular back and arms, and knew his anger was directed at her.

The noses of three concerned canine chaperones pressed against her legs, vying to be the most comforting.

"I'm sorry I surprised you like this," Buck murmured as he edged her back toward the bed. "Sarah loved you. Her last words—she cried out to you before she fell, Cat."

Caitlin recalled the image of Sarah on Shepherd's Rock that last summer. No two friends had understood one another better. She missed the warmth and humor, the secrets and good times. Caitlin sobbed against Buck's shoulder at the thought of Sarah crying out to her, at the thought of not being there in that last desperate moment. "Please, Buck, no more. No more. I just want you to go." She sat down on the mattress.

It was Farley who jumped onto the bed and stepped onto her lap and tried insistently to push her hands away from her face with his muzzle. Buck attempted to pull the dog away but the Lab was riveted to the spot.

"No, Buck. Leave him." Caitlin brushed tears from her cheek. "Farley's just worried. It's natural—for dogs."

She watched Buck reach into his dresser drawer and pull out a white handkerchief. As he tucked it into her clenched fist, she looked up and caught a glimpse of Buck's haunted expression and turned away, unwilling to absorb the ricochet of his anger and grief. Her own soul was still unraveling.

While he gathered the sleeping bag and clothes, Rusty's fiddle began a heartbreaking lament that started her tears anew. At last, she heard the bedroom door close and allowed herself to edge toward a tormented sleep. She was thankful he hadn't attempted to comfort her. That would only have made her decision more difficult.

Tomorrow she'd make other sleeping arrangements. Tomorrow she'd weigh the possibility of leaving Echo Creek and Buck Rawlings forever.

Buck set a breakfast tray on the bedside table and stood back a moment before waking Caitlin from her fitful sleep. He was tempted to leave the coffee and roll by the bed, and avoid all possibility of another confrontation. His anger had festered through much of the night.

Last night, he'd simply meant to be honest about his feelings, but something had gone very wrong. He'd ambushed her, in much the same ruthless manner his own father had used on him since Sarah's death. Is this what grief did to the Rawlings men or did he purposely want to sever his ever-growing attraction for Cat O'Malley?

Bending down, he shook Caitlin's shoulder, making no attempt to be gentle. Even in the mist of awakening, she eyed him with a look of contempt, totally void of warmth or recognition, then sat up, draping her knees over the edge of the bed. She glanced at her watch. "Hell, I never wake up this late, Rawlings."

"Louie sent you a Continental breakfast," he said matter-of-factly, handing the black-and-gold Laurel Burch mug to her. "Lester said to tell you this is a double tall Amaretto skinny with extra foam."

She sipped the cappuccino and sighed. "The power must have come back on."

"Klyde got up early and drove the generator over to Doc Morrow's place. His caretaker took a look at it and fixed the problem."

"So the storm let up?" She glanced toward the window then set the mug back on the tray. She tossed her head and brushed the hair back from her face. With her chin tilted, her heart-shaped face was awash with diffused morning light.

"The storm..." Buck felt entranced by the sight of her uptilted breasts, straining against the fabric of the bright teal thermal top, their full curves silhouetted against the light-colored sheets. "It's still wet and windy but the sound-and-light show is over."

"I don't want to sit here eating breakfast and discussing the weather. Last night changed everything, Buck."

"I had to be honest. I don't think our conversation is finished though, Caitlin—"

"But *we* are, Buck. I need to call my father in Missoula to discuss the possibility of turning this shoot over to another professional."

"You fought to convince me you were qualified to replace him."

"I am qualified, Rawlings, but I can't work with you. Not after last night. And every time I look up at Shepherd's Rock—I can't bear the thought of going out there today."

"I've been staring at that accursed rock for seven years, O'Malley."

"If I leave, I don't want Dad to lose his insurance benefits, understand?"

"You make me out to be a heartless bastard."

"If you find a replacement for me, then Dad will be forced to share the income."

Buck realized she was reasoning aloud, arguing with her sense of duty to her father.

"Forget it. You're not going anywhere, O'Malley. The road is blocked by a tree two miles north of the Morrow place. You can't even get to Twodot—and the phone's still not working." Buck stepped to the window and pulled the curtain aside. He wasn't entirely surprised by her desire to leave but found himself torn by his own mixed emotions. "The truth is, I don't want you to leave, Caitlin. Not under these circumstances. I was pretty harsh last night."

"It was nothing short of a brutal verbal assault."

"Hey, I apologized. Now if you're interested in completing your father's assignment, we've got a crew of tired, hung-over models waiting for you to make an appearance."

"Hung over?"

"They threw an all-night poker game. Louie's a few hundred dollars richer, as usual."

"And you expect me to photograph them today?"

"I figure it's a good day to shoot rain gear."

Caitlin pondered for a moment. "Rather than posing, I guess you could pull out the chain saws and have them cut up the tree on the porch. The light would be good in that area and most of those mountain parkas and ponchos have hoods to hide the effects of the morning after." She paused and gave Buck a pointed stare. "The morning after," she repeated. "I guess we're all suffering in one way or another."

"So you'll stay another day?"

"Sounds like I have to. There's a tree blocking my exit, Rawlings, like an act of God."

"An act of God? Is that the *only* thing keeping you here?" Buck glanced down at the untouched tray beside the bed. "What about us, Caitlin? Last night, you talked about qualities that attracted you to me. Is there anything left? Any feelings?''

"Why do you ask? Are you so desperate for female companionship, Buck, that you'd settle for someone you despise, someone who can never hold your trust again?"

Buck ignored her sharp response. He didn't want to get mired in talk of the past, of what might have been. Clearing his throat, he nodded toward his closet. "I'll have Lester bring your clothes, cameras and gear down from the third floor. I want you to use my room—"

"I'd rather sleep upstairs."

"You don't have a lot of options, O'Malley. The workmen from town have to cut through that fallen tree on the road in order to get here to repair your room. When they accomplish that, you can expect the repair work to take a few days at least. There are two rooms on the third floor that are habitable and I'm giving those to the workmen. Chase will be here tomorrow most likely so I can't give his room away. Your only other choice is sleeping on the pool table. Pete slept there last night after the poker game—"

"Don't joke about it, Rawlings. I slept there seven years ago. Green felt and lonesome strays don't make for restful nights."

"You think I slept easy last night outside in the hallway? Tonight I'll sleep in here by the fireplace."

"I'd be more comfortable if we weren't sleeping in the same room."

"Why can't we just call a truce, O'Malley, and make the best of it until your room is repaired?"

"How can I make the best of it when you say I bring out the worst in you, Buck? Last night certainly wasn't the church camping trip you promised."

The woman was exasperating. Buck was tempted to sleep alone downstairs but he felt some infernal need to protect her. He recalled a time his brother Chase put a snake and a bumblebee together in a jar and shook it up. With a sigh, Buck thought how it must have felt to be one of those ill-fated critters. Cat O'Malley had a stinger no sane snake wanted to tangle with.

"We'll mend some fences tonight, Caitlin," he said, with a hint of venom, before he turned and left the room.

During a short break for sandwiches, Caitlin left the crew on the porch of the lodge and walked alone to a clearing overlooking a vista of Medicine Bowl Lake and cloud-topped mountains. Farley and her collies stuck close, as they had since her confrontation with Buck the night before.

"You dogs must think we're a couple of ill-mannered mongrels, huh?" She spoke in a high, excited voice as she clapped her hands. "Fighting during valuable sleep time then dancing carefully around each other the next day. I wonder who the *real* dumb animals are around here?"

Farley shook his whole body in response. Caitlin smiled, knowing it had secretly annoyed Buck to see his dog side with the enemy and ignore his master's attempts to win him back. She turned to her largest collie.

"C'mon, I know the big beefy Burrito baby knows best. Hey, tell me what well-bred dogs would do in this sticky situation. What's the answer, girl? Do I pack up and leave, or do I—" Here, away from the stares of the men at the lodge, her voice cracked. "Or do I follow my gut feelings and give Buck another chance?"

Burrito barked three times, then sat and offered her paw. The gesture touched Caitlin. She felt raw and empty today, scoured by Buck's ruthless accusations. Kneeling in wet grass beneath a cottonwood, she stroked the white fur on the dog's throat then buried her face in the thick black ruff of Burrito's neck.

"I want to stay at Echo Creek, girl, but not like this." She lifted her head and touched her nose to the dog's muzzle. "I want it to be just like it was before everything went wrong."

"Miss O'Malley?" Lester's familiar drawl interrupted her private moment. "Louie and the boys wanted me to bring you some lunch."

"How thoughtful." Straightening, Caitlin inhaled sharply and looked at the tailor's inquisitive expression. "Lester, did you hear me talking to my dogs?"

"I heard 'nough, but I'm not one to repeat a person's musings. It's jes' not my way."

"Do you understand the situation—what's happening between Buck and me?"

"Well, now, I pride myself on my understandin' of men and women." Lester took a bite out of the sandwich he'd brought for her and chewed it thoughtfully. "But, you see, I'm also pretty smart about stayin' outta a body's personal business. Learned that in the lingerie factory in Chicago thirty years ago. Two feet of elastic can be turned into a mighty powerful weapon. I'll show ya my scar sometime, but that's another story."

"I'm sure it is," Caitlin said with a chuckle. She picked up a stick off the ground and tossed it toward the clearing beyond the cottonwood, then smiled when the trio of canines raced past her in pursuit. "I admire your personal code of not getting involved in Buck's affairs, Lester, but it's a real shame because you probably know Buck Rawlings better than anyone else."

"Miss O'Malley, I swear Buck's got a black belt in being mysterious. Course I'm so much like the man that I could answer your questions blindfolded and blind."

Lester's colorful expression only served to remind Caitlin of her father's retinopathy and the doctor's prognosis of blindness. She had to stay at Echo Creek. Her honor was at stake, as well. She'd agreed to substitute for Sean O'Malley. She'd given her word. Backing out of a business agreement would tarnish her sense of honor. How she would spend her days *and nights* peaceably with Buck was the real question here.

Lester took another bite of her sandwich and gazed out at the cloud-enshrouded vista. "Behind that wall of mystery is a man who wants to hold you, protect you and show you some tenderness, Miss O'Malley. But ya move away like a skitterish mare and keep yourself all busy with your fancy camera gear. At meals, you sit on the end of the bench givin' your dogs more attention than you do Buck.''

"I thought I was being more subtle than that."

"I'm the expert at being subtle, Miss O'Malley. Tailors know all about takin' a nip and a tuck. You've seen me work my magic. Nothing rash or dramatic. Life's kinda like this big piece of fabric. Some things like nap and bias and texture...well now, let's just say that's what the dry goods man gives you. The basic package. But you still got a lot to say about the pattern you pick out and if you want your life to be casual or constrictin'. See what I'm sayin?"

"I think so."

Lester finished the last of her sandwich. "Of course, the fabric of life isn't about clothes. It's the whole bolt of cloth. If you're wantin' to be with Buck, like ya were tellin' Burrito, you gotta put your bolts side by side and see what happens. Now, in my personal view, Buck's black leather. He's rawhide.''

"Lester, this is foolish—"

"No. Askin' your critter for advice on a man and woman romance is *foolish,* Miss O'Malley."

Caitlin laughed and tossed the stick a second time.

"Okay, now," Lester continued, sticking a toothpick in the corner of his mouth, "maybe you've lived in Montana some, and ya love Echo Creek clothing, but, Miss O'Malley, you are silk, silk the color of magnolia blossoms, and you are pearls, cultured and feminine. Nothin' you do can hide that part of you."

Caitlin felt her hackles rise at his remark. All her life, she'd fought labels, such as well-bred, aristocratic and refined. She wanted no reminders of her mother's blue-blooded family who'd never approved of the easy-mannered Sean O'Malley. After her mother's death, they'd passed sentence on her progeny, as well. Young Caitlin had been forced to suffer through every conceivable lesson on etiquette and grace, dressage and French cooking, ballet and ballroom dancing, opera appreciation and Latin languages. Where her Irish grandmother had nestled her close and told her romantic stories of daring women in pursuit of almost mythical men, her proper Bostonian grandmother Covington had judged her every word and movement in her never-ending search for signs of poor breeding.

Would she ever rid herself of the Covingtons' early influences?

"So, Lester." She attempted to keep her irritation from showing itself in her voice. "I stick my bolt of silk next to Buck's bolt of black leather. What does that prove?"

"You gotta test the fabrics together, maybe baste a few seams . . . nothing permanent at first. You need to understand how Buck has shaped his life—and why. I've seen leather and silk work in real life and in the movies. What about the Sundance Kid and that schoolteacher? And then there was Bogie and Hepburn in *The African Queen*."

"But Buck and me—we're not people of epic proportion, Lester. We're not battling a river in Africa or running from lawmen in the Old West."

"It's clear you two are runnin' from something." He took the toothpick out of his mouth and gestured with it. "Grief is a powerful thing, more powerful than a rogue river clear on the other side of the world."

"Sarah's death has had more impact on Buck than I realized, Lester."

"Damn straight. He won't even say her name. Never has. But I suggest you put that tragedy aside or find some way to overcome it. The man *will* say *your* name and I betcha someday soon he's gonna say it with tenderness, like he used to."

"Thanks for your insight, Lester."

"S'been a pleasure, Miss O'Malley." He tipped his hat rakishly. "I reckon we best get back to the lodge."

"I'll be right along." Caitlin watched the wiry man take a meandering path through a patch of wildflowers, then glanced down at Echo Creek's combination compass and

thermometer on the zipper of her mountain parka. Buck
had slipped it on this morning against her protestations. She
turned in a circle and watched the needle of the compass
spin, then stopped abruptly and observed the needle's search
for direction. Not unlike her own search, she mused.

After calling the dogs, she began walking, following Lester's path through a vibrant bouquet of red and yellow. She
had a feeling things would heat up quickly with Buck if she
decided to allow him to show his "true colors." There had
been a look of longing in his eyes, a hint of challenge in his
deep voice when she'd photographed him in hunter green
rain gear this morning.

Once again, Buck had impressed her with his fairness.
Though he was angry with the crew for drinking and playing poker all night, he'd made his feelings known in a brief
announcement then organized the cleanup effort with his
usual compelling presence. The more hung-over men were
given light work and less conspicuous poses in the photo
layouts.

So he played fair with other men. Would that same sense
of honor carry into his personal dealings with her? Could
she trust him with her heart? Half a dozen years ago, he'd
taken a scissors to their relationship without her consent.
She looked down. The needle on the compass grew still and
pointed at her. What she decided today could change the
tenor of the shoot for the next two weeks—or change the
rest of her life.

Leather and silk. The images that came to mind more
than intrigued her. It had worked once long ago. They'd
woven their fabrics together in a sweet, sensual tapestry.
Would it work again or had Sarah's death unraveled their
rich design forever?

Why had the advice of a toothpick-wielding tailor touched
her so deeply? Buoyed by a vision of Katharine Hepburn at
the helm of the *African Queen,* Caitlin felt newly committed to completing the Echo Creek catalog and opening herself to Buck's long lingering looks.

* * *

Buck finished giving instructions to the two-man work crew from town who'd arrived after lunch to repair the damage to the third floor. As he walked down the second flight of stairs, he glanced through the open door of his bedroom and paused, his stomach lurching. Just outside the window facing the front of the lodge, Cat O'Malley was perched precariously on a high limb in his ancient oak.

Holding on to his Stetson, he took the stairs three at a time. His boots hit the planks of the front porch seconds later, startling crew members who backed away from the base of the oak, mumbling to one another in hushed tones.

"O'Malley!" he shouted, leaning over the porch rail and staring up through the tree's foliage at a pair of Echo Creek's steel-gray Laredo twill trousers. She didn't even know how to dress for tree climbing! The woman was insane and would soon threaten *his* sanity.

Swearing loudly, Buck bounded over the rail and slid down the short incline into a gnarled root at the base of the ancient tree. Pressing his palms against the trunk, he assessed the situation from a new vantage point. She was clearly in danger. "What the hell are you doing up there?"

"I'm perfectly safe, Buck," she retorted sharply.

"You didn't answer my question!" Grabbing hold of a lower branch, he began to climb.

"I needed a wide shot of the crew." Her voice gained volume.

"The shot sheet shows men on the *ground*. It doesn't call for any bird's-eye views or any damn *wide* shot."

"Stop where you are, Buck. I'm almost finished."

"Oh, no you're not! You're not finished with *me*, O'Malley." Adrenaline shot through him as he climbed within a yard of her, following the familiar path of limbs and whorls he'd used as a boy.

"How can I get my shot with you shaking the tree?"

"Put the camera down and hold on. You're not getting paid to risk your neck."

"Don't start with your overprotective blatherings, Rawlings. I'm an expert tree climber—"

"I really doubt that and right now I don't want to have to turn into an expert at rescuing a woman who holds that foolish notion." Inches from her perch, Buck stopped when he encountered her boot blocking his path.

"In fifteen years, you haven't changed a bit. Move your foot," he demanded, "or I'll toss your boot into the next county."

"Before you make a fool of yourself, Rawlings, why don't you look down? See, there's a big opening in the foliage here and it gives me the perfect view of the—"

"I don't care if you see the Four Horsemen of the Apocalypse down there. You're going to reverse your sweet little behind and climb back down this tree with me, O'Malley. Nice and slow and safe. If you were an expert tree climber, you would've realized you're sitting on a limb weakened by last night's storm. This oak lost a hefty-size branch and some minor branches, as well. *That's* why there's a big opening in the foliage!"

"I was aware of that and tested every limb before putting my weight on them. I simply thought the catalog needed a wide shot of the damage to make sense of the shots of the men," she continued as if she hadn't heard him, "to pull the story together."

"The story? We're selling clothes, not telling stories for our customer's entertainment. O'Malley, get your butt moving—*now!*"

She appeared too hesitant. With one final thrust, he hoisted himself up to a limb opposite her.

Buck was unprepared for the sight of her. She held her camera protectively in one hand while grasping a tree limb with her outstretched arm. The crucial fourth button on her crimson corduroy shirt had come undone, allowing him an expansive view of her lacy red bra and the swell of her full breasts. Several strands of lustrous chestnut hair had worked loose from her braid and waved around her delicate heart-shaped face, flowing to the tops of her breasts.

Caitlin's large golden eyes reflected calm. He found none of the rancor her voice had displayed while he'd stormed her treetop fortress. Looking into her serene features, he felt his anger dissipate, replaced by an unexpected sense of quietude. In the green cocoon of intimacy created by the oak's lush foliage, she looked ethereal, like a mythical creature come to work her magic...on him.

"What am I going to do with you, Cat?" he asked, tipping the brim of his hat back with his thumb.

She spoke matter-of-factly and looked into the camera's viewfinder. "Right now you can move your boot three inches to the right so I can finish this wide shot."

He shook his head and decided to comply. "All right, get your infernal shot. Hey, guys," he shouted to the men on the ground, "get back into position. O'Malley's taking your picture."

He watched her knit her brows and bite her exquisitely shaped lip as she focused on her work. Moments later, she dismissed the models, snapped the protective lens cover in place, slipped the camera's strap over her shoulder and looked at Buck expectantly, her head tilted playfully. "Now what? Are you going to let your testosterone get the better of you, Rawlings? Plan to drag me down this tree trunk by my hair?"

He let her smug smile stand for a thin minute before he reached out and caressed the satin of her cheek with his work-roughened palm. "You've always looked at home in dangerous places, Cat. Straddling boulders, rafting grade-five rapids, sitting in treetops, and the most dangerous place of all—" he slid his fingers down her jawline and tilted her chin to face him "—lying in my arms."

"Buck—" her voice was a raspy entreaty "—the men—"

"Damn the men." He dragged his callused thumb across the sensual curve of her lower lip and smiled at the sudden darkening of her tawny eyes. Her lips parted under the pressure of his thumb. There was a change, a willingness in the set of her shoulders, the tilt of her head, that hadn't been there before.

And within his own being, some gate opened, a portion of his resistance melted away.

"I had a thought this morning, O'Malley. About us."

Like some moonsick fool, Caitlin felt tethered to his every word. The sensible businesswoman in her wanted to flee the intimate confines of this canopy of leaves and the hex of Buck Rawlings's mesmerizing touch. Some aching, empty female part of her yearned to shut out the rest of the world and surrender to the dark man in the black leather vest.

Leather and satin. Perhaps this was the moment. The beginning of a new tapestry. Or the final unraveling of the old. Gently she stopped his fingers from continuing their tantalizing pattern on her mouth. She curled her fingers through his and captured his hand in her lap. She let the silence stretch, studying the firmness of his jaw, the challenge in his eyes.

"I was willing," he continued, the lines of strain around his mouth softening, "to go beyond a truce, to take a chance on seeing if things might work between us, but then you climbed the tree."

"Are we back to that again?" She released his hand. "I told you I tested every branch."

"If a bridge were weakened by a hurricane, would you test its safety by driving out on it one yard at a time?"

"That's an extreme example, Rawlings. Last night was hardly a hurricane."

"The storm was strong enough to do visible damage. Lord only knows about the damage we can't see."

"Trees, lost limbs, danger. The storm is over, Buck. I'm sitting up here and I'm safe, so give it up. I don't want to talk about the whims of nature. I want to talk about us."

"Last night—" he took off his hat and raked his fingers through his wavy dark hair "—there was another kind of storm. Between us, Cat. With visible damage. And maybe some damage of the unseen variety." As he slipped his black Stetson back on his head, his mouth became a thin wary line. "And I get the feeling every time we bring up the past, it'll be another gully washer or maybe worse."

"So do we get in our cars and test the bridge, one yard at a time, or do we sit on opposite shores for the rest of our lives ... wondering if it would have stood our weight?"

"I'm willing to drive out that first yard, Caitlin, but only if you promise not to take any more risks."

"Didn't you just say I look *at home* in dangerous places?"

"Yeah, but that doesn't mean I want to *see* you taking risks. It was just an observation."

"Great! Then you can observe me climbing down from here, Rawlings. I'm glad you dumped me seven years ago, mister, because if I had married you, I'd be a very safe but very frustrated woman by now!" She turned and found sure footing on the next limb down. Her only dilemma was climbing past the man she'd just insulted.

Reaching out without warning, Buck dragged her up hard against his chest and captured her mouth in a slow plundering kiss that made all memories of his previous kisses pale.

Caught off balance, she was forced to grasp his neck and wedge her lower body awkwardly between his legs.

"Buck." His name tore from her. He caught her soft cry against his mouth and took her lower lip between his teeth. A storm of sensations whirled about her but she pushed against his chest and broke the kiss.

"S-stop," she hissed. "You're the one—the one talking about bridges and gully washers and visible damage. I won't let any man put senseless limits on what I can and cannot do. I'd rather burn the bridge and stay on the opposite shore ... forever, without you!"

Buck wrapped his fingers in her hair and held her pinioned against him. His green eyes turned glacial as he studied her in stony silence. "Fine, O'Malley, it's your choice."

He spoke her name as if he were choking on ground glass. "But I'm still your employer. I have the right to set restrictions. So stay out of my tree and out of trouble, lady, or next time, I *will* drag you down by your hair."

Chapter Six

Buck lit another oil lamp and blew out the match with a sigh of exasperation. It had clearly been the longest day of his life. Long enough to make a man glad it was almost over. He made a mental list of disasters: early-morning generator repairs, a barely functional crew stricken with hangovers, a photographer bent on climbing trees and working his last good nerve, a new surge of wind and rain and a betrayal of every promise he'd ever made to himself regarding Cat O'Malley.

Now at the twilight of his own personal doomsday, the generator chose to go on the blink a second time, leaving the lodge once again without power and the inhabitants with a terminal case of cabin fever.

Picking up the enameled coffeepot from atop the wood stove, Buck poured himself a cup of fresh brew and added a finger of whiskey for good measure. Lingering by the stove for a moment, he allowed the lethal combination of

Fogcutter and Scotch to join forces and warm the cold dread settling in his chest.

That accursed kiss had been his undoing. How could the ethereal mood evaporate so quickly? His hopes for renewal had dissolved like mist. Back on the ground, the two of them barely spoke.

In the uppermost limbs of his family's sacred oak, he'd asked Caitlin to make a simple promise, assuring him she would avoid taking risks. Yet O'Malley's daughter had gone on to make a number of reckless choices while wrapping up the rain-gear shoot. Before the afternoon light deepened to dull gray, she'd climbed the porch rail and braced herself against a roof support with scant inches to anchor her boots. The woman had scrambled up a slippery incline, falling twice. Was she purposely tossing caution and wisdom to the wind to defy his request?

"Hey, boss, the door to the game room got accidentally locked. You seen the key?" Klyde stood waiting anxiously in the kitchen doorway.

"It's in my pocket." Buck patted the back pocket of his black jeans. "I think y'all had enough poker last night. It's time to find some alternatives to gambling when bad weather hits."

"Without power, there's no television or radio, and it's too dark to read," Joe protested from the opposite doorway. "Rusty's fiddle is one thing but when Lester starts singing his torch renditions of Patsy Cline and Hank Williams, we all get a little homesick for better times."

"Or better singers." Klyde lowered his voice to a conspiratorial whisper. "Right now, Buck," he added, "Miss O'Malley's out in the Big Room trying to cook up interest in some *group project.*"

"A group project? Really?" Buck took a second sip of coffee. Entertaining the troops. Was this her way of apologizing for her earlier behavior? "Well, let's give her a listen."

Buck slipped into a shadowed corner by the stone fireplace, his eyes drawn to the statuesque figure of Caitlin burnished by firelight and the faint glow of hurricane lamps situated throughout the living room. She held up magazines and spoke with a good-natured urgency, addressing Louie, Lester, Pete, Carlos and Rusty. Looking sheepish, Joe and Klyde shuffled in begrudgingly, folded their arms and narrowed their gazes at her. Farley, the world's most traitorous Labrador, kept his liquid-brown eyes trained on her every movement.

"A goal collage is just a collection of images and words that illustrate your dreams." She opened a magazine. "You can focus on one aspect or many aspects of your life and include career, family, fitness, wealth, prosperity, to name a few. There's a side benefit to the project that might surprise you—personal growth."

Goal collages? Oh, Lordy. Buck studied the faces of his men, easily recognizing the reluctance and wariness he expected from any red-blooded male forced to take scissors in hand to cut up magazines in the name of personal growth. How did O'Malley's daughter manage to dream up this especially cruel torment?

He gave silent praise that his position of authority made him exempt. He'd rather take a wrench to the blasted generator than make his goals and dreams public. Hell, today's kiss and subsequent deep freeze had been public enough.

"If you've got magazines in your rooms or scattered around the lodge," she continued in a soft indulgent voice, "you might want to contribute them to the cause. I've got scissors and glue ready and I've cut up some packing materials to substitute for poster board. Any comments?"

Stunned silence followed her question. A number of his men sent pleading glances in Buck's direction. He hid his smile by taking another sip of his whiskey-laced coffee. Personal growth with Caitlin O'Malley as goal guide seemed a fitting punishment for the crew's night of drinking and gambling.

Lester stood up. "I just want to thank Miss O'Malley for organizin' this project. I'm planning my daughter's weddin' dress for the big event this fall, so I've got a stack of bride magazines I'm willin' to share with you bachelor types."

"Got any magazines to contribute, Buck?" she asked moments later after the group of grumbling men, many visibly dragging their boots, dispersed to ferret out reading material from their rooms.

"We keep plenty of fishing and sporting magazines around the lodge, O'Malley." He spoke matter-of-factly as he stepped out of his shadowy alcove next to the fireplace. "In the den, I've got old issues of *Business Week, Time* and *Life.* I dropped my subscription to *Reckless Women* seven years ago, so I won't be able to supply you with images of rash and wild women for *your* goal collage."

He watched her bring the pile of magazines up protectively against her chest. "I'm sure I can rustle up a wolf or a boar for *your* masterpiece, Rawlings."

"Forget it. I'm not participating. It's not my style."

"Oh, really?" She put her boot on the raised hearth and stared into the flames. "I'm sorry to hear about your lack of interest. I thought it'd be *nice* if everyone at the lodge got involved. I've done this with my friends in New York and—"

"I'm *not* nice and I'm certainly not one of your cultured East Coast friends. This is a mountain lodge, and we're here to do serious work."

"Not every waking hour. There appear to be some hours left over for more pleasurable pursuits, Mr. Rawlings. For a moment today, I thought we might pursue the pleasure of getting reacquainted, but that was before you started asking for conditions."

"Today was an out-and-out disaster." He turned from her and headed to the entryway, grabbing his hat and jacket off the coatrack.

"Why did you have to put conditions on our being more than friends, Buck?" she asked from the doorway.

"So, now you're saying we're friends?" He settled the Stetson on his head and slipped into the field jacket he'd modeled earlier. "Friends. Well, that's a step up from last night anyway."

"Do you want to start back at square one, arguing semantics?" She lowered the stack of magazines to waist level. "We can't change what happened today, Buck. You can ignore it if that makes you more comfortable, but I *won't*. I just want to move forward. I'm ready."

"I've had to get used to discomfort around you, O'Malley."

"Personally I'm glad it happened, Buck. It was time you stopped looking and started showing me your feelings." She walked back to the fireplace and set the magazines on the coffee table and bent to arrange the scissors and glue. "So are you slinking outside while I get to know your men better?"

"I've got a generator that won't stay fixed. If you want your fancy cappuccino tomorrow morning, you'll thank me for the work I do tonight."

"Are all men in Montana this arrogant, Rawlings, or did I just get lucky?"

"Maybe you're looking for one of those boys from *Bonanza* after all. We've both changed a lot in seven years, Caitlin."

"That's becoming more evident by the minute." She bristled at his remark. He was the one who'd changed, becoming more bitter and remote and unapproachable.

"So, are *you* planning to make one of these goal collages, O'Malley?"

"Why do you ask?" She narrowed her gaze at him and took a step backward.

Buck grabbed a handful of Echo Creek catalogs off the hall table and tossed them onto the nearest sofa in the Big Room. "If you need images of yours truly, this will give you something to choose from."

Caitlin set the last of the completed collages up along the ridge of wainscoting on the far wall in the living room then stood back and surveyed the results proudly. Crew members crowded around holding oil lamps and muttering among themselves.

"Who wants to go first?" she asked in a nonthreatening voice, not wanting to intimidate them further. Collages could be a risky business.

Wild-haired Louie's boots sounded noisily on the polished wood floor as he stepped in front of the others. He pointed to a picture of an elderly man with a lap full of children. "I want to get better hearin' aids so I can listen to my grandchildren. I don't want to miss a single word. They're my second chance 'cuz I messed up pretty bad with my own kids."

"You got great kids, Louie." Carlos put a hand to the older man's shoulder.

"No. What I got is a bunch of kids willin' to forgive me. Luck of the draw, I guess," Louie countered before pointing to an elegant image of Trout Almondine and continuing to go over his images.

On down the row of collages, the men took turns talking of goals, dreams, mistakes and second chances. More than once, Caitlin reached up to wipe away a tear or laugh wholeheartedly. She could now understand why it was so difficult for Buck to contemplate firing these men in favor of replacing them with young, handsome models.

Baseball fanatic Joe dreamed of visiting the Hall of Fame in Cooperstown. A large map of New York state dominated his work. He identified a handpainted red star on the map as his own personal Mecca. "Baseball is the one thing I shared with my dad," Joe the humble pilgrim explained.

"We still have that in common, so I guess I'll have to bring him along or face being disowned."

Lester surveyed the group thoughtfully. "The way I see it," he drawled, "there are goals and there are dreams, and it's good to always have a new dream waiting in the wings. Me? I really want to get the opportunity to design female clothin' for Echo Creek Outfitters. Now I know Buck Rawlings doesn't agree on the feasibility of this venture but I believe in it. When ya run into a mountain, ya find a way around it. That's what I aim to do.

"Back at home, I'm spendin' every extra hour fixin' to make my daughter look like a princess in satin and lace for her weddin'." The tailor nodded toward a photo of a laughing bride in an elegant gown. "Lettin' go of someone you love, someone you've protected, well, it makes me feel like an old dress form—all hollow and sad, and without a need for arms 'cuz I won't be the one holdin' my baby girl no more."

Caitlin heard a cough and spotted Buck sitting in shadow near the fireplace. She chose not to draw attention to his presence, unwilling to put a damper on the men's sharing by making them feel censured. She wondered if he was as touched as she was by the confessions of the crew.

Pete the avid fisherman had splashed scenes of fishing, boats and waterways across his work. His dark skin shimmered handsomely in the lamplight as he pointed to the figure of a man working at a computer. "I'm writing a book about my distant grandfather who was a Buffalo soldier and about his struggle to resettle his family in Montana. It might get published someday, but that's not why I chose to write it." Pete paused for a moment then made eye contact with every person present and smiled broadly. "I couldn't let his diaries rot another year in my father's attic. His words echoed something inside of me. So when I'm not approving bank loans, I'm researching and writing."

Rusty planned to enter a national fiddling contest while Klyde hoped to reconcile with his estranged wife and kids.

Carlos was the last man to stand next to his collage. He revealed his plan to save every extra dollar he earned as an X-ray technician to sharpen his skills at a seminar for magicians being held in Minneapolis. "I work with a lot of pediatric cases and use sleight of hand to put the little ones at ease." Carlos gestured to pictures of wide-eyed solemn children. "Lot of 'em arrive tremblin' and too scared to even cry. I can't help rememberin' some pretty frightening things that happened to me as a kid. I know how it feels to be alone and scared." He pointed to a second grouping of children, all laughing and smiling. "So I tell myself I'm going to make every single child smile." Carlos motioned to Caitlin. "And now, I believe it's Miss O'Malley's turn."

Caitlin felt so moved by Carlos's unselfish ambitions that she found it hard to step up to the gallery of collages. Each image on these squares of cardboard now told a story, was now imbued with an emotional intensity that had not been there hours before. The narrow ledge of wainscoting held so much hope and promise and concern for others that she felt intimidated as she approached.

Turning, Caitlin looked across the room at the shadowed figure on the sofa, paging through magazines, the three dogs grouped around him. She felt a tingle of panic. She hadn't planned on Buck's presence. How would she dance around the images of a bride and children on her collage? Their shared kiss and stormy confrontation that afternoon made her hesitant to share her feelings about marriage and motherhood. She'd spent the past few hours amending such dreams, and had even contemplated editing out the hope of sharing a life with Buck Rawlings.

Caitlin began slowly, speaking softly of climbing peaks, mountainous and otherwise. She listed specific magazines she wished to sell to, honors she sought, celebrities she admired and hoped to photograph.

"You all know my father, Sean O'Malley, and you know he's more than a parent to me. He's always been my good friend and mentor. I moved back to Missoula a year ago to

be close to him and close to Montana." She smoothed her
fingertips over an image of two hands intertwined, one pair
gnarled, the other yet untouched by time. "Soon it'll be my
turn to be the strong one. One of my goals is to offer my father my strength when needed and get him to accept it.

"Another of my goals is to nurture myself." She paused
before a photograph of a mother nursing her child. "My
mother died when I was an infant and I know it's impossible for most people to remember scenes from babyhood but
for some reason I have this impression of being at her breast
and feeling absolutely safe and loved and comforted." Her
throat tightened and the rest of the room fell away. She
stood alone with her images and felt her heart tear a little at
remembrances of being a lonely little girl. "As long as I can
recall, I've yearned for that sensation, that sense of being
nurtured. D-Dad always wanted me to be the brave little
soldier at his side, to be fearless.

"But I'm not fearless. I may take risks and appear to be
unafraid of anything, but I have my fears and weaknesses.
Like thunder and lightning and windstorms, haunted castles . . . abandonment and loss."

"Miss O'Malley," Lester interrupted when her pause
stretched into long moments of silence. "Well, now, it seems
t'me when a person's all growed up, they need a bit of help
with this nurturin' business. Why does a pretty, intelligent
woman like you feel like ya gotta do it alone?"

Unprepared to answer the tailor's question, she grasped
for ways to sidestep the issue. "I guess it's like washing hair,
Lester. Some people love to go to a salon and have an expert shampoo them." She grabbed a handful of waves from
her shoulder and ran her fingers over their length. "I could
never lie back and enjoy that. I prefer to take care of my
own hair."

"But hair ain't anythin' like the part of you that needs this
nurturin'," Lester argued. The other men nodded in agreement. "If we're talkin' the same language, Miss O'Malley,

I take it t'mean things that make the very soul of you feel good. Like someone who takes your hand without askin'."

"Someone to make you one of them latte da things," Louie added. "That damn citified brew would never touch these lips, but I can see how it must give comfort to a refined woman like yourself, Miss O'Malley."

"Fer all of us here, Miss O'Malley," Lester added, "I jes' wanna say we've all taken care of our share of orphaned critters and such, and we're here t'help if you need it."

Orphaned critters? Caitlin was shaken by the comparison, but moved by the offer of nurturing from this ragtag band of middle-aged men. Chivalry was alive and well at the Echo Creek Lodge. If only the dark knight in the corner...

Caitlin put her problems with Buck Rawlings aside and concluded her collage presentation with comments about the success of the project and how she felt closer to everyone present. As the men climbed the steps to the second floor to make up for sleep they'd lost the night before, she overheard comments and inquiries that told her they felt the bonding among themselves, as well. She stood alone for a moment, arranging the squares of cardboard and hope on the ledge.

"Well, well, that was insightful." Buck's deep voice echoed through the room.

Her back still turned, Caitlin heard his boots on hardwood and dreaded his approach. Feeling the need to protect her visions of the future from the man who'd destroyed her dreams seven years ago, she stepped in front of her work and slowly turned to face him.

Buck was surprised by her stony mask. She'd been so warm and open with his men. Did her resentment run so deep that she was unwilling to share the intimate details of her life with him?

"Trying to hide something from me, O'Malley?" He stopped in front of her, leaned forward and placed his hands on either side of the wall behind her, lightly trapping her. She hadn't mentioned love or marriage and he had to wonder how she felt on those subjects. If she wasn't willing to open up to him, he might have to exact her trust with a little forceful persuasion.

She met his gaze, chin tilted defiantly. "You were eavesdropping, no doubt, so you already heard me talk about my goals, Buck. Show's over."

"I don't know. I see a lot of interesting pictures up here that you purposely ignored."

"Such as?"

With one hand, he pulled the cardboard out from behind her and set it farther down the narrow ledge where he could study it in its entirety. "There's a wedding dress here you didn't elaborate on. What's all that about? Do you plan to photograph weddings now or could it be a simple desire to wear white?"

She turned to look at the image his finger rested on. "I plan to marry someday. It's not unusual for a woman—and even some men—to dream of love and commitment." Her voice had a wistful quality that made him hesitate to push the point further.

He studied the images scattered over the fair-sized square. There was a dark-haired, green-eyed baby that looked suspiciously like photos of himself as an infant.

"You didn't mention children in your little speech, but I see a pile of rather small people here."

"I want children." Her tone was flat, emotionless. "Two or three."

"And you're going to put your camera bags down long enough to hold these needy little bundles? Long enough to hold the man who makes it possible to create the babies?"

"I can juggle a baby and a camera any day. As for men, I'll just slip the camera strap from my shoulder for a minute. It doesn't take that long with most of the male species."

"You better exclude present company on that one."

She gave him a cryptic little smile. "Present company excluded."

Still he wondered at the bitterness in her tone. "Have there been a lot of men since that last summer with me, Caitlin?"

"I've done my share of traveling."

"I was kept informed of your travels by your father. I'm asking about a different kind of map. How often did you slip that strap from your shoulder?"

She edged away. "I've said enough. If you're looking for answers, study the collage, Buck."

"I don't see my image here. I gave you the catalogs—"

"And you assumed I'd include you in my dreams?" Her laugh was edged in bitterness. "There are images of men but I thought it was wise to leave it unspecific."

"Unspecific? An unshaven man in black? A laughing man in white?"

"They're symbols, Buck."

"What's this little country cottage doing here? Is this symbolic, too?"

"I want a home to return to after my many adventures."

"There's no room for the babies, or your symbolic men. And what's this photo of a woman on a mountain peak? Does that represent you, Caitlin?"

"One of my dreams is to use my photography and personal experience to spread awareness of the accomplishments of women who've conquered the wild." She ducked beneath his arm and started to pick up magazines off one of the many sofas surrounding the fireplace. "As a group, their exploits aren't chronicled in the same fashion as those of men."

Irritated, he swept up the collage and followed her. "Don't you think spreading that message is dangerous?" Buck tapped the back of his fingers against the image of the woman that disturbed him so much. "Women don't have the upper-body strength needed to challenge most wilderness situations."

"There are plenty of *men* who venture up mountains only to encounter problems because of a lack of physical conditioning." She lined a portion of the magazines she was gathering into neat piles on the coffee table. Straightening, she put a hand to her hip. "I'm not advocating any and all women take up climbing, kayaking, rafting or trekking without skill or preparation. But I believe women are capable and would benefit from challenging themselves.

"As a kid, I sometimes traveled with my dad when he was on assignment, photographing national parks and wilderness areas. We met incredible women, Buck. I started reading about female adventurers and even wrote letters to them. I guess that's why it's not in my nature to limit myself. Or allow *you* or anyone else to set limitations for me."

"If you were my woman, O'Malley, I couldn't condone that philosophy."

"These are core beliefs I hold, Buck. They're part of me—a total package. Do you intend to get a scalpel and cut out any viewpoints I hold that rival your own?"

"I'm a little more evolved than that." He lowered the collage until it rested against his calf. "I simply want to know you're safe. Try to understand. I lost two women in my family, two skilled and physically capable women, to adventure."

"Two?"

"I know you and Sarah occasionally joked about being two motherless waifs. I envied the two of you at times. You gave each other strength and support. I was motherless, as well."

"But Sarah said your mother drowned."

"My sister never told you *how* or *why* Mom drowned?"

"Never. She might have said it was an accident, at least, that's the impression I was left with all these years."

"It was no accident. Mom had an annual birthday ritual of hotdogging on water skis, showing her friends and family she was still young. We were picnicking at a small lake up north of Missoula. She hit a submerged log."

"Oh, Buck, I'm so sorry."

"I was twelve. I've always resented her need to prove herself. She was almost thirty when she married.Dad so I guess—I don't know. It was purely selfish. She didn't give a thought to her children. Hell, Sarah was seven and Chase was only four. He doesn't have a single memory and the way I figure it, he's probably better off for not remembering her."

"Buck—"

"I want you back in my life, but you have a choice to make, O'Malley. How important is it for you to conquer another mountain or trek through Alaska? You had the nerve to put *babies* on your collage." He pressed the sheet of cardboard into her hands. "You talk about searching for comfort and safety in your life because you lost your own mother so young. Knowing that, are you willing to chance leaving your children behind, feeling lost and motherless, in order to fulfill your own need for glory?"

"Now isn't the time to argue this, Buck."

"When do we hash it out, then? After we decide to try again and become so physically and emotionally entangled that we can't let go without tearing each other apart?

"Just being here at the lodge is difficult for me," he continued. "I have memories of family summers at Echo Creek before Mom's death. Then my sister died at the foot of Shepherd's Rock and her ashes are scattered in Medicine Bowl Lake. For me, each ripple on those waters stirs a painful memory of Sarah. Now can you understand, Cat, why I can't afford to watch another foolish woman, a woman addicted to adventure, die?"

Caitlin saw grief, raw and unforgiving, etch years into Buck's features. She was tempted to reach out to comfort, to offer her understanding. But she was certain now that renewing their relationship would be impossible, would only lead to deeper pain and despair than it had years ago.

Was now the time to reveal Sarah's secret to Buck? she asked herself. Would reading the letters and understanding the crisis in Sarah's life give comfort or add to his burden?

"I need to let the dogs out. I'll probably walk awhile," he announced solemnly.

"Buck," Caitlin began, "there's something you should know—"

"Don't say a word, O'Malley." He cut her off. "You're right. Now isn't the time to talk about decisions. Go upstairs, start a fire in my room, get in bed."

Caitlin felt disappointment. Would there ever be a perfect time to reveal the truth about Sarah? Perhaps when Buck returned from his walk.

"There's no need for you to sleep outside in the hall tonight, Buck."

"What are you saying?"

"You could sleep by the fireplace in your room."

"Don't wait up," he snarled.

For the second time that evening, she watched him grab his hat and coat and turn his back to her. Caitlin stood alone, listening to the thudding of her heart. His revelation changed everything . . . and nothing. She was still unwilling to let go of old dreams. Would her life remain one of regrets and reaching out for a man who wasn't there—physically or emotionally?

To calm herself, she picked up the remaining magazines scattered about the room and stacked them neatly on the table. One of Lester's magazines lay on top, a smiling bride teasing her with illusions of white lace and forever. Not with Buck. His black leather and grief would suck the happiness out of any marriage. Why start with a deficit, with a known strike against the promise of happiness?

Caitlin noticed a few torn pages on the sofa where Buck had sat watching the group present their collages. Picking up the ragged sheets of glossy paper, she was startled by the first image. An elegant Victorian-style house. Some half a dozen years ago, the two of them had planned a future together. In this very room, they'd foraged through magazines looking at homes. When she'd chosen the quaint

charm of a Victorian, no-nonsense Buck had surprised her
with his enthusiastic agreement.

The remaining images she found were of men alone in the
wild. Lone figures set against an unwelcoming world. A
solitary tent, a fly fisherman casting with only his shadow
for company, a single set of footprints in the snow.

She'd left her own collage propped against the back of the
sofa after Buck had thrust it into her hands. She glanced at
it now, pulled in by the warmth and color, and promise of
sharing. The solemn man in black and the laughing man in
white were the two sides of Buck she'd known and loved
long ago. Had these two opposites grown farther apart?

Her optimistic grouping of images contrasted sharply
with the dark, foreboding pages Buck had chosen. She held
his goals of solitude and independence in her shaking hands
and realized they would never mesh with the dreams she held
so dear in her own heart.

She slipped the photo of the Victorian into her pocket
then stood and fed the rest of his torn pages into the fire and
slowly watched the flames consume her hope of a future
with Buck Rawlings.

Buck leaned back against the bedroom fireplace and inhaled sharply on the cheroot he'd borrowed from the box
Rusty had left on the kitchen table. On long rides into snow-
laden mountains, he sometimes indulged in such sinful lux-
uries, but never in the company of women. But then, how
often did he share a bedroom with the likes of Cat O'Malley? He was tempted to pay the repairmen from town a little extra to linger at their work, to delay the final touches on
the third-floor restoration, just so he'd have the opportunity to watch her sleep, her finely sculpted features soft and
unaware.

How dare she paste symbolic men on her collage when he
was here in flesh and blood? After returning from his walk
with the dogs, he'd sat in the Big Room studying her square
of cardboard in private.

Half a dozen years ago he hadn't given much thought to the differences in their backgrounds. That final summer, those lines were blurred by passion and optimism. Now he had to wonder. If Sarah's death hadn't destroyed their relationship, would Caitlin's love of finer things and his need for wide-open spaces have interfered?

There among her images on her collage he found all the trappings of marriage to a woman of good breeding and sophistication: formal dinner settings with candlelight shimmering on fine china and silver, diamonds and fancy flower arrangements, lacy lingerie.

Is this truly what he wanted? He'd long imagined spending his life with a true Montana woman, a woman satisfied with ironstone plates, wildflowers and an heirloom ring etched in a pattern of wheat and simplicity. And the lacy lingerie... well, that would suit his tastes just fine.

He walked over to the four-poster bed and stole a glimpse of O'Malley's daughter. He watched a thin fist of smoke rise from his cheroot and curl over the yellow gold light of the oil lamp on the bedside table. His sleeping bag waited, unzipped, back by the fireplace. Perhaps tonight their dreams would mingle in the vaulted timbers above his bed and they'd come to an understanding no amount of talking had accomplished.

Cat O'Malley was his woman. He'd branded her with a look almost fifteen years ago when he'd first seen her coltish walk and mesmerizing golden eyes. He'd claimed her fully over half a dozen years later in this very bed. Was it time to claim her again, once and forever?

Booted footsteps sounded on the stairs. Farley growled low in his throat but Buck quickly silenced him with a hand command. Instinctively, Buck stepped to the foot of the bed, forming a protective barrier between the bedroom door and Caitlin's sleeping form.

The ornately carved door opened and in the faint glow of the oil lamp, Chase Rawlings stood, one hip canted to the side, scowling as he took in the scene.

"What the devil...?" his younger brother asked gruffly.

Buck swore beneath his breath. He'd hoped to have his problems with Caitlin resolved before his second headache arrived.

Chapter Seven

"**I**s this how you take care of our business interests, big brother?" Chase asked pointedly after Buck had motioned him out into the hallway and closed the door. "I'm working my butt off hauling horses and supplies up this godforsaken mountain—" Chase gestured wildly with his hat "—while you're sleeping with O'Malley's daughter in Grandma's bed. Dang! That's practically a family shrine, Buck."

"That's rich, coming from you. How many times have you brought women up here for wild weekends, Chase?"

"*My* bed isn't a family shrine."

Buck smiled at his brother's exaggeration. "You're overreacting, as usual. And Caitlin and I weren't having sex."

"Sure. I suppose you want me to believe you didn't inhale on that cigar, either. Right?"

"I sure as hell don't need to explain anything to you," Buck shot back. He slapped his hand firmly on the second-floor banister. "Let's take this conversation downstairs." He started down the darkened staircase and heard his brother's insistent footsteps directly behind him.

If only Chase weren't so much like himself. Intense, emotional, quick to anger. For a time, his younger brother had set up residence in Buck's home and Buck's housekeeper had complained not only about the daily fireworks but about the difficulty of keeping two wardrobes of almost entirely black clothing separate in the laundry room.

Chase paused on the landing. "When Sean O'Malley broke his leg and I hired Caitlin, you didn't even want the woman to stay the first night. Now she's in your bed. What happened to the time limit you gave her? Wasn't there some business about her proving herself before I got here?"

"She's proven enough. Now if *you* agree, it'll be official, Chase. We can tell her in the morning."

"Hold on. Did we just have a business meeting back there on the landing?" Chase asked when they reached the bottom of the staircase. "I don't think I got to vote."

"I voted for you," Buck snapped. "It was unanimous. Cat O'Malley stays."

"And there's another thing." Chase pressed a finger into Buck's shoulder. "Caitlin's on payroll. *You're* the one who set up the rules against fraternizing with employees."

"Those rules apply to a factory setting. Let me refresh your memory, college boy. You tend to infiltrate the troops now and then to hand select your prey. And don't forget the paternity suit—"

"Hey, I proved my innocence."

"At great expense to the family's legal fund." Buck stormed into the kitchen and groped in the dark for an oil lamp.

"Here we go again." Chase followed, cursing in the dark. "*I'm* the low-down rat preying on the production-line innocents and you're the lofty brother who travels to the purity of the mountains to prey on a woman you heartlessly dumped eight years ago."

"Seven," Buck corrected, striking a match from the box above the stove and lighting a hurricane lamp. "It was seven years ago. Did you unload the horse trailer?"

"I let 'em loose in the corral for a little exercise. We'll have to give 'em all a good rubdown and put them in the stable later. So you admit it was heartless?"

"Cruel." Buck said the single word without hesitation. These few days with Caitlin had given him the chance to see his actions for what they were. He lit the wood stove and started a pot of coffee. "I'll concede to cruel but I wasn't intentionally heartless. And I didn't sleep with her tonight or any other night since her arrival."

"Then what the hell were you doing next to the bed with a cheroot hanging from your lip, your boots beside the bed and that heartsick look on your face?"

"Some detective you are. Those were Caitlin's boots." Buck tapped his heel against the planked floor. "I still have my boots on, Chase."

"You could have made love with your boots on. Goes along with the Rawlings mystique, I guess. Hell, I don't know anything about the lovemaking techniques of *old* men."

"At eight years your senior, Chase, I'm hardly infirmed," Buck responded with a short derisive laugh. The brothers often teased one another about their age difference. Without Sarah, the middle child, to bridge the gap, the chasm seemed wider and harder to cross. He set two mugs on the table and began to rustle up sandwich ingredients.

"You look like you haven't slept for days. Somethin' other than O'Malley's daughter been on your mind?" Chase grabbed a slice of roast beef off the plate Buck set down and stuffed it into his mouth. "Or have you discovered you still love her? Sometimes old feelings die hard."

Buck paused before he opened the jar of mustard. "If I love anything, maybe it's the memory."

"You're not the kind of man who'd be satisfied with a fading memory."

"Who said the memory was fading?"

"You need a flesh-and-blood, here-and-now, in-your-face woman, old man. You need Caitlin O'Malley back in your life."

Buck glanced up and watched Chase take off his hat and casually toss it a few feet onto the kitchen table. The younger man leaned his long frame against the wall beside the wood stove, his arms folded against his chest. A look passed between them that made further conversation on the subject unnecessary.

Buck returned his focus to the sandwiches he was preparing. Outwardly, the two men were similar. They shared the raven hair and dark coloring of their mother's distant Shoshone ancestors, the forest green of their father's eyes and the same last name. But inwardly, they couldn't have been more different.

While Buck tended to brood when confronted with a problem, Chase reasoned aloud or reacted angrily. Buck spent his leisure time enjoying the solitude of mountains and lakes. In his off-hours, Chase gravitated toward honky-tonks and rubbed elbows with movers and shakers. The two brothers rarely shared managerial philosophies or a view to the future of Echo Creek Outfitters.

"So how's the shoot going?" Chase asked.

"The last few days haven't been a picnic, Chase," Buck explained with a sigh. "I had a major storm to contend with, and we ended up with extensive damage to the third floor and a portion of the porch."

"I saw the spot up the road where someone cut through a tree that had fallen across the road. You hire those guys from town to make repairs here?"

"Yeah, but the generator went down for a second time this afternoon. Come to think of it, weren't you supposed to check it out when you were up here three weeks ago?"

"My apologies, big brother. I was too busy desecrating the shrine on that particular trip to even think about repairing that blasted antique. I'll fix it come morning."

"Very funny. And on top of everything else," Buck continued, slapping slices of tomato atop the beef, "the crew stayed up all night drinking and gambling and tonight—well . . . tonight, Caitlin had this asinine project. Goal collages."

"No, not that. Not *goal collages*." Chase feigned disbelief. He picked up one of the sandwiches before Buck could slice through it. "Damn, I'm starving. You want to put some salsa on this roast beef for me? Is that coffee ready yet?"

"Hey, I'm not here to wait on you, Chase. Give the coffee five more minutes and get your own damned salsa."

Buck was reminded of the many times he prepared lunch or supper for his motherless siblings on the housekeeper's day off. Chase's impatience was legendary. So was his appetite.

He took a bite of sandwich, and in the golden glow from the lamp on the table, watched Chase relish his third mouthful. His brother had a gift for savoring even the most simple things in life. Follow Chase Rawlings for half a day and you'd think you'd stepped into an advertisement for the best things about Montana—or light beer.

Chase was salsa. Hot, unpredictable and sure to surprise. Buck was mustard, albeit one of the darker blends with horseradish but mustard just the same. Dependable, honest and none-too-fancy. He didn't feel jealousy toward the younger man, but he had to confess to some resentment about preferential treatment their father had shown Chase since Sarah's death.

"Coffee's finally ready," he announced after they'd eaten in comfortable silence. "When I told Caitlin you had a birthday this week, she insisted on planning a little party. Course, you'll have to act surprised."

"Thanks for the warning. Has she changed much?"

Buck smiled to himself. "Now she's into wearing Echo Creek clothing tailored to fit her curves. She's still a tomboy with a rebel heart, Chase."

"I still insist we do a feasibility study on starting a line of women's clothing, Buck." Chase's tone turned business-like. "There's a big market out there and it sounds like O'Malley's daughter is the perfect example. Lester's champing at the bit to start on this. I know you're resistant but we've got to work this out."

"Work this out usually means doing it your way—"

"I've got the MBA, the expertise in marketing."

"You've got a million fancy names to stick on everyday office procedures and methods of handling production line and employee problems, Chase. I've got the common sense." Buck curled his hand around the cup of coffee.

"Face the truth, Buck. You're losing interest in the company. You want to start your wilderness guide business—"

"I want to find a way to do both! Dad found a way to keep the ranch and the factory. I just need some cooperation from you, Chase."

Buck watched while Chase steepled his fingers against his chin, his dark lashed eyes growing remote. Another impasse. They stared at one another for several seconds before Buck picked up his coffee and took a sip.

"When we're done here, Chase," he said quietly, "let's take some lanterns outside and get those horses rubbed down. You have any trouble with the horse trailer on the way up?"

While Chase listed a number of problems with storm debris, Buck thought about this year's catalog shoot. It was cast in shadow, mired in complications. Old hurts and issues with Caitlin, Sarah and Chase loomed larger than the tallest peak in the Crazy Mountains. His need to reconcile with Chase on management issues was his highest hurdle. The family business was at stake. Would Buck's desire to start a wilderness guide service be shoved to a back burner—again?

Buck decided to find the time and energy to resolve all the problems and to put old ghosts to rest. He was thirty-five, and though Chase teased him about his elder statesman status, he felt the rumblings of the big four-oh loom on the horizon and felt the need to cleanse his life of unanswered questions.

Watching his crew stand up and speak bravely about their lives had made him think. Problems never solved themselves. When life got crumpled, you had to iron out the wrinkles yourself. Of course, Cat O'Malley was more than a complication or a simple wrinkle in his plan. Far more.

Buck filled their coffee mugs a second time then laid a hand on his brother's shoulder. "You're a pain in the butt, Chase, but it's good to see you."

"Yeah, same here," Chase muttered, wrapping his hands around the warm cup. "Of course, you may not be thinking that tomorrow after O'Malley's daughter realizes she's got a younger, better looking model to make her job easier. She'll probably want me to model all the underwear, all the swimwear, anything that calls for brawn. Dang! The woman will probably work my butt off, brother Buck." A grin spread across Chase's handsome features. "And maybe, just maybe, while you watch her photograph *moi,* you'll realize how much you care for that filly…or you'll step aside and let me take a chance at winning O'Malley's daughter for myself."

"Oh, yeah?" Buck took a sip of coffee and stared into the darkened corners of the kitchen. "This ain't no horse race, brother," he said quietly.

Caitlin drew her woolen jacket closer to her body as she stepped out onto the porch. She allowed her eyes to adjust to the inky blackness on the cloud-covered sky before attempting the long set of weathered steps. A light wind rustled through the oak, adding to the eerie atmosphere of Echo Creek at two in the morning.

Twenty minutes earlier, she'd been roused from sleep by the sound of male laughter. A glance outside Buck's bedroom window was all the explanation she needed. A portion of the family's large horse trailer was visible. Chase

Rawlings, Missoula's one-time wunderkind, had arrived, bringing with him the horses needed to complete the catalog shoot.

She wondered what effect his rambunctious presence might have on Buck and the rest of the crew. The last time Caitlin had seen Chase, he'd been twenty, dressed in preppy gear and anxious to return to Yale. He'd also appeared anxious to turn his back on the ways of Montana.

Did Chase share Buck's view of blaming her for Sarah's death? It was unlikely, she reflected. The man had allowed her to pinch-hit for her father, had trusted her with the most important catalog Echo Creek Outfitters had ever produced. Still, she had to wonder if grief and loss had put a bitter edge on Chase's view of life as it had Buck's.

She heard a faint nicker as she approached the stable situated a stone's throw from the lodge. Through the open double doors, the soft radiance of lantern light created an aura of welcome. Stepping over the threshold, she beheld a world of warm-toned woods, gleaming leather and the burnished brilliance of glowing straw. Four horses stood in their stalls, munching quietly on molasses-drenched oats. The bittersweet smell of their late-night meal assaulted her senses and drew her closer. Buck's chestnut stallion and Chase's palomino mare raised their noses, curious about the intruder. The striking bay in the far stall was foreign to her, a new acquisition for the Rawlings family's small herd, no doubt.

Like the gaming room in the lodge, this building held memories of stolen moments of passion with Buck. It was a tinderbox looking for a lighted match. Images of his tanned muscular body and sinewy hands, and impressions of her fiery responses, flittered through her mind, halting her step and causing her to catch her breath.

But it was grief, swift and fierce, that stabbed her as she leaned over the stall closest to the entrance and ran her fingers over the familiar star on the face of Denim Hank, Sarah's blue roan. As the horse's limpid brown eyes studied her,

Caitlin recalled the many afternoons she and Sarah had ridden side by side on country roads and well-marked trails near Missoula. Those summers at Echo Creek, they'd roamed through alpine meadows ablaze with wildflowers, and here in the stable they'd spent endless hours talking as they groomed their mounts.

Caitlin recalled the pain of selling Moonlight, her good-natured palomino, when she moved to New York. Life was full of bargains made with others and one's self. What had she sacrificed to put distance between herself and Buck Rawlings? What was she willing to sacrifice now to renew her relationship with the man?

"Hey there, Hank," she whispered in a voice choked with unshed tears. "I've missed you, buddy." She grasped the horse's mane and drew his cheek alongside hers. Just that evening Buck had revealed to her for the first time the whereabouts of Sarah's ashes. "Good Hank. You and me— we'll go riding. Huh, boy? We'll go visit the lake together. Just like old times."

Caitlin closed her eyes and searched for solace in the scent and heat of the large animal. Those old times were gone, never to be relived. How many times would she have to face that harsh reality before she let go of Sarah—and possibly Buck? She thought she'd released the pain two nights ago when Buck had made his brutal accusations, but it remained, like a sliver in her heart, refusing to heal.

Muted laughter sounded at the far end of the stable. Mingled with the sweet scent of hay and the pungent odor of the horses was the distinctive aroma of whiskey. Her attention was drawn to the black-clad figures of Buck and Chase Rawlings. Both men stood with their backs against the frame of the smaller door on the opposite end of the L-shaped stable. Their heads were thrown back, their laughter full-bodied and infectious, as each swirled a glass of amber liquid lazily in his hand.

Her father had said it was her Irish blood that made her appreciate the pure lines and well-defined stature of a thoroughbred. Could there be some truth to his claim? Was it the song of Celtic ancestors in her own lineage that drew her to the primitive mystique of horses and to the even more primal charm of men of dark beauty and tribal fire? With a swift movement, she wiped a tear from the edge of her eye, patted Denim Hank's cheek one last time, and stepped into the aisle where both men could see her.

"Dang, would you look at Caitlin O'Malley!" Chase straightened then removed his hat. "All growed up and no place to go, except maybe into these big arms for a hug. Come here, darlin'—" He glanced sidelong at Buck. "Darlin'—*ma'am.*" He added the afterthought with a wicked grin that gave the formality an even more intimate implication.

"You look good, Chase. How're you doing?" Caitlin allowed him a quick embrace then stepped back and folded her arms across her chest. Her emotions were still too frayed by her encounter with Sarah's horse to dredge up memories of the younger brother who'd once been a part of her daily visits to the Rawlings home in Missoula.

"I thought you were going to take Wall Street by storm, but lucky us. Montana has a way of calling the best people back home, doesn't it?" She kept her tone playful.

"Yes, ma'am." Chase rubbed the glass of whiskey along his upper thigh. The amber liquid sloshed onto his hand. With his gaze riveted on her, he lifted his thumb to his mouth and licked it. "It's hard for some of us to ignore the call of the Big Sky Country."

"Or the demands of Big Daddy August Rawlings," Buck added solemnly, his face shadowed in the lamplight by the brim of his Stetson. The shadow of his beard added to his desperado pose. He tipped the glass in his hand up to his lips and finished the whiskey with one swallow.

A single droplet of liquor remained on Buck's lower lip, glistening softly in the lantern light, and Caitlin found her attention riveted there. Suddenly she longed to enfold herself in his powerful embrace, her creamy silk against his black leather soul, and to kiss that pearl of moisture from his mouth. She wanted to experience once again the intoxicating thrill this man and only this man could arouse in her.

As if sensing her thoughts, Buck ran his tongue along his lip, capturing the droplet and sending her heart skidding past resentment, past reason and straight into the unfamiliar grip of willingness. Buck had done everything possible to scatter the embers of their passion the past few days and she'd played her part in that effort, as well. But a single ember remained and a single ember was all that was required to start a fire.

Looking down, relieved to break eye contact with both men, Caitlin struggled to find a safe topic. The subject of Chase's return to Montana seemed to stir unease in both men and she chose to ignore it.

"My father said you two decided to add horses to the catalog shoot about three years ago," she said matter-of-factly. "I think they give the layouts more of a wilderness feel. I like it."

"Helps to sell our expanded line of equestrian gear, too." Chase handed his whiskey to Buck, walked over to a storage area, ripped open one of the cardboard boxes stacked there and pulled out a woolen blanket patterned in southwestern pastels. "We're introducing this new Navajo print this fall. Double felt liner, all wool with one hundred percent lambswool fleece next to the horse. Buck negotiated an exclusive contract on these and I think it's really going to pay off with Christmas orders. They're really special."

She watched Buck's eyes light with the fire of pride at Chase's announcement.

"Exquisite." Caitlin hefted the horse blanket in her hands before lifting it to her face. "Any thoughts on how you want me to photograph these, Buck? These pastels would look beautiful against Denim Hank's coloring."

Buck watched Caitlin place the blanket against her cheek. He recognized something achingly feminine about the action and about the tender expression on her face. He'd forgotten about her love of horses, and had mistakenly figured years of urban living had erased such interests forever.

There was something incongruous about the mix of leather and lattes, about Caitlin and himself for that matter. Here in the warm golden glow of the stable he realized a part of her still clung to country ways. Her Echo Creek wardrobe was more than window dressing or an attempt to adapt to Western chic. It was part of her upbringing. Sean O'Malley had always had a passion for horses, remote cabins, the outdoors. His Irish friend held fast to old-fashioned notions of family, honor and duty. It was only natural for Caitlin to embrace those same loves and concepts.

If that were the case, he pondered, New York must have felt like a land of exile to Cat O'Malley. And this simple Echo Creek stable, with all its memories of lovers and friends, must feel like a homecoming.

Perhaps he'd been taking the wrong approach. Perhaps he needed to stop thinking of Caitlin as a woman with one foot in New York.

"You're right. Hank would be the best candidate for these blankets," Buck agreed, "but Kodiak should model the jewel-toned patterns. Nothing like a chestnut to bring out those colors."

As Chase brought out more samples, Buck watched Caitlin praise the quality and choice of their products. They discussed a variety of settings and shots before Chase stretched and announced his need for sleep.

"Get to bed, brother. I'll finish up in here," Buck volunteered, helping Caitlin place the blankets back in the boxes.

"Thanks, Chase—" Caitlin held out her hand "—for trusting me with the job."

"Oh, by the way, we're going to let you stay, ma'am," Chase drawled, casting a knowing look in Buck's direction. "It's official. You can sleep easy tonight. Now if you'll excuse me, I'm heading back to the lodge. See y'all in the morning."

Buck watched Caitlin's face flush with obvious irritation. She put a hand to her hip and confronted him.

"How and when was this decision made, Rawlings, and on what merits was I judged?"

"Calm down, O'Malley." He continued stacking boxes in the storage area. "We're both professionals. My decision was based on your expertise and your ability to handle the crew. On top of that, you've found ways to work around foul weather to save time, and in my business, time is money."

His half-truths seemed to calm her. She dug her hands into her pockets and tapped a bale of hay with the toe of her boot. "And there's no longer a question of my compromising quality?"

"Forget it." He brushed his palms together then rubbed them against the back pockets of his black denim jeans. "It was a bad judgment call on my part." He shrugged slightly, uncomfortable with admitting his error. "I should never have assumed you'd cut corners." He offered his hand to her. "I'm sorry. I'd like to apologize, Cat."

She pursed her lips and seemed to study his hand as if to expect words written on his palm. "Apology accepted," she murmured after long moments of hesitation.

As she pulled her right hand out of her pocket, a folded piece of paper fluttered to the straw-strewn planks, landing at his feet. He glanced at Caitlin whose eyes held a sheepish expression, then bent to pick it up. Unfolding the paper, he recognized its content immediately. He'd forgotten the magazine page he'd torn from the house and garden magazine while Caitlin and the crew displayed their collages. Had she found it and crumpled it in anger?

"What was this doing in your pocket?" he asked.

"It was in the Big Room—" she explained coolly. "I—I've always loved Victorians and this house is especially nice."

Buck hesitated for a moment, knowing what he had to say might hurt her deeply. "It's a photo of my home in Missoula."

Caitlin felt something tighten in her gut and blossom outward to every part of her being. How could Buck buy such a house knowing the two of them had included it in their dreams of the future? Their failed future. How could he stare at its gingerbread edging day after day and not recall the night Caitlin had chosen just such an edging from a similar magazine? Worst of all, how could he dream of living there with any other woman but her?

"I—I don't understand," she stammered. "This was obviously torn from a magazine."

"They did a feature on people who chose to restore houses doomed to be torn down." He flattened the magazine page against his thigh then handed it to her.

Caitlin stared at the fanciful design of the bay window.

"When did you buy it?"

"Five years ago. Decades back, it was in my family. My great-grandmother sold it to people who couldn't afford to keep up with repairs. I couldn't stand the thought of it being demolished."

"It's beautiful, Buck."

"There's still some work that needs to be done, but I'm really proud of the exterior."

"I guess I don't understand how you could scoff at the little cottage on my collage when you have a monster of a house waiting when you return home from *your* adventures?"

"I wasn't ridiculing anything. You chose a Victorian cottage, Caitlin. It made me remember how much alike we can be." His deep voice softened. "When I bought the Victorian, I don't know—maybe I believed there'd be a day when you'd return. And with every room I've restored, I've kept a mind to the colors you liked, the little touches you'd mentioned seven years ago. Wishful thinking, I guess."

Wishful thinking. Caitlin turned from him, grasped a post support and closed her eyes briefly. It was hard to imagine rawboned, tough Buck Rawlings indulging in wishful thinking yet his words were as tender and revealing, as convincing as a kiss. Could she allow herself to be taken in by his apology and heartfelt confession? The tranquil image of Buck's home hardly reflected its brooding owner. And too many questions remained. How could a man who blamed a woman for his sister's tragic death truly yearn for that same woman to return and share his home? Add *that* sticky question to the paradox that was Buck Rawlings.

Tonight's revelation made her ponder once again the time she'd spent in New York and Europe, so far away from her true heart's desires. The money, prestige and international exposure had been crucial to her career, but could she have achieved the same success working from a home base in Montana?

"Cat?"

Caitlin felt Buck's fingers on her shoulder gently urging her to turn. When she didn't respond, he stepped around to face her, gently unfolded her hand from around the post and pulled her into his arms. She closed her eyes once again and felt herself melt against the hard planes of his chest. But her questions wouldn't dissolve. They remained a wedge between them.

"Once I commit to something, O'Malley," he murmured as he wove his sinewy fingers through the loose waves of her hair, "I put all of my energy into it. But I just need to know, to have a guarantee, that you'll make an effort to agree to my—"

"But you committed yourself to our future seven years ago," she countered, surprised by the bitterness in her own voice.

"Hush." He pressed the tip of a single finger against her lips. The heat of the callused millimeter of skin coursed through her.

"Buck, I can't forget what happened between us the last time I stayed at Echo Creek." She gripped his wrist, but the sensual dance his finger was creating on her mouth and mind continued. "I don't think I can ever forget."

He lowered his head and touched each of her eyelids with a kiss. His unshaven jaw rasped against the arc of her cheekbone, reminding her this was not one of the smooth-faced, stereotypical New York men she'd dallied with. Buck Rawlings *was* an individualist who defined himself and set his own style.

"Well, then, somehow, some way, I'm going to have to make you forget," he said, his husky voice vibrating against her skin and sending a frisson of warning through her senses.

Caitlin damned the warnings and chose the risk. Caught up in her hunger, an escalating need that had built steadily since her arrival, she caressed his face with both hands and brought his mouth down on hers. Like a burst of wildfire, Buck Rawlings responded with a deep and desperate kiss and caught her in an embrace that corralled her, body and soul. His tongue was hard and searching, and she arched on tiptoe to accept its depth and the shivering pleasure that resulted.

Buck wrestled with demons, old and new, as he held O'Malley's daughter and kissed her a second time. The touch of her warm palms against his cheeks signaled her willingness and branded him with a desire to make right all the wrongs of the past.

He leaned his long frame against the stall and hauled the sweet length of her up against him, savoring the ripeness of her firm high breasts against his chest. His hands dropped to cup and caress her rounded backside, bringing the V of her legs against the bulge in his jeans with mind-boggling accuracy. With each plundering exploration of his tongue in the sweet recesses of her mouth, a rush of stampeding blood crashed against his own urgent need, pumping erotic messages to his brain that would make the most hardened voluptuary blush with amazement.

She wanted to feel his naked flesh beneath her fingertips. Awash with the fine fire of unleashed passion, Caitlin unfastened each strategic button on Buck's shirtfront and let her hands roam over the washboard contours of his midriff, then splayed her fingers over the broad expanse of his well-muscled chest. Buck Rawlings was no present to be unwrapped slowly and savored. He was familiar ground, tested and true, and she wanted him willing and ready, and she wanted him now.

With a groan, Caitlin shrugged the woolen jacket from her shoulders and let it drop to the straw beneath them. Immediately Buck's hands cupped her bottom roughly and drew her up against the hardened outline of his need. The nicker of a horse, the soft glow of the lantern, the bittersweet aroma of hay and molasses-drenched oats, the fiery echo of this man's knowing touch—all swirled together to create a fever within her.

"It's been so long, too long," he whispered into the hollow beneath her ear.

Caitlin felt his fingers outline the circle of her breast through the filmy nightshirt she'd tucked into her jeans before walking out to the stable. Her nipple grew taut under the pressure of his thumb and the softest part of her feminine self clenched in response. Never in her dreams had she imagined an interlude in which Buck would discover the hastiness of her wardrobe choice or in which his hands would evoke such a plateau of pleasure.

Buck felt the bite of her nails on his shoulders and for a heartbeat, smiled in remembrance. Cat O'Malley had always made good use of her nails. Beneath the cool sophisticated exterior and proper manners lurked a most improper woman. The years had done little to tame her or curb his hunger for her savage responses.

But everything was happening too quickly. Buck drew back slightly; his hand stilled upon her breast. It took every ounce of his control to pull the reins on his raging arousal. The overpowering sensations had momentarily brushed aside the black pall of bitterness and grief that had taken up residence in his soul for too many years. Was it fair to use his desire for Caitlin to drive out his demons?

Lips parted, model-perfect cheekbones flushed, she was more beautiful than ever. Keeping his gaze riveted to her tawny eyes, he sucked in air and brought his hand up to caress her cheek tenderly.

Above the thunder of his heart, a voice of reason and honor whispered through the fog of desire. He'd promised her a future together years ago and then shattered her world with his selfish need to place blame. Until he knew for certain that she was willing to agree to his condition that she stop risking her life, it wouldn't be right to promise her anything. One day, two days, a week. It didn't matter. He couldn't deceive her again.

"Cat." He nearly groaned her name, holding her at arm's length. "I can't go any further, not knowing. Tell me—can you promise you'll stop taking risks?"

Her features became a pained mask of disbelief. She straightened, then stumbled backward, tripping on the jacket she'd dropped earlier. He took an eager step forward to catch her, but she pulled her arms up and stepped swiftly out of his reach. Gasping for breath, she bent to retrieve the puddle of plaid wool from the straw then stood, her back turned to him, as she shrugged it on over her shoulders and thrust her arms angrily through each sleeve.

"What was it you said about that article they wrote about you, Buck? You're a person who chose to renovate a home rather than tear it down? Do you feel the same way about relationships, or is this benevolent attitude of yours limited to large inanimate objects?"

"Caitlin, benevolent and charitable are hardly the way I'd describe my feelings for you."

"Would 'off and on, according to your whims' be more accurate, Mr. Rawlings?"

"Hell, no! I don't want to hurt you again. We can't get physically involved with each other until we know if there truly is a future."

"You're beginning to sound like a business person checking out the safety of an investment. What were you doing a few minutes ago—checking out my assets, investigating the desirability of the account?"

"Dammit, Caitlin. You're trying my patience."

Speechless with anger, she watched him button his shirt with sure, brisk movements. Was it the whiskey, the late hour or indifference that enabled Buck to exhibit such calm? It was evident he wasn't experiencing any of the turmoil that rollicked through her now, each tempestuous wave sending her further and further from any desire to reconcile.

"This isn't easy on me, either, O'Malley," he added before she could speak. "I like things neat and easy and in their place."

A shiver of white heat coursed through Caitlin at his arrogant tone, so similar to the cavalier manner used by his brother to announce their decision to allow her to stay at Echo Creek. Had they made that decision with the same offhanded approach? Did Buck take her seriously in matters business or personal?

"I think it's best if you bunk with your brother tonight, Rawlings." She backed away from him toward the double doors of the stable, unwilling to break eye contact while expressing her rage. "You'll find your sleeping bag and your high-strung, disobedient dog out in the hallway."

"No one kicks me out of my own room, lady!" With the stealth of a predatory animal, he moved towards her. Caitlin found herself captured between the hard boards of a stall and the even more ungiving wall of Buck's chest.

"It's your call, O'Malley. I don't want to rush you. But if you feel half the passion I do, I think eventually you'll agree to my terms. Everything—what we had together in the past and what we might find in the future—everything hinges on you."

"You're asking me to change my very nature, Buck, to suppress my inborn desire to be challenged by adventure. I can't stop being what I am."

"I'm not asking you to change your nature. I'm simply asking you to stop and think before you take a risk, to weigh the consequences. Maybe it's selfish of me, but I just want to know you're safe, O'Malley."

He watched her close her eyes and he felt mesmerized by the sweep of her dark lashes against the heightened color of her cheek. Lowering the arm that imprisoned her, he stepped away until his back was against the opposite wall. In the silent minutes that passed, he made a decision of his own. He would not rush into a renewal of their relationship no matter how much his body pulsed for her.

"I want you so much right now." She spaced the words evenly in a breathy wisp of a voice. Opening her eyes, she studied him wistfully. "Which means this is the worst of all possible times to make a decision. I can't be swayed by passion, Buck. But you're starting to make sense. Either that, or you've simply found a new way to package your plan. I can almost see myself agreeing to it."

Her words were like a shower of petals, cool and light, after a heavy rain. Some part of him uncoiled, relaxed.

Buck looked down at the straw floor and gave thanks that she was coming to her senses. Even if the woman decided there was no hope for their relationship after thoroughly testing it, at least she'd recall his warnings each time she was tempted to test her limits foolishly.

"Great," he said quietly. "And maybe you're right. It's probably best if I move my sleeping bag into Chase's room for the night."

She gave him a puzzled stare. "That isn't necessary. We could relax the rules while I'm in the process of making my decision."

"It's the honorable thing to do."

"Honorable? This isn't like you, Buck."

"I've always been told I have two natures."

"And I'm very familiar with both, Buck. Brooding and really brooding."

Ignoring her comment, he continued on in a low voice that made it clear he intended to have it his way. "Since you've made your decision to allow us to get reacquainted, I thought it only fair that we start out slow. I'm going to court you, Cat O'Malley. Flowers, dancing, moonlight swims, sitting side by side staring into the fire."

"Buck, the only thing you've ever courted in your life is trouble. With a capital *T*." She closed the distance between them and slipped into his arms. He could see straight down the V of her nightshirt to the shadowed valley between her breasts.

He averted his eyes and tried to paint a picture of courtship, Rawlings-style. "Tomorrow night, you and I are going to saddle up a couple of horses and have ourselves an innocent little supper just above the lake, Caitlin. There's a field of wildflowers."

"Am I supposed to put on a gingham dress and style my hair in a couple of braids?" Her tone was sarcastic. She reached down and brought his hand from her waist back down to her derriere. "What happened to the wanton man that challenged me here in the stable tonight?"

Buck whipped his hand back to her waist in a swift prudish motion. It took all of his control not to cup her sweet bottom and take her right there. "Oh, that man's still here— don't worry about that. Some things can't be rushed, Caitlin. Seeing you here tonight with all the trappings of country life, I realized how complex you are."

"Trust me. I'm not that complicated, Buck."

"You may have lived in New York, you may have gotten used to fast men and rush hours, but this is Montana. I know a lot of outsiders are moving in and trying to speed things up, but the truth is—we take our time around here."

"I assumed we'd be starting out where we left off seven years ago," she protested, her fingers toying with a button he'd just refastened.

"You expected to make love *tonight?*" he asked with mock surprise. "You were going to allow me to peel this nightshirt from your hungry body and do unspeakably wonderful things to you?"

"That's enough. Stop the act, Rawlings. I know you want the same thing I want."

"We've both changed a lot, O'Malley. There's a lot about you, lady, that I want to rediscover slowly, safely."

"How slowly?" she asked, her voice edged with desire. "One day, two days, a week?"

He lowered his mouth to a hairbreadth of her lips and stopped. "This time I want to be sure, Cat." He raised his head, and stepped back from her. "You just better get used to the thought that I'm going to woo you just like Grampa wooed his woman."

"You, Missoula's original bad boy, will woo me?"

"Yes."

"And how will we know when the wooing has worked and it's time to move on to more serious pursuits?"

"We'll just know," he answered with a shrug.

"Fine. Then bunk with your brother tonight, Rawlings." She backed away from him toward the double doors of the stable. "Like I said before, you'll find your sleeping bag and your high-strung, disobedient dog out in the hallway."

"Caitlin—"

"Don't worry. When I slam the door, I'll do it slowly— Montana-style!"

Chapter Eight

How hard could it be to make a decision about a man who'd been on her mind for almost fifteen years and in her heart for seven? Caitlin reflected as she closed the door to the library, locked it and set her address book and coffee on the sleek oak desk. All day she'd grappled with the pressure put upon her by Buck's ultimatum. To keep what was left of her mind occupied, she'd put all of her energy into today's work on the Echo Creek catalog, pushing the shoot even further ahead of schedule.

Buck had been a disturbing presence all day. He'd cast long smoldering looks in her direction, making her wonder if he was serious about the innocent picnic planned for tonight. Erotic images from their summer of passion paraded through her thoughts without invitation.

She took a sip of her latte and sighed. When a person was stuck at a crossroads, they sought direction, she reasoned. She dialed her father's hospital room and frowned when she heard his lackluster greeting.

"Dad, you don't sound like a man who's ready to burst out of those hospital doors and climb a mountain," she teased.

"A very small mountain, perhaps," he said without enthusiasm. He sidestepped all of her questions about pain, medications and blood sugars in a matter-of-fact tone.

Caitlin had stolen away for a few moments daily to read the books and articles on diabetic retinopathy she'd brought with her to the lodge. She no longer felt so utterly helpless at the prospect of her father's loss of sight. There was hope. Heartened by reports of recent advances, she shared the news with him now and mentioned a doctor in Seattle who'd had success in dealing with macular degeneration.

Sean O'Malley's voice perked up only slightly.

"I wish I could be there, Dad, or you could be here. You're worried about more than your health. I can tell. What's bothering you?"

"Ach, I've called five companies to reschedule assignments for the next few months and two of them wanted to cancel on me." His cantankerous tone returned. "On top of that, the leg's not healin' as well as expected and there's a bit of infection where the doctor stitched my arm."

"But you've always healed well. I'm sure it's just a temporary setback. Let the antibiotics go to work. By tomorrow, things could turn around—"

"Stop playin' with me, Cat, treatin' me like some frightened child a person lies to so they feel comforted and safe—especially when they have real reason to be afraid."

Caitlin bit her bottom lip. Never in all these years had she confronted her father about her childhood, about his technique of insisting she be fearless, or his need to constantly demand proof of her courage.

"Is that what you did to me, Dad?" she asked softly in her most nonthreatening tone. "Did you lie to me so I wouldn't feel I was a burden to a single parent? Did you belittle my fear by telling me any normal ten-year-old would love to spend the night in a haunted castle?"

"Caitlin Grace O'Malley! You're talkin' to your father, girl!"

Caitlin heard the creak of bedsprings and heard him groan. She wasn't being cruel or hurtful in confronting him, she tried to convince herself. She'd meant to ask him about these things for years. With her own life in chaos, she couldn't put it off any longer. Her father might offer valuable insight about herself no one else was capable of.

"I have absolute respect for you, Dad, but this whole confrontation with Buck Rawlings has me thinking about why I am the way I am. Why can't I admit fear or sense danger? Why do I seem to be addicted to taking risks?"

"And you want to blame your poor lame father for all of that?" Sean O'Malley roared into the phone. "I dare you to come here and say such things to my face, daughter! I sacrificed for you, Cat. And I didn't raise you to question a father's duty."

She wanted to remind him that she'd always been a dutiful daughter. While living in New York, she'd always opened her doors and rearranged her schedule when he paid one of his impromptu visits. Now that she'd returned to Missoula, they shared a duplex and a darkroom. But she knew none of those reminders would convince her angry father of her loyalty. In his eyes, she'd questioned his parenting skills. It was best to hold her ground. In the O'Malley clan you fought fire with fire or faced the flames.

"Calm down, Dad," she said sternly. "Believe me, I love you dearly and I'm *not* blaming you. I'm just trying to understand what makes me tick and to find out whether I can change—enough to please Buck."

"If I hadn't taken you with me on my wild journeys, Cat, you'd have been smothered in fancy petticoats and French lessons. If I hadn't brought you to Montana with me, your witch of a maternal grandmother would'a turned you into a spoiled snob. You would'a turned against me."

"Turned against you? Never. We're too alike." Caitlin stood and faced the wall. A topographical map of the area hung on the wall. She'd studied it soon after her arrival, in search of scenic points. Now the rugged ridge where Shepherd's Rock was located drew her eye.

She turned back around quickly, away from thoughts of Sarah's last adventure, and stared blindly at the top of the desk, at the objects caught in the glare of the green banker's lamp. Sarah was a risk taker, but the circumstances were different, she told herself. No one would ever know for certain if it was desperation brought on by her disease or plain bad luck that plunged Sarah to her death.

"So Buck Rawlings wants to change you? You know better than to believe you can change yourself to please any man, daughter." Her father's voice quieted but his brogue deepened. "Ach, people can't change—unless it benefits them, as well. How exactly does Buck want you to be different, girl?"

"He says he wants me to constantly keep a mind to safety, but I get the sense that means never taking a risk. A few days ago, he stated flatly that he didn't want me climbing trees, but that could have been the heat of the moment."

"It's utter nonsense. In our business, risk is necessary, Cat. Otherwise you lose your edge. Would I have caught my famous picture of the eagle in the Rockies if I had not chanced death or injury? I'd be disappointed in you, daughter, if you kept hugging the tree and forgot about going out on the limb."

Caitlin sat down and sank against the high back of the plush leather chair. On a whim, she'd sought direction from her father. Rather than assist in her dilemma, his comments only served to complicate matters. If she held her impulsiveness in check to please Buck Rawlings, she would disappoint and alienate her father.

And what about her own sense of self and what she wanted in life? What about the images on her goal collage? How much was she willing to sacrifice for Buck?

Buck took a sip of wine, stretched out on the picnic blanket and watched Caitlin feed carrot sticks to Kodiak and

Denim Hank, the two horses they'd ridden up to the meadow above the lake. He'd cursed himself repeatedly since the start of their romantic supper. This wooing business might be fine for a man without memories of lovemaking with Caitlin O'Malley, but he'd never forgotten a single detail. Time had only embellished the erotic images forged seven years ago.

Putting the brakes on his desire was wearing down his willpower, putting a kibosh on his appetite and making him feel like howling at the moon.

He did have a dual nature—that much he knew—and he'd hoped to put his best side forward this evening. Problem was, both sides—the good Buck and the bad Buck—were ready to pull out the stops and put the pedal to the metal.

Pouring himself another glass of wine and wishing it were a cold frosty beer, he smiled wryly and secretly toasted his arousal. "At least you're showing your true nature," he muttered.

"You say something?" Caitlin asked, her cheek still pressed against Hank's face. The blue roan seemed to be leaning into her embrace, smiling, and taunting Buck's empty arms.

"Come back over here, O'Malley. This blanket's getting cold without you."

She gave the horses one last pat and turned toward him. In her all-white Western shirt, red belt and indigo jeans, she looked heavenly and pure with just a touch of trouble—like every cowboy's dream woman. The collar of her shirt was edged in rhinestones, the front and back yoke trimmed with long white fringe beneath lavish embroidery. She'd explained that it was a gift from her father who liked to indulge her with embarrassingly feminine garments.

As she walked through a carpet of Indian paintbrush, Buck thought of the filmy ladylike clothes he'd like to buy to drape on her slender but curvaceous figure. Not one item would remotely resemble the practical, durable Echo Creek Outfitters gear she favored.

Caitlin settled on the blanket beside him and accepted her half-finished glass of wine from his hand. "I didn't know this place existed, Buck. You never brought me here—before, you know, last time."

It was awkward dividing their history into prepassion, postpassion and the present—the slow burn.

"It's a secret place. Grampa called it Libby's Pocket after my grandmother. He used to bring me here when I was a kid. We'd talk for hours and he'd always be whittling."

"Sounds like he was special to you, Buck."

"Gramps was a true romantic, a member of a dying breed. He grew up in my Victorian house in Missoula when his father, a rancher, divorced his mother." Buck watched in fascination as the first hint of gold from the setting sun cast a soft glow on Caitlin's heart-shaped face. "He ended up working the ranch anyway, which was another kind of romance in his way of thinking."

"This is the same man who built Echo Creek Lodge." Caitlin stretched out on her side to face him. The long silky fringe on her shirt parted and curled around the mound of her breast.

"Yeah, with the help of his brothers. Incredible, isn't it? Always loved to work with his hands. Made my oak bed and Sarah's willow bed. Grampa's the one who encouraged my father to start a business in outdoor gear." Buck couldn't take his eyes off the white fringe on her shirt. With her every movement, the stuff floated and resettled around the rise of her breasts. It was the sexiest damn thing he'd ever seen.

"Last night, you said he courted your grandmother properly?"

"You might call it the old-fashioned way." Buck paused to gather his thoughts. "He told me all about it, acted as though winning her love was more of an accomplishment than working a ranch or building a log cabin. She wanted nothing to do with him in the beginning.

"Well, he knew she liked wearing hats and watching birds and canoe rides. He was young and struggling with hard times, but he bought her a hat he couldn't afford and made her a birdhouse and borrowed a canoe. One of his brothers taught him to dance out in the barn. He started taking her to dances and turned out to be quite the hoofer.''

"How romantic. How long did it take for your grandfather to convince Libby to marry him?''

"Two years. But it didn't end with their marriage. The man took special care to find out what pleased her until the end of their days.''

"Those were different times, Buck. And we're different people.''

"Not so very different.'' Buck took Caitlin's hand in his and ran his callused thumb over the smooth satin of her palm. "Maybe that's what's wrong with a lot of couples these days. They feel they've got to keep up with the frantic pace of the rest of the world. Some things can't be rushed. When there's a problem that needs to be talked out, you can't schedule it for a half hour on Wednesday night. You've got to drop everything and take care of it.''

He brought her hand to his lips and kissed the backs of her fingers. Her lips parted, her golden eyes widened, but she said nothing, allowing him to caress her hand and weave his fingers through hers.

Buck wondered what was possessing him to talk so much. He'd always practiced an economy of words. It was just his style. Perhaps it was memories of long talks with his grandfather, tucked in the peace and beauty of Libby's Pocket, that prompted him to empty his heart to Caitlin.

"You know, people are calling Montana the last best place.'' He pondered aloud after long moments had passed. "Not just because of the natural beauty but because of its ideals. I want to hold on to that.''

"Are you one of those people who wants to keep all outsiders out?''

"That's impossible. Besides, there's room for a lot of different people here, Caitlin. I'll be happy as long as I'm able to recreate some of the simplicity my grandparents spoke of. But I've discovered simplicity has gotten pretty complicated. I found that out when I began to restore the Victorian. And this past week, when you came back into my life."

The sun had turned crimson, staining her white shirt with a sensual pink flush. The rhinestones on her collar sparkled like a necklace of pure light, spreading an aura of dusky rose on the slender column of her throat. The row of fringe turned a deeper pink, like raspberries mixed with cream. Buck released her hand and picked up a silky loop. Curling it around his finger, once, twice, three times, his fingertip met the soft resistance of her breast.

Caitlin laughed softly. "If my father knew how you were using the fringe on the shirt he gave me—how you've turned it into a weapon, he'd have your hide."

"You're wrong," Buck whispered. "My lips are the only weapon I'm going to use tonight. The only weapon I'll need." With that comment he lowered her to the blanket and brought his mouth down on hers for a thoroughly arousing kiss.

His resolve to move slowly melted. He wove his fingers through the cascade of fringe and felt the long loops give way over the mound of her breast. "I haven't been able to take my eyes off you all night, Cat," he said against the arch of her cheekbone. "I can see where my plan might lead to a good deal of frustration on my part."

"On your part?" She closed her eyes for a moment then opened them and fixed him with their tawny depth. "You aren't the only one feeling the savage pull of desire, Rawlings. But now that I understand where you got these notions of romance and courtship, I'm willing to go along.

"I guess I want whatever modern-day variations you can give me on the canoe rides and the birdhouse and kitten in a basket, Mr. Rawlings. But I don't want it to take two years. I doubt if I can stand two days, but there's something exhilarating about the wait."

Her words took away his chance to change his mind, to join her in the great oak bed tonight and pick up where they'd left off seven years ago. Buck kissed her gently, then simply held her in his arms. Across the horizon, above the vivid stripes of sunset, a scattering of stars were visible.

"You brought a jacket?" he asked.

"The thick wool with the hood," she answered, settling her head in the curve of his neck. "It's at the foot of the blanket. You're thinking of staying out here a little longer?"

"I want you to see the stars from my mountain, Caitlin."

"I remember your diamond skies, Buck. You showed me your stars once before." She skimmed the edge of his jaw with her fingertips. "Have they changed all that much in seven years?"

"I wouldn't know," he said quietly, thinking of the precious time they'd lost. "I just started noticing them again—tonight."

Buck relished the sweet satisfaction of their embrace. Tomorrow he'd take her fishing before dawn. Perhaps he'd challenge her to a game of pool, but he doubted she'd accept. As his mind raced through romantic locations around the lodge, another part of him wondered if he could withstand that much togetherness.

In the distance, a coyote howled. Caitlin tensed and drew closer. Buck smiled to himself. There was uncertainty between himself and Caitlin, but here, in the embrace of his beloved Crazy Mountains, he was certain of one thing. This is where they both belonged.

"The Tush Push?" Caitlin put a hand to her hip. "You've got to be making this up, Lester Owen."

"God's honest truth, Miss O'Malley." Lester made an imaginary X over his heart with the tip of his finger. "There is a country-western dance named the Tush Push, and you've jes' got t'learn it fer Chase's party. Your tired old two-step won't cut it anymore. You learned that when you were sixteen."

"I know. Okay, teach me the Tush Push. What other crazy steps do you have on that list in your hand?"

"There's nothin' crazy about these dances, young lady."

Caitlin watched as Lester pushed another chair away, making ample space on the tiled floor of the gaming room for dancing. "I know you had ballroom dancin' lessons and such. Jes' name me some of the dances you learned back there when you lived with that grandmother, the one who thought your Daddy was no good."

"That was a long time ago, Lester."

"I don't care. You offended my Western sensibilities. Now you just give me some of them names."

"Mambo, foxtrot, tango, waltz, modern jazz, quadrille—"

"Well, now, those names sound a whole lot crazier than what I plan to teach you. You ever tried the Ten Step or Slap Leather, Honky-Tonk Stomp, or the Cowboy Motion? Everyone's heard of the Achy Breaky but what about the Cotton-Eyed Joe or the Sixteen Step?"

"I didn't know there'd be so many."

"See, there's partner dancing for a man and a woman, and then there's country line dancin' where you don't need a partner. Everyone just up and dances. When you figure we got a lodge full of men and one tall glass of water—"

"Tall glass of water?"

"That's you, Miss O'Malley. It's a compliment." He turned on the cassette player. A slow country tune filled the room. "Okay, let's start with somethin' simple like the Cowboy Motion. It's a line dance. We jes' stand side by side here. Ready? Start with the vine—sideways right and sideways left, and uh, huh, that's it, now backward vine. Yes, ma'am. Three steps—one, two, three—and touch." With each movement, Lester's reed-thin body took on an energy that made Caitlin feel she was in the presence of a line-dancing master.

"Heel tap double and single, switch feet. Then you're goin' wanna bump. Twice," he continued. "Hands in front, thrust hips forward—no, you got to *thrust* the hips forward while pullin' your arms back."

"It seems . . . very suggestive."

"That's because *I'm* doin' it. My ex-wife always told me that I have a natural earthiness. Try it again. Uh-huh."

Caitlin asked him to start from the beginning. Again and again she watched and copied his steps until she felt sure of herself. As he forwarded the audiotape to teach her the Tush Push, she reflected on the past two days. Stargazing, fishing, long walks, picnics, flowers by her bedside. Buck Rawlings was no slouch at courting, but the strain was evident. He was a man used to long hours of solitude. It seemed as much a need to him as food or rest.

But it was wrong. They were pushing aside the real issues of Sarah's death and Buck's need to control her, and were reliving the courtship of his grandparents. Buck called it "a return to simplicity." Caitlin called it "avoiding the inevitable."

"What good will these dance lessons be if none of the men know how to do them?" she asked Lester after ten minutes of Tush Pushing.

"Every one of 'em knows all of these dances. See, there's never any females up here on the mountain. During the catalog shoot, the men always go into Harlowtown to the Beef 'n Brew to dance. I've been teaching 'em over the years. Last year, I started bringin' a few of my instructional videos. We didn't want the men of Echo Creek to look like fools, Miss O'Malley. Now let's work on the Ten Step. It takes a bit of practice."

Caitlin followed Lester's lead as he swiveled and demonstrated a stomp clap and a pivot.

She remembered the dances they'd had at the lodge when she and Sarah were in their mid-teens. Buck had been a frequent partner even then and his bad-boy attitude and dark silhouette had always intrigued her. There was something magical about the way music brought out his duality. The dangerous lone wolf had loved nothing better than to display his wicked little two-step. On the flip side, he'd used a choirboy demeanor to draw Doc Morrow's wife onto the floor for a sweet country waltz.

"What about Buck?" she asked Lester. "Does he still go into town—to dance?"

"Oh, yeah. He's the best of the bunch. A real natural. Seems odd, doesn't it? Secretive type like Buck letting loose. He is really goin' t'appreciate you learnin' these dances, Miss O'Malley."

"There's something else I could use your help with, Lester, but only if you're willing. The party is only two days from now."

"Ask away."

"I want you to help me create a feminine-looking outfit for the party. A miniskirt, maybe, and something snug and sexy on top."

"Thank you, thank you for trustin' me, Miss O'Malley." Lester went down on his knee, grabbed her hand and kissed it. "I've got designs on paper that have been beggin' to be released for years. You want frills and ruffles or—"

"No, I want to look like a bad girl, as much like an outlaw as Buck."

"I tol' you before, Miss O'Malley, that you were silk and Buck was black leather. You might be fightin' your true nature if you do this."

"Lester—" She held up her hands. "Even the most virtuous of women get the urge to look naughty now and then. Very naughty."

Buck swatted a drifting balloon from in front of his face and ducked beneath a birthday banner suspended from between two rafters. "Raise this up an inch or two before someone gets banner burn on their neck," he called up to Klyde who stood atop a ladder in the center of the Big Room. "Anyone seen Lester?"

Buck sensed a nervous undercurrent among the crew. Caitlin and Lester had been absent from the group more than a few times during the past forty-eight hours.

"Are you guys trying to keep secrets from me? I'm not the brother you're supposed to surprise."

The men looked at one another sheepishly, then shrugged or shook their heads.

"And where is Lester? Is he your chief conspirator?"

"He's more of a coconspirator," Rusty offered, looking up from tuning his fiddle. "It's complicated, Buck. Let's just say we've been asked to keep things under wrap."

"You lookin' for me, boss?" Lester's familiar twang echoed across the vast room. He stood at the bottom of the staircase, a yellow tape measure draped over his neck. The band of elastic that circled his wrist was topped with a bright red pincushion.

"Lester, I've been looking for that pair of black Sundance jeans I modeled the first day of the shoot. I'd planned to wear them tonight. I checked the inventory in the storeroom without any luck. Have you—"

"Well, now, I'm sure they're around here somewhere, but when a man's in charge of several hundred items of wardrobe, it's possible to have one missin'." Lester looked down pensively and fussed with the pins on the tomato-shaped cushion. "Course you always did look good in those Laredo jeans with the cowboy cut. The black would be 'specially appropriate for tonight's small but festive gatherin'. It's not like you're hard-pressed to find a pair a'black pants in that collection of yours, boss."

"Thanks, Lester. I'll take a second look in the storeroom."

"Fine. As soon as I'm done with things down here I'm going upstairs to prepare myself for a well-deserved evenin' of fun. I'll be lucky to get five minutes to do that!" Lester sniffed. "I swear, no qualified tailor should have to endure what I go through for two weeks out of the year. Now I'm being asked questions like I'm somebody's personal valet."

"Lester, I'm sorry." Damn, Buck felt like a heel. Courting Caitlin slowly had put him on edge, making him as irascible as Louie. Thank God he worked with a very forgiving crew. He'd make amends tonight when he announced they all had tomorrow off for a day of rest. Thanks to Caitlin's efficiency and Lester's organizational skills, the shoot was almost two days ahead of schedule, easing concerns about going over budget.

After Buck changed into the Laredo jeans, a black vest and shirt, he helped Joe move sofas and roll up a number of handwoven rugs, leaving a good portion of the immense hardwood floor open for dancing. The thought of holding Caitlin in his arms to the rhythm of a sweet country song only doubled his edginess.

He helped Klyde move the upright piano in place then stood with his elbow propped against the top while Klyde warmed up with a few bars of a ballad. Rusty's fiddle responded to the mating call and the two polished a short duet then stopped to talk about the evening's musical agenda.

"When do we expect Chase back, Carlos?" Buck asked the part-time magician who was busily preparing for his magic act. The three dogs sat watching his every move with worried expressions. He pulled a Ping-Pong ball out of Farley's ear with a chuckle then made it disappear into thin air, which sent the three hounds searching through the room.

"We sent Chase to town about five o'clock, told him we were clean out of coffee. I called ahead and told Ed at the grocery store to keep Chase talking for about half an hour, which will make it about seven at the latest," Carlos calculated aloud, then glanced at his watch. "It's almost eight, which means he'll be here in fifteen minutes or so."

"Great." Buck found himself walking about the room, checking last-minute details, monitoring Louie's progress on the buffet table and the decoration of the three-tiered cake.

With a smile, Buck recognized the familiar pattern that played itself out on June first of every year. After their mother's death, it was left to Buck to organize and stage Chase's birthday parties. He'd felt woefully inadequate the years his younger brother turned five, six and seven. He'd been trying to duplicate the typical backyard party their mother would have planned, all the time realizing no one could replace her.

When Chase's eighth birthday arrived, Buck was fifteen. With the help of two friends' mothers, he took the celebration out of the backyard and down to the local pool. Each year, the parties varied greatly, but always they were away from a home haunted by memories of a mother forever lost to her children.

Twenty years had passed and he was still the older brother, trying to make up for Chase's loss of childhood. For the past seven years, Sarah's death and their father's bitterness had shadowed the celebration further, making it an event Chase preferred to celebrate alone, away from family. In a way, Buck was looking forward to the opportunity to once again make his brother's birthday a family celebration. To both Buck and Chase, five aging models, a wild-haired cook and a torch-singing tailor were family. Buck was saddened only by the fact that Sean O'Malley was absent from the group.

"Has anyone seen Caitlin?" Buck asked after dimming the lights. He noticed a number of men staring at a point just beyond his right shoulder. Turning, he spotted her, standing on the landing, her cheeks flushed, golden eyes glowing as she watched him expectantly. Her hair flowed loose in lustrous waves from under her black Stetson, its red highlights captured like faerie fire in the glow of lamplight.

O'Malley's daughter was dressed from neck to thigh in girl clothes. Feminine, sexy, amazingly formfitting girl clothes that contrasted sharply with the practical, masculine attire he'd come to expect. There was some obvious pirating of Echo Creek clothing designs, but he'd be hard-pressed to identify the style names or catalog numbers.

"You look incredible, O'Malley," Buck murmured aloud, pushing the brim of his Stetson up with the tip of his thumb.

Her upper body was caressed by a reinvention of a man's ribbed knit top in a soft muted gray. The round collar had been altered dramatically to scoop low above the rise of her full, high breasts. A black leather vest emphasized their alluring fullness all the more.

A row of small pearlized buttons, the top two left open to create an inviting V, drew his focus downward to Caitlin's impossibly narrow waist, belted with black leather and studded with buffaloes fashioned in silver. How he'd love to put his arms around her and start a stampede among those frozen silver critters.

Instead, he restlessly shifted his weight from one boot to the other and savored the view. He knew he was staring rudely, unabashedly but he didn't give a damn. She was his woman, had always been his woman. Circumstances beyond his control had never allowed him to take full possession and to make her feel that she was his, but Caitlin was his all the same.

His starving eyes were riveted on her long shapely legs, a view afforded him by the black denim miniskirt that hugged her hips so enticingly. Her deerskin cowboy boots completed her provocative appearance.

At the edge of his consciousness he heard the front door open and glanced away to find Chase in the doorway of the Big Room gazing in an enraptured fashion like every other healthy male present at Cat O'Malley.

The silence stretched several seconds before Caitlin smiled back at Chase. "Surprise! Would you like the first dance, birthday boy?" she asked descending the stairs.

"Surprise..." The crew joined in two beats late in a dispassionate chorus.

Rusty began a raucous country standard as Chase ran his fingers over the brim of his hat, flexed his shoulders and started moving across the floor toward Caitlin. The crew voiced their approval with catcalls and whistles.

Buck folded his arms across his chest, smiled and shook his head in amazement as Chase took Caitlin's hand, placed a hand on her shoulder and began a spirited Cajun two-step, circling the room, shifting her in and out of the more intimate promenade position.

"Well, now—" Lester joined Buck on the sideline "—that is one mighty fine woman. Miss O'Malley is a real pleasure to work with."

"So my suspicions were right." Buck looked down at the tailor he also considered a close friend. Lester wore a crimson shirt emblazoned with the black silhouettes of wild horses, three to be exact, racing across the narrow boundaries of his sunken chest. "Did you intentionally transform her into a country-western vamp, Mr. Owen?"

"Vamp? Well, no, sir. Now that is not how I would describe the look I was goin' for. I myself would use the word *enchantress,* or perhaps somethin' stronger, like *seductress.* It felt real good, Buck. I love bringin' out the best in the female of the species."

Buck felt a flare of minor jealousy. Lately, Caitlin had looked like a flower taken from the shadows and exposed to sunlight. She was opening, unfurling and searching for more sun.

For the past few days, her oblique golden eyes shimmered with an unearthly glow even in the dimmest of light. Her sassy walk had grown sassier. Gone was the flawless French braid, replaced by wild waves lassoed into a ponytail or allowed to flow freely down her back. He'd like to believe himself partially responsible for the changes in O'Malley's daughter.

"I felt like Professor Higgins preparing that street urchin Eliza Dolittle for the royal ball in *My Fair Lady,*" Lester continued. "See, on top of riggin' up an outfit, I taught her some of the better country steps and she caught on real fast. Course, Miss O'Malley is far from being some gutter-snipe with her fancy background, and she certainly didn't need no elocution lessons or such, like in the movie.''

Thank God, Buck mused.

"She jes' wanted an outfit for the party that'd make her look and feel sorta—sorta naughty. Wanted to open up some eyes, she said.''

Naughty? Buck wondered what Caitlin had on her mind. Had she come to a decision about their future?

"Well, Lester, she certainly accomplished her goal.''

"Recognize those Sundance jeans you were lookin' for earlier?''

Buck narrowed his gaze and studied the short black skirt and its shapely cargo as Chase and Caitlin circled the room again. Since the dance started, Caitlin had glanced frequently in Buck's direction, stirring his possessive longings to a slow boil. He was ready to cut in then and there as the couple passed, but it was Chase's birthday, after all. Let him have the first dance. And maybe Lester was entitled to the second dance.

What Buck really longed to do was waltz her onto the side deck to dance in the open air. He'd see if her comments to Lester about looking and feeling naughty were idle talk or a fantasy waiting to be fulfilled by a dark prince.

"Nice work, Lester. Very nice.'' He complimented the man at his side.

"I consider it my first female ensemble for Echo Creek Outfitters.''

Buck only nodded. He didn't want to touch on the volatile subject of a clothing line for women. Let Lester enjoy his moment of glory. Besides, Buck reasoned, it was impractical for a company devoted to the rugged outdoors to produce anything as frivolous as a miniskirt.

So what did it mean? he pondered. Was letting her hair down and putting on seductive clothing an attempt to hurry the courting process? Or was it her way of announcing she'd reached a decision?

Buck straightened, tugged his hat down until the brim shadowed the penetrating glances he cast in her direction and wondered how he could wait until evening's end to find out what Cat O'Malley had up her sleeve.

Chapter Nine

Grandmother Covington would have vapors if she were to see her well-bred granddaughter now, Caitlin thought as she performed a frantic Cotton-Eyed Joe to a rockabilly duet played by Klyde and Rusty. For ten straight songs, she'd danced with every member of the crew and the two burly workmen from town. Everyone but Buck had promenaded her around the spacious dance floor. Through every tune, she'd searched for his black Stetson in the dimly lit circle of hat-wearing men and always found him watching her intently, while allowing the other men to step forward to dance.

His damnable generosity and need for fairness only built her anticipation to a fever pitch.

Rusty announced the musicians' need to take a break and explained the group would be listening to recorded songs for twenty minutes. Caitlin watched a number of men amble onto the floor and position themselves for line dancing, the perfect formation for half a dozen men and one woman.

Lester had shown her one of the instructional videotapes he'd brought to the lodge but he'd warned her the video couldn't compare with the thrill of the actual group experience. At the moment, the only thrill she was truly interested in was that of dancing in the protective arms of Buck Rawlings. Seven years had been too long a hiatus. She did a perfunctory search of the room and found the man nowhere in sight.

"Miss O'Malley," Lester said, motioning her to a space beside him, "you'll wanna get yourself in the center of this first row next to me. I'll help you through any rough spots. Ready, boys?" he called out to the group. The men responded with good humor, encouraging a few stragglers onto the floor.

"Let's slap some leather!" Joe called out.

The men's laughter and ribald comments faded as the music started, a rhythmic ballad from the dark side of romance, a side all-too-familiar to Caitlin. She hooked her thumbs in her belt loops and tried to visualize the steps to the Slap Leather. The group began performing the vine in unison.

"Back three steps, then hitch!" Lester prompted her after she'd fumbled on the double heel. "Great. Now swivel and do the star! Toe, front, side, back, side!"

Caitlin completed the move by slapping the toe and then the heel of her boot with the palm of her hand. When everyone did a half turn and performed the line dance a second time, Caitlin found herself keeping the moderate tempo and going through the steps without having to think of their order. Chase Rawlings reached out from the next row and playfully tapped her shoulder, winking and giving her a thumbs-up sign.

After the group turned in unison to their original position facing the fireplace, Caitlin glanced up in time to see Buck Rawlings step out of the shadows, looking like an ebony cowboy who'd slipped through the smoked mirrors of time.

"Vine," she whispered to herself. "Heel . . . step." The sight of his black-clad body destroyed her concentration.

Buck's shadowed eyes were riveted on her every move. Lester had described him as black leather to her white silk. Never had that stark label been more appropriate. He was clothed in the somber shade of midnight. The room's lamplight, diffused by parchment shades, glinted off the silver conchos on his hat band and leather vest, giving him an aura of danger and mystery.

"One, two, three, hitch." She raised her knee.

He gave her a cryptic smile and ran a finger along the brim of his hat as if striking a match. Caitlin felt something within her ignite. The fire spread along an unmapped pathway of nerves until she tingled with the anticipation of what might happen this evening. The man wanted to court her in a slow, easy style, a style popular a century ago, but half a week was long enough. No one would dare label her an innocent with a need to be slowly introduced to his lone-wolf ways.

Then and there, she decided that she'd seduce Buck Rawlings tonight.

"Swivel. Toes and heels." She recalled Lester's instructions, voicing them aloud to keep herself focused. As she thought of how his bare chest would feel beneath her fingertips, she hooked her thumbs deeper until her belt loops strained.

Buck began moving toward her. One look at his sexy rebel walk and Caitlin felt as though it were high noon and she'd left her guns at home.

"Star. Toe, front—" Her trembling words held no volume, only a shiver of breath, as he stood facing her like a sensual shadow mirroring her every step.

"—side, back, side." Buck completed the instructions in his deep commanding voice.

In unison they slapped the toe and heel of their boots, completing the eight-part sequence. The country ballad's bass guitar and throaty songstress echoed Caitlin's longings. An unseen but palpable force bound her to Buck. She felt tethered to his every movement, a puppet animated not with strings but with the arch of his brow, the full curve of his lower lip, the echo of his heartbeat. The trendy line dance had become a mating ritual with the heavy promise of an erotic climax. Once, twice, three more times, he stood before her through an entire sequence, stirring her desire with the graceful movements of his sleek silhouette.

Buck was transformed. His moves were fluid, his rhythm flawless. Caitlin could hazard only one explanation. While she'd been a young girl afloat in white lace and gloves in training for the cotillion, Buck had wandered in wild moonlight. He'd learned to harness the darkness and mystery of the night and bring it indoors, to clothe himself in midnight and magic and to effortlessly cast his enigmatic spell on women.

She'd heard the stories of his youth. When Buck Rawlings walked through the door of the Black Bear Café, a fight would soon erupt. Since she'd never witnessed such an event, she had to wonder if it was his ability to ignite a dance floor and turn female heads that caused those notorious rumbles.

A second song started. Wordlessly, Buck pulled Caitlin out of the front row and, taking her right hand in his, placed his other hand on her shoulder and began moving her about the floor in a classic two-step. The rest of the men continued line dancing in two rows, murmuring loudly among themselves as their boots struck the wooden floor in unison, creating a feeling of tribal unity.

Buck guided her gracefully into the promenade position.

"Lester taught you well," his silken voice rasped beside her ear, "but there are a few moves I plan to teach you myself, O'Malley."

Sliding his hand down her arm, he lifted his own arm up and Caitlin found herself being pulled into the circle of his arms, her back nestled against his chest in a cozy maneuver Lester had neglected to demonstrate.

Just feet away, crew members applauded. "And what is this called?" she asked.

"Some call it the Cuddle. I call it the Corral. We'll be doing it often. I like my woman facing forward rather than dancing backward."

My woman? Corral? His choice of words annoyed her. She liked to believe she belonged to no one but herself. No man could ever possess her fully or fill every chamber of her heart. Perhaps that was why she found it so hard to agree to Buck's condition about taking risks.

Yet, no matter how much she resisted his labeling, a tender ache filled her as he held both her hands, cradled her in the circle of his arms and guided her along the dance floor. In this arena, he was the expert, she was the novice. She felt captured by his strength and the gentle power of his words, but she'd never be *his woman.*

To demonstrate that fact, Caitlin slipped out of the cozy confines of the Cuddle and floated free of Buck for a moment before resuming a woman-facing-man dance position, her chin held at a proud tilt, her arms keeping him at a distance. After all, a woman couldn't properly seduce a man without watching his eyes.

But she'd forgotten the power and intensity of Buck Rawlings's eyes. Green flecked with gold. Savage pride mingled with an unspoken sadness. She didn't want to be called *his woman* but the man could brand and hold her captive with one of his smoldering glances, and tonight the fierce fire in his eyes was unmistakably possessive.

How dare she think she could mimic his dangerous outlaw airs with her simple skirt and vest? Caitlin straightened her shoulders and increased the distance between them by the scant inches possible. She wanted to take the reins in her hands and feel the man respond. Buck was the one who wanted to woo. She was the one who wanted to conquer. Before this night was over, she intended to play the seductress fully and bring him to his knees.

* * *

Even as a kid, he'd had a problem with sharing, Buck reflected. Tonight he'd discovered how little he'd changed in thirty-five years. Watching Caitlin move so freely between his men had made him feel ill at ease and irritable. During Carlos's magic act, he'd watched and clapped cordially, but in truth, he'd been seething with impatience. As he lit each candle on Chase's birthday cake, he'd been so captivated watching the soft golden glow of candlelight brighten Caitlin's eager features and illuminate the low scoop of her top, he'd burned his fingers. Twice.

Klyde and Rusty began a sultry tune suitable for slow dancing, and Buck spirited Caitlin through the Big Room's open double doors to the side deck. Gone was his desire to keep it country, to follow a sequence of time-honored steps. He wanted his movements to echo the intense hunger thrumming through his veins, to a primitive rhythm older than time. He pulled her body roughly up against his.

"I heard from the illustrious Professor *Lester* Higgins that you'd commissioned him to create something naughty for tonight's party." He held her firmly in his embrace as they danced, stealing occasional glances down the V of her shirt into the shadows between her breasts. "Any truth to that?"

"Lester does love to talk." When confronted, she appeared to sidestep the issue. "What a lovable character."

Buck brushed a stray tendril away from her cheek and brought his thumb back to rest in the hollow of her perfect cheekbone.

"Don't change the subject," he chided. "We're not discussing Lester's character. We *are* talking about the magic he can work, turning a pair of Sundance jeans into a strip of pure temptation." He lowered both his hands and ran his palms slowly over the curve of her bottom. "Oh, Lord, too tight, too short, too much. Whatever was on your mind, O'Malley?"

"We tried your style of courting for a few days. I thought it was my turn."

"Your turn to do what?"

"To speed things up a bit. To show you what I'm feeling, Buck."

"Feelings? Is that what this scandalous, naughty outfit is all about?" He pressed the issue. Caitlin didn't respond. She lowered her head, causing her hat to block his view of her eyes. Their slow intimate dance came to a standstill. Buck lifted the hat from her head and tossed it onto the nearby wicker settee. He bent to brush his lips lightly across her mouth. "What exactly are you feeling, Cat?"

She threw up her hands then let them fall against his chest. "I feel like jumping out of my skin half the time. I'm putting all my excess energy and frustration into my work so I don't have to think about—about us."

Buck didn't have the heart to tell her there was no "us." Not yet. He couldn't commit to her emotionally until the road was clear for a definite future. Even then, even if she promised to uphold his condition, there was no guarantee the relationship would gel.

"You're right, Caitlin. I set the ground rules these past few days. I have to play fair. It's your turn to set the mood. Any ideas?"

"I have several." Her responding laugh was deep-throated, sexy. He'd been mildly aroused since she'd made her surprise appearance on the staircase. Now her nearness and the alluring curve of her rump beneath his hands brought him to full hardness. He ached with his need for her until it became a potent weight guiding his hands to press her against him wantonly.

O'Malley's daughter had a power over him that robbed him of his control. He'd had enough of playing suitor. Chaste picnics and conversations about the virtues of Victorian living had him climbing the walls and taking early-morning swims in Medicine Bowl Lake. Buck would let her set the mood but he'd be damned if he'd allow her to fully take the reins from his more than capable hands.

Caitlin watched the play of emotion on Buck's normally guarded features as the sultry tune ended. Did he realize how determined she was to take control of the evening? Was he feeling threatened by her aggression? The sound of Lester singing a bittersweet Hank Williams tune filtered from the Big Room through the balcony's open doors. Buck took a step back and inhaled sharply, seemingly grateful for the change of pace.

"Since I'm taking the lead tonight, I want you to indulge me with a waltz," she whispered, "like you did with Doc Morrow's wife all those years ago."

Caitlin smiled as he brought one hand up to her waist and took her hand in his for a classic waltz. Cheek to cheek they danced in wordless surrender to the forces that had brought them together—then and now.

"What else do you have on your list, O'Malley?" he asked when the music concluded. "I hope it's short."

"Actually it encompasses the next few days. I heard your announcement about the crew having a day off tomorrow."

"Uh-huh."

"We could saddle the horses and ride up to an alpine meadow—"

Buck put a finger to her lips. "After we sleep in late."

She studied his eyes to see if he was serious. His dark visage remained unflappable. A skitter of heat coursed through her. This game of seduction was fun as long as the dice remained in her hand. Why did the man feel a need to steal a turn?

"You make it sound as though we'll be sleeping in together, Buck, which means we'd have to sleep *together* first."

"That's the logical progression in these things. There are variations on that theme, of course."

"You always did like variations, Mr. Rawlings. What did you have in mind? You haven't built a birdhouse for me yet. And I don't recall you giving me a big floral hat or taking me on a canoe ride."

"I confess I don't have the patience my grandfather had. I want you, Cat, now. Tonight. There ain't no doubt about it."

Caitlin hesitated. Her plan was working faster than expected, but there was a single hitch. "What about me having to make my decision before we . . . take that step?"

"We'll table that discussion." He picked up her hat off the settee and placed it on her head, then paused to straighten it. "I'm forgetting. This is your night. It's your turn to set the tone."

She smiled and nodded toward the furniture on the deck. "I doubt any of that wicker will hold the two of us."

He placed a hand at the small of her back and began walking her in the direction of the double doors. "I want you to say a polite goodnight to the boys, to walk up the stairs to my room, and to wait for me. Start a fire. Light some lamps. And take all your clothes off. I want you ready and waiting—"

Caitlin felt an angry flush rise from her throat and warm her cheeks. How dare he order her to his bed? The man was infuriating. First of all, he made the whole prospect sound so shameful, something he wouldn't want his men to know about. And secondly, he didn't even want to undress her slowly and experience the sweet anticipation. Whatever romantic feelings she'd been experiencing moments earlier turned to dust.

"You have a lot to learn about wooing women, Rawlings." She moved away from the pressure of his hand at her back and turned to confront him face-to-face. "You want me to go to your room, strip and wait for you? It'll be a cold day in hell before I follow a sexist asinine directive like that."

"You little—" His hands balled into fists. "I was trying to protect your virtue, O'Malley. If we blatantly announce our intentions and walk up the stairs, you might find it difficult to live among these guys and get them to cooperate for your photographs."

"You don't have to worry about your crew, Buck. They're not living in the last century like you are."

A solitary balloon floated in from the Big Room and landed on the planks of the deck. Caitlin stared down at it for a moment as another wave of anger washed over her. With an impulsive kick, she sent it flying upward. She'd have preferred to crush it beneath her boot.

"You're being hotheaded and stubborn, Caitlin." Buck took another step.

"No, I'm being smart for the first time since I arrived at Echo Creek and *you're* being your usual arrogant self." She took two steps back, feeling for the rail with her hand. "Lord knows what kind of orders you would have given me once you arrived in your cozy little master suite."

"Look, I admit my approach was a little crude but my intentions were pure. We both want the same thing, O'Malley." He stood a few yards from her, hands on his hips. "The only difference is that I don't dance around. I'm honest and direct."

"You told me it was my turn to set the tone. Then you took charge. You always want to be the one at the helm."

"I ordered you to my bed, lady, because I want to be there with you and because you made it obvious that's where you want to be—" He took off his hat and ran his fingers through the shock of hair at his forehead. "Are you going to admit that much?"

Caitlin closed her eyes for brief seconds and leaned back against the wooden rail of the deck. She could hear raindrops hitting the foliage that lined the path alongside the lodge. Buck wasn't the only lone wolf on this balcony. She often shared his need for solitude—and now that need loomed up and overwhelmed her. Her plans to seduce the man had taken a disappointing twist. Seduction didn't come naturally to her. She needed time to rethink her plan.

Was she overreacting to his comment? Maybe the real problem was the thought of being in his bed again. She'd slept there alone for a number of nights and felt certain until now that she'd exorcised the ghosts of their past.

But so much was left unsaid and unresolved. Just this morning, she'd glanced at Sarah's letters, tucked away in a pocket of her camera bag, and pondered when she could reveal the truth to Buck. More important, she'd asked herself how that revelation would change what was happening between Buck and herself.

Perhaps it was best that things had gone badly tonight and she'd been forced to rethink her strategy. She didn't want to be the virginal innocent being awakened to the mysteries of lovemaking by Buck Rawlings. She'd been there, done that. The role of aggressor was far more intriguing. Risky and appealing. But she'd prefer to distance herself from the man first.

"I need some air. I'm going down to walk by the lake for a while." Caitlin swung a leg over the narrow railing and straddled it while looking down to gauge the long drop to the path below. A steady rain was falling. She'd have to allow for the possibility of damp vegetation and estimate how far she might slide in the slick new men's boots Lester had loaned her from wardrobe.

"Don't you dare jump, O'Malley!"

She looked back to see Buck frozen in place, his face pale and stricken, his arms stretched toward her. Not wanting to chance another emotional encounter, Caitlin slipped her other leg over the rail and leapt into the darkness.

In the heart-thumping seconds before Caitlin jumped, Buck was hurled back in time to the day of his sister's death. Once again, he was submerged in the utter sinking terror of that moment at Shepherd's Rock. Sarah's cry for Caitlin, the terror in her eyes as he grasped her hand, the rending of his being as her sweaty fingers clutched, struggled then slipped soundlessly out of his desperate grasp. The final look passing between them—the miraculous sense of calm that came over her features in the final seconds before she plummeted almost one hundred feet to the rocks below.

In those fatal seconds, Buck's life was altered forever. Forever.

Buck expelled the air he'd been holding in his burning chest and rushed to the rail. He looked down hesitantly, fearful to witness tangled broken limbs and—

O'Malley's daughter had landed squarely on her feet, only muddying her palms slightly as she bent forward to break her fall. Her hat had slipped off and rolled down the embankment and with an ache, he recalled Sarah's weathered felt hat caught in a draft and drifting down the rock face in the aftermath.

Watching Caitlin willingly climb the rail and leap defiantly away from him was another reminder of the woman's stubborn impulsiveness, her spontaneity, her damn spunk. He hated these things about her. Had she been playing the safety-conscious innocent while he courted?

He didn't have room in his life for her antics. Was she willing to stop taking chances? He'd tighten the screws and wring a decision out of her tonight.

He leaned over the rail. "Stay where you are," he commanded in his deepest, gruffest voice, hoping the tears that had choked him moments earlier were not in evidence.

"I told you before I'm not taking orders from you, Rawlings," she retorted loudly, brushing the palms of her hands on the wet grass, oblivious to the hell she'd just put him through. "I'll do as I damn well please during my free time. And don't you dare follow me."

Furious and deeply shaken, he clutched the smooth wood beneath his palms and watched her scramble down the embankment to retrieve her hat. Setting the Stetson on her head, she hurried through the ankle-high grass toward the path that led to the lake and away from him.

Buck ground his back teeth as he stalked through the Big Room and gathered a large plaid blanket from the back of a sofa.

"Where are you going?" Chase asked, stepping out of the line dance to grab Buck's shirtsleeve.

"I'm taking a walk with Caitlin," Buck muttered.

"That's odd," Chase said with a shrug. "I thought Caitlin was on the side deck. I haven't had a chance to thank her for planning the party."

"She *was* on the side deck." Buck paused and took in the inquisitive glances of his crew. Rusty and Klyde stopped playing and the men fell into a circle around Buck. The three dogs rushed to the door and wagged their bodies excitedly. How would it look to these old-fashioned males if he explained Caitlin's hasty departure? "O'Malley got sort of a head start."

"You want I should rustle up a latte for Miss O'Malley?" Louie asked quietly. "She didn't drink nothing with her cake. Might be a bit parched, you know."

"It's pourin' heaven's hardest out there," Lester said from the front entry where he held the door open. "It's no kind of weather to be walkin' a woman in."

"And Miss O'Malley's not dressed for rain. That skirt—well..." Carlos shook his head and made fussing noises as he took a raincoat off the coat tree in the hall and handed it to Buck. "Get her covered up."

"The woman jumped off the railing," Buck announced to the gathering of overly solicitous men. Reaching for the light panel, he flipped the switch to light the path to the lake. "If you want to hand out sympathy, give it to me, dammit!"

Footfalls sounded on the path behind Caitlin. As she turned, her body was enveloped in a heavy cloak of wool. She felt large, insistent hands on her shoulders and held back her urge to scream. She freed one arm, and pulling the fabric back from her chin, looked up.

Buck towered over her on the path, his hands holding the edges of a large blanket together. "Don't ever run away from me again, O'Malley."

"I never run from anything, Buck." She struggled to free the rest of her body from the confines of the voluminous blanket. A gust of wind swept rain across her face.

He pulled the wool together again, holding it tightly with his fist. "You could have broken your leg jumping from that railing. That's a drop of ten feet. Just what we need. Two O'Malleys in casts."

"I weighed the risk, Rawlings." She ignored his protective gesturings with the blanket and tried to walk past him.

"You didn't have time to weigh any risk. You're never going to change, are you?" Buck blocked her path again.

She stomped each boot firmly on the path to demonstrate the soundness of her legs. "Nothing is broken. And please, I don't need a blanket, Buck, and right now, I don't need you."

"It's cold and wet and you're barely dressed."

"That's my concern. Being angry keeps me warm." She slipped past him and continued on the narrow trail to the lake, leaving him standing with a handful of blanket.

He caught up with her in seconds, a bold shadow on the darkened path. "Do I have to pick you up and carry you back to the lodge—fireman-style?"

She gave him a scornful laugh. "At the moment, Rawlings, there is no fire. Not even a spark. You've spoiled everything. I have no desire to carry out my plans."

"What plans?" He sounded genuinely concerned.

"To take control, for once." She hesitated to divulge the full scenario. "To have things my way." She'd reached the upper shore of Medicine Bowl Lake. With a sigh, she ducked under the overhang of the abandoned shack next to the old corral and leaned her back against a roof support, far away from the imposing silhouette of Buck Rawlings.

Watching her shiver in the chill of wind and rain made Buck feel a fierce surge of protectiveness, but he forced himself to step past Cat O'Malley, to ignore the urge to lift her onto his shoulder and carry her back to the comfort and warmth of the lodge. Instead, he stepped inside the weathered shack. Taking the blanket from his arm, he tossed it over the straw in the one remaining stall to dry. His grandfather's old red lantern had hung in the small spot since Buck was a boy. He found it easily despite the darkened interior. Striking a match, he lit the wick and illuminated the ancient stable, abandoned years ago in favor of the larger, more efficient accommodation closer to the expanded driveway and turnaround in front of the lodge.

The straw was kept fresh and the interior clean for use as a background locale for the catalog shoot. Lester's clever use of props gave the old building a nostalgic feeling of simpler, easier times.

He walked to the doorway and studied the shadowed figure of Caitlin, standing beneath the overhang but close enough to the steady downpour of rain to reach out and wet her hand. Her rigid back and the defiant set of her shoulders were testimony to her stubborn pride and the intensity of her anger at him.

There was more than one issue at hand here. He'd have to take things in order.

It had been very male and very foolish to order her to his room. What had possessed him to do such a thing? And how could he undo the mistake?

"I messed up tonight," he admitted in a clear concise voice that rivaled the soft roar of the downpour. "Why don't we set aside what happened and just start over?"

She remained a lone sentinel facing the rain but shrugged one shoulder as if to shake off an irritating fly. Buck felt a shudder of annoyance. He'd give his effort two minutes at most; then he'd douse the lantern and leave Caitlin out here in the dark and cold. Could any woman, even O'Malley's daughter, be worth this much trouble?

With his thumb, he edged his hat back slightly, set the lantern on a ledge and leaned his body against the doorjamb.

"My grandfather had the right idea when it came to courting, Caitlin. There are some benefits." Buck watched her shoulders turn slightly, saw the cant of her head and guessed that she was listening rather intently. "These past few days have given me a chance to learn more about you. Important things. Like your favorite authors and your political views, and your thoughts on the changing future of Montana."

Some moments later she angled herself around to face him. In the faint light of the lantern, he could see the distrust etched in her features. He was the one responsible for putting the wariness in her soft golden eyes, the hard edge in the curve of her mouth. Buck felt compelled to erase any vestige of doubt.

"But I've also learned the little things, Caitlin. The way you laugh while playing tag with your dogs, what songs on the radio make you wistful and what songs make you sway your hips just a little wantonly." He chuckled to himself. "I've watched you communicate with the horses without uttering a single word and I can only guess it's some brand of Irish sorcery."

Her expression softened.

"You like to sit and watch Louie smoke his pipe on the porch and you're teaching him how to use your fancy coffeemaker. In fact, he's developing quite a taste for cappuccino with an orange slice."

"That's Klyde." She stepped toward him, then stopped, looking down and creating a circular pattern in the straw with the toe of her boot. "Louie likes a triple espresso laced with Frangelico with extra foam and a dusting of cinnamon."

"You're the expert. I stand corrected, O'Malley."

"What else have you learned?"

"You're a sucker for fields of buttercups in sunlight, but you never use butter. In fact, you like cake without frosting, toast without jam, meat without gravy, and you eat your potatoes naked."

"I've never eaten a potato naked—"

"That came out wrong. Meaning *the potatoes* have nothing on them."

"Some things can't be improved upon." She smiled and stepped to the doorway, edging her hands under his vest and around his waist. Buck drew her closer and kissed the hair at her temple.

"Why don't we start again, Buck?" she asked softly.

"If I remember correctly, we were waltzing to the sound of rain on the deck."

Buck took her hand, tucked his arm around her waist and whirled her out in the wide-open space beneath the overhang, humming the same tune that had been playing when their dance had ended so abruptly almost an hour ago.

The passion that had seized him while holding her on the lodge's side deck ignited again and flared through him. He sensed it in Caitlin, as well, in the welcomed grasp of her hand on his back and the way her fingers slipped possessively into the back pocket of his jeans to pull his lower body up against hers.

After five minutes of swaying rhythmically to the music of their bodies, Buck guided her from the exposed area under the overhang into the shelter of the stable.

"Your clothes are soaked, Caitlin, and you're shivering." He peeled the wet leather vest off her body. Her gray ribbed top was drenched. The thin fabric caressed her full high breasts like a second skin. Onionskin. Transparent. The sight of her taut nipples straining against the ribbed knit sent a ricochet of desire through him. "We better get you into something dry."

"You're wet, too, Buck."

"I wasn't out in the rain as long as you were, but then I chose a more conventional method to leave the lodge." He had to bank his urge to give her hell about her recklessness. This wasn't the time. The woman was shivering.

"There's nothing for me to change into but that blanket," she said with a shrug.

"We've got a storeroom in the back. Lester keeps props there and spare items from wardrobe have accumulated over the years." Setting the lantern on a shelf beside the door, he opened the ancient creaking door and stepped inside. "Let's see what we have here. Chaps, overalls, hay apron—" Images began to form in Buck's imagination that were not entirely pure.

Caitlin remained in the doorway watching Buck search through the chaotic clutter. He chose a ridiculous multicolored shirt with gold fringe.

"Branding irons, horse whips, spurs, bridles, reins, harnesses." She began her own inventory. "Why does Western gear always seem so damn earthy and mysterious and somehow linked to things sexual?"

"Sexual?" Buck turned and fixed her with a bemused smile. "Spoken like a true greenhorn and ex-city dweller." He stepped up to the doorway and squeezed in beside her, his legs spread wide, a foot in each room, as he pressed his body against hers. "I should make you wear that really sexy leather hay apron but this will do the trick."

"That shirt's a monstrosity." Her laughter ended with a small groan as she felt his hand sneak between their bodies and stroke her ribs. His thumb moved over each bone until it reached the underside of her breast. "You don't carry that style in the catalog, Buck." Her breath caught. She nodded toward the gaudy clothing in his other hand. "What's it doing in your storeroom?"

"It's left over from a trick we played on Joe," Buck whispered hoarsely as he placed a gentle kiss on the arch of her cheekbone. "Lester made the ugliest shirt possible, dog ugly, and we got Joe to believing he had to model the damn thing."

"Poor Joe. I recall my dad mentioning your cruel trick." She struggled to keep some semblance of normalcy in her voice but the feel of his hand on her rib cage, his thumb stroking the curve of her breast, made it waver.

"And you—" He tossed the shirt back into the storeroom while keeping his compelling eyes locked with hers. His thumb did an unstructured line dance up to her nipple and stopped. "You choose *not* to wear this Lester Owen original?"

"I'd rather wear nothing at all...." Her entire being was focused on the slight pressure of his thumb as it hovered like a tiny hummingbird's wing on the tip of her breast.

"Nothing, O'Malley?"

"I'm a snob when it comes to fashion."

"Lucky me."

"Stop teasing and please, just touch me, Buck." She thrust her body forward, pressing her breast into the palm of his hand. "Touch me."

Buck responded to her breathless entreaty by gathering the hem of the damp top in his hands and lifting it over her head in one quick movement.

"Sweet Lord," he muttered. Her breasts were cupped in red satin and lace. Amidst the sharply contrasting surroundings of weathered wood and limp straw, this wisp of sexy red elegance enthralled him and reminded him hotly of the differences in their worlds.

He watched as Caitlin reached up and unfastened the front clasp then left the rest of the unveiling to him. Buck lowered the thin straps then peeled the lacy confection away from the smooth ivory curves of her breasts until they were completely free.

For seven years, he'd depended on his inexpert memory to recall the shape, taste and texture of her breasts, but this was real. He gathered their elegant contours in his hands, testing their weight in his palms, marveling at her perfection, stroking his thumbs across the rosy tips, enjoying the texture of her pebble-hard nipple beneath his touch.

Bending his head, he took one of those pebbles into his mouth and suckled gently while his hands moved down to unbuckle her belt and unzip the front of her short skirt. The black denim hit the floor with a soft satisfying thud. With one hand, he reached around her hip to caress the enticing curve of her bottom while the other hand skimmed down her flat silken belly.

He could only guess that the scrap of satin and lace that covered the soft mound of her sex was as crimson and filmy as her bra. That thought set him to swirling his tongue over the crest of each breast. Caitlin moaned softly, her fingers weaving wildly through his hair and pressing him closer to her breast. He blew a soft hot wind across her glistening nipples and heard her sharp intake of breath.

Buck looked up at the torment in her tawny eyes, at the suggestive O of her half-parted mouth and realized the doorway to the storeroom had grown far too small for his intentions.

Sweeping her up into his arms, he crossed the stable and stopped before the single stall lined with straw where the blanket lay drying. Caitlin kicked off her boots and he smiled at the determination on her face. He set her down gently, then stepped back and took a moment to admire her wild beauty.

With her regal grace, long neck and elegant curves, O'Malley's daughter was born to wear pearls and silk. Again the contrast of this refined woman and his rugged masculine world struck him. But she waited for him, eyes glistening with desire in the faint glow of his grandfather's antique lantern, resting on his father's traditional tartan plaid blanket. With a ragged breath, he shrugged off his vest and shirt, kicked off his boots and reached for the zipper of his jeans. It was time to reclaim his woman.

Caitlin felt drugged by the heat of Buck Rawlings's smoldering gaze upon her near-naked body. When he whipped off his shirt and vest, exposing his muscular chest to the lantern's soft golden glow, she realized time had been very good to Buck. When he stepped out of this black jeans and narrow briefs, she thought it was time for Buck to be very good to her.

A woman couldn't make love to a memory, but for seven years, she'd done just that. How often had she stood in a crowd and spotted a tall dark man with a haunted restless look and felt her body physically react? How many nights had she awakened with the all-too-familiar surge of heat and a desperate ache that no amount of sheep counting or warm milk could put to rest?

It was this man and this man's body she'd ached for. Buck stood before her, naked and fully aroused, and for a fleeting moment, she felt fear—not physical, but emotional fear—and scooted back on the blanket.

How could the commanding virility he displayed while dressed in black seem even more apparent when he removed his bad-boy uniform and desperado hat? In seconds, he was beside her on the blanket, his mouth edging down toward hers. Caitlin's cry was lost as his unshaven jaw rasped against the tender flesh of her jawline, and one of his sinewy work-roughened hands caressed her breast.

"Buck—" She gasped as his thigh crossed over her legs, pinioning her to the blanket. His hand skimmed over her belly and lower, his nails raking trails of fire over her flesh. When his fingers dipped into the triangle of lace and touched her silken folds, he paused.

"You're so wet." He spoke in a broken whisper as he nuzzled her throat. "So ready for me." He slipped the panties over her hips and sat up to pull them over her legs and feet. Lifting one leg in the air, he kissed her calf and spread a series of tantalizing kisses toward her thigh. "Do you remember our first time, Cat?"

She'd anticipated such a question. "Of course I remember. But that person no longer exists."

"You're seven years older—"

"And seven years wiser. I'm not the virgin you took to your bed some half a dozen years ago, Buck," she said calmly as she rose up on her elbows. It was time for the seductress to awaken and play out the rest of the game. "I know what I want and how to get it."

"What the hell does that mean?" His tender whisper rapidly escalated to a low growl.

Caitlin laughed as she rolled up on all fours on the opposite side of the blanket. "It means I'm in charge tonight. I set the mood. You agreed to this at Chase's party."

"I agreed to a waltz. I agreed to let you set the mood. This is different, Cat. Lovemaking is best if the man has the upper hand."

"You've even less evolved than I thought." Playfully she motioned him to the center of the blanket. "There'll be plenty of opportunity to show me your commanding presence and control later, Mr. Rawlings. Or you can just keep poking along with your courting if you choose. But at the moment, I want you on your back and at my mercy."

Feeling chagrined, Buck threw up his hands and smiled broadly as he followed her directive, scooting to the center of the blanket. "Why do I get the feeling you've given this a lot of thought, O'Malley?"

"I don't think we should think just now." Her tone held a warning. "Let's just relax and enjoy." She leaned over his chest and snaked her tongue over each of his nipples then blew on them softly. The resulting heat made Buck lift his back off the blanket. With the pressure of her hand, Caitlin coaxed him down again.

Her tongue and fingernails trailed lazily down his midriff and set a tormenting pace over his abdomen. Her long hair skimmed over his sensitive flesh, heightening his awareness with an agonizing acuity. When her fingers curled around his shaft, Buck swore softly.

"Enough is enough, O'Malley."

Ignoring his pronouncement, she pressed her hand against his chest in mild restraint. Buck closed his eyes.

When at last she lowered her head and took him in the warm recesses of her mouth, he moaned loudly and grasped handfuls of blankets. "No," he murmured faintly, melting against the expert machinations of her tongue. He'd been her first lover, but never had he introduced this particular brand of lovemaking to their repertoire. "Where did you learn *that?*" he demanded.

Caitlin didn't answer. Instead, she straddled his hips and looked down at him with a triumphant expression that brought him swiftly up into a sitting position. She'd carried this business far enough. He'd waited years for this moment. Could he really allow her to steal his thunder so easily?

"I brought protection." Stretching, he grabbed his jeans and pulled them close enough to fish one of the gold foil packets out of the front pocket. "Look at me for a minute, Cat. I want both of us to be sure about this."

The fire in her amber eyes spoke more than words. Still holding his gaze, she took the packet from him, tore it open and answered his question with the agonizing movement of her fingers.

"We've been apart so long, Cat. I want our bodies close when I claim you for my own again." With his hands on her slender hips, he positioned her over his hot, aching arousal.

"Claim me?" she repeated, almost choking on the words. Then taking the control out of his hands, she guided herself onto his shaft, and sank onto every electrified inch of him. "Never," Caitlin whispered as her arms went around his neck. "Never."

Chapter Ten

Caitlin reveled in the hot, satisfying sensation of surrounding his silky length with her womanly warmth. With each lift of her body and downward movement, she further welcomed him and clasped him anew, tightening her reins on his control and driving Buck deeper into submission. It was her turn, her night, her Echo Creek rematch.

She gloried in the closeness of his body and her ability to test the texture of his heated flesh. The rasp of his unshaven jaw on her shoulder and his woodsy male scent fueled the melting fire of ache within her. She was captor and captive, possessor and possessed.

Caitlin closed her eyes as Buck's hand moved between their bodies, igniting the small nubbin of pleasure in her nest of curls. She responded to his stroking with a sweet wild cry and he echoed with his own sensual moans.

The smells of his masculine world of oiled leather and pine boards wafted around them, reminding her of his dominion, and her invasion of that dominion.

Never in the past had she felt such freedom in his arms, such reckless abandon, such bewitchment. His thrusts quickened and became more powerful. Caitlin felt rocked to her very soul each time he lifted his hips and drove into her.

Rain slapped against the weathered boards of the old stable and the unrelenting sounds of nature spurred her on to match his pace and intensity, to follow his rhythmic rocking motions.

"Caitlin, my Cat." He murmured her name, the word a soft rumbling caress, a throaty affirmation of his need.

Caitlin smiled at the sweet nonsensical birdsong of their lovemaking. Tucking her chin into the crook of his neck, she stopped trying to define who was in control. The line blurred. The thing that had waxed and waned between them for all these years, this living breathing undercurrent of attraction and caring, was the great leveler.

She began to convulse and spasm around him. Wanting the moment to last forever, she fought the final spiral.

"Let go, darlin'," he urged. "Come home. Come home to me, Cat."

The sound of his commanding, quicksand voice sent her over the final crest. With a cry of rapture, Caitlin was swept helplessly toward a timeless oblivion.

Buck closed his eyes against the last shuddering vestige of his own shattering release and rested his head against Caitlin's damp forehead. Murmuring soft assurance, he stroked damp tendrils away from her face and looked into the hazy torment reflected in her large golden eyes.

He'd scripted this moment in his mind since her arrival at Echo Creek. Never could he have imagined O'Malley's daughter stealing his thunder and taming it. With her own magnificent sorcery, she'd swept him through a storm of ecstasy that made him glance around in search of smoke and mirrors. The woman amazed him. She was magical, unforgettable, simply amazing.

A sudden realization sent a shudder of another sort down his spine. Caitlin's impulsive nature, the daring spirit that made him reluctant to commit to a relationship without conditions, was the very thing that made her appeal to him as a woman.

If he did anything to dampen that spirit, what would become of the long-ago girl who'd first turned his head with her outrageous behavior and the wonderfully unpredictable woman she'd become?

Buck splayed his fingers across her slender back and slid them over the narrow tuck of her waist and downward, to caress the soft curve of her bottom.

There was a second dilemma. He'd always yearned for a woman who would depend on him—financially, physically, emotionally. He'd honed his skills in life in preparation for that role of protector. He prided himself on his liberal policies toward women in the workplace but in truth, he was a man who needed to feel needed. And Cat O'Malley had made it abundantly clear she needed no one.

Wind slammed against the stable door unexpectedly and Caitlin jerked to full alert in his arms, then pulled away fearfully.

"Buck—"

"I think we're in for a small storm." He stroked her cheek then brought the ends of the blanket up around her shoulders to protect her naked body from the cool rush of air. The lantern flame flickered, sending haunting shadows over the walls of the weathered stall. "We're safe out here."

"But I don't feel safe." She shivered and rested her cheek against his.

Caitlin's words sent an ache through him. A woman couldn't get any closer to a man, and yet his nearness and protective embrace were seemingly no comfort to her.

Then he recalled her fear of storms and her comments the night she'd displayed her collage. There'd been a listing of her greatest fears on that occasion. Following on the heels of thunder, lightning and wind storms was the mention of haunted castles.

Lightning flashed, illuminating the cobweb-coated wooden beams overhead. Thunder followed brief heartbeats later, crashing like a gutterball skidding across the roof.

She gasped softly, her eyes glancing furtively at the ceiling. "These beams—they have the same look. Sinister. Forbidding."

"Caitlin, tell me about the castle. What happened, to make you so afraid?"

She began slowly, telling him in halting words of her father's assignment to shoot haunted castles in Ireland and his increasing expectation of courage and calm from his ten-year-old daughter.

"The last castle was the creepiest, Buck, the most frightening thing I'd seen in my short but well-traveled life. We arrived late—at nightfall—and it loomed above the landscape like a dark hand of doom, one evil finger pointing ominously to the threatening skies.

"I didn't want to go inside," she continued. "As we traveled to each new location, my father told me of the specific ghost or haunting associated with the castle. This place was at the top of the list for horror potential—a multitude of ghosts, inexplicable music and tales of Irish Druids and human sacrifice. It was like someone had made a list of the top ten childhood nightmares and found one place to house them all."

Buck tightened the blanket around her shoulders and stroked her hair lovingly.

"When we got to the wooden door that marked the entrance, I argued and resisted. Dad was already behind schedule. He tried to calm me down, to assure me, telling me he was there—he'd protect me. But there are some things no one can protect you from."

Buck raised his brows at that remark. Did Caitlin feel that way as an adult woman? Was that belief the thing that gave her impetus to protect herself and not reach out to others?

"Did you actually spend the night in that place?" he asked quietly.

"We were there almost a week! But that first night, a storm came up. Thunder and lightning like I'd never seen. Like I haven't seen since. Dad was delighted to get exterior and interior shots with the lightning streaking around and adding to the already eerie feel. He put me to bed in a remote alcove and reassured me before leaving to get additional photos. I was too terrified to sleep, of course. I got up to look for my father and that's when I got lost."

"Oh, Lord, Caitlin." Buck drew her closer. In their own present-day world, the storm picked up. Wind rattled the windowpanes and sent the lantern's flame fluttering.

Buck felt as though he were looking into the haunted, fearful eyes of a child. Her voice had become small and frightened, her phrasing hesitant. Though he ached because of the fear that had followed her all her life, a flush of satisfaction washed over him. At this moment, Buck knew Caitlin needed him.

"I was terrified, Buck. I hadn't seen anything this frightening at the other castles we'd visited. I'd been plenty scared by noises and cold spots but I'd almost developed a sense of bravado, so I left each location with a proud little strut." Caitlin smiled faintly. "I'd conquered my fear a bit each time.

"But at that last castle, all of the promised horror came true. Some strange things do exist in this world, Buck. I can testify to that."

He kissed her cheek. "I believe you."

"The place was a maze, a dark, cold, massive maze, and I was getting hopelessly disoriented and farther from my alcove. I was so crazy with fear that I tried squeezing myself against the walls but they were damp and clammy—like the skin of a slimy beast. I sobbed and sobbed and curled into a little ball on the floor.''

Buck's hand rested on her shoulder where he held the blanket tight around her body. She shifted in his lap. His thumb touched the base of her throat, and there he felt the jackhammer rhythm of her pulse. The rapid rise and fall of her chest and her pale color further concerned him.

"You're getting too upset, Caitlin," he cautioned. "Don't tell me the rest of the story if it's going to upset you so much."

"I want to finish, Buck." She leaned against his chest, tucking her head between his shoulder and neck. "I'm almost done."

"Did you find your way back to your room?"

"I don't know. The last thing I remember is clutching a wall and seeing a child, a ghostly child. I'd never considered the possibility of a child dying, much less haunting a castle forever in a tiny body. Seeing that little girl made me feel absolutely vulnerable, terrified beyond belief. It was at that point that I made a conscious decision."

"What kind of decision?"

"I decided to talk aloud to the images I saw, to challenge them, to tell them I was not afraid and to ask for guidance to return to my room."

"Hell, O'Malley. You challenged dead Druids and Lord knows what?"

"I challenged myself."

"What happened?"

"Like I said, I don't recall. A member of the staff found me the next morning. I was unconscious, lying on the cold hard stones in a corridor not far from my room. I developed a fever within hours and a doctor was called. I hovered near death for a few days."

"What do you *think* happened, Cat?"

"I think—" Before she could resume her story, lightning blossomed around the darkened building, followed by a more distant thunder. Buck felt an instant tensing of her body. Shuddering, she glanced up at the beams overhead.

"It's like a memory just beyond my reach." She put her fingertips to her temple. "When a storm comes up, I feel torn between wanting to remember and wanting to forget. The truth could be too much to bear."

"How did your father feel, Caitlin?"

"Guilty. Neglectful. The man prayed by my bed the whole time. Says he promised me a field of ponies and my own camera, but when we got back to the States, Grandmother Covington had found out about my brush with death and she was livid. She petitioned for full custody of me and there was a nasty court battle that was almost as scary for me as the night in the castle."

"What was decided in court?"

"Grandmother was given partial custody. My dad couldn't leave me in convent schools when he was away on long assignments anymore. The judge wanted me to have a stable home and a more consistent school life. That's why Grandmother Covington got her way about all those wretched lessons. Her house in Boston became my second home."

A fresh onslaught of lightning and thunder left her looking stricken.

"Lord, Caitlin, you're still so afraid. Back at the lodge, the night of the big storm, you thought Farley was a wolf in the bathroom. You were out of your mind with fear."

"But that same night, I managed to help board up the front windows where the limb from the oak hit the front porch. I always manage, Buck."

The harrowing story was over but she still sounded so vulnerable, so childlike that Buck couldn't resist rocking her in his lap. That motion and the enticing feel of her bare skin against his thighs sent fresh flames of desire shooting through his loins. He let the blanket drop back off her shoulders and lowered her to the ground, leaving her glorious body open to his view. Her nipples tautened against the cool air. Buck bent his head to tongue the dusky rose tip of her breast, then positioned himself above her.

"I'm thinking of something we could do to forever link the sound of thunder and lightning in your mind with something far more pleasurable."

"There could be a drawback, Rawlings. What if I don't want to spend the rest of my life remembering, uh, oh, yes, s-such intimacy whenever a storm comes up?"

"You choose to remember ghosts and haunted castles when you could associate bad weather—" he thrust into her when the next bolt of lightning illuminated the room and rocked her to the rumble of thunder "—with the feel of me inside you?"

"This is very unconventional therapy, Rawlings," she gasped. "And strangely appealing."

"It could be the only thing that might help you get over your fear." He kissed the edge of her jawline and brushed his mouth against hers as their mutual rhythm became more insistent. "It's purely scientific, you understand."

"I always did love science."

Wind whooshed against the latticed window and it rattled furiously.

"My technique is working, O'Malley. You hardly flinched."

"But there are other fears, Buck."

"Such as?"

"Emotional . . . being hurt by you."

"Never. I'll never hurt you," he whispered into the hollow at the curve of her throat as he felt her silken fire constrict. "Never."

Caitlin felt a disquieting sense of déjà vu as she lay in the curve of Buck Rawlings's body and slowly came awake to the new reality of their relationship. The first light of morning filtered through the oak tree outside Buck's window and, with a soft glow that seemed to vibrate before her sleepy eyes, kissed the silvered logs that made up his bed-room walls.

She could argue with herself as long as she wanted about not belonging to Buck, about not being Buck's woman, but at the moment her body felt harnessed to him in immeasurable ways. Unwillingly, she found herself enjoying a few of those aspects.

The slight throb between her legs was testimony to his vigorous approach to lovemaking, in the stable and later, here in his imposing heirloom bed.

Intimacy had brought out the subtle humor in Buck that she had missed so much. Life was serious enough. She wanted someone to understand her quirky flights of fancy and... this amazing man had the patience to listen to her rambling tale of misbegotten ghosts from her childhood and to actually believe her. She'd been thoroughly touched by his attempt to rid her of her fears. His sensual brand of exorcism had achieved miraculous results. Either that or she was too dazed by her multiple climaxes to react to thunder, lightning or the rush of winds.

Caitlin snuggled deeper into the curve of Buck's body and sighed when his arms moved protectively around her. Let the man slumber. She wanted to savor this delicious moment of calm, knowing it might be short-lived.

They had issues that couldn't remain under the table for long. The blame for Sarah's death hovered over them like an unseen force. During the next few days, Caitlin would have to tell him the truth about what really happened at the cliff and why. She wanted the whole complicated business unraveled and put to rest.

In her vision of hope, she would stand on the shore of Medicine Bowl Lake and wish her forever friend, Sarah, a peaceful farewell. In the outer mist of her vision, Buck would stand beside her and they would put their grief to rest before leaving the lodge and returning to Missoula.

"Cat? You awake?" His gruff voice startled her. He moved aside, giving her space to roll onto her back, then bent to brush a kiss against her cheek.

Caitlin looked up into his green eyes. Gone were the shadows of grief and suspicion, replaced by a strange new light.

"You all right this morning?" he asked softly, his hand skimming over her midriff and resting on the flat plane below her navel. "I'm sorry if I got a little rough last night."

"I was about to apologize myself," she countered, allowing her hand to follow a similar journey past his midriff to his lower abdomen. "Your back has to be crisscrossed with proof of my satisfaction. Are *you* all right this morning?"

"Watch out." He chuckled, raising his buttocks off the mattress. "You'll start a thunderstorm with those inquisitive fingers of yours." He rested his head back down on the pillow and moaned. "I can't tell you how good it feels to wake up next to you, Caitlin. It's been a while."

"It was too soon before. Seven years ago, I was pretty young to make decisions about my entire life."

"What about now?"

"I've given this issue of your conditions a lot of thought, Buck. I can't be pressured to make a decision before I'm ready."

His head rose off the pillow a few inches. He turned her chin with the gentle pressure of his fingertips until their eyes met fully again. "Hasn't making love made a difference?"

"Please, don't take this the wrong way. Last night was wonderful but the truth is—sex is a temporary fix. We're still in limbo, Buck. Making love has changed everything and nothing."

His fingers slid down her neck to embrace her shoulder.

"Can you at least make an effort not to take unnecessary risks, Caitlin, for the rest of your stay at the lodge?"

"Is this a test? Isn't it enough for the two of us to see if we're compatible on other levels of life? Does everything have to depend on your need to be assured?"

"I'm not asking for a promise, Cat, just an effort."

Caitlin pondered his request. Values were important to her. Above all, she valued the meaning of her word. If she could test his condition without making a solemn promise, she could get some sense of how restrictive it might be.

"All right, I'll make an effort."

The shadow of suspicion crept back into his eyes. "How do we define risk?"

"On a case-by-case basis." Caitlin tucked the sheet tightly over her breasts. She didn't want this discussion to get sidetracked.

"Last night on the deck, when you straddled that railing and looked down, did it occur to you that it was a fairly steep drop?"

With an exasperated sigh, she rolled away from him. "I weighed every possibility, Rawlings."

He tucked the front of his body against the back of hers and held her tenderly in his arms. "And in that case, the risk won?"

She couldn't resist a smile. "No, the desire to be as far away from you as possible won."

"Oh, Lord, the snake and bumblebee in a jar."

"Snake and bumblebee? What's that supposed to mean?"

"You and me, lady. Someone just shook the jar again." He kissed her shoulder blade, then nipped the same spot gently with his teeth.

"Do I have to get treated for snake bite now?"

Buck nudged her with his arousal. "I have the cure right here."

"Sorry, Doctor, I have to get up and get dressed." She struggled playfully to get out of his embrace.

"I gave the crew the day off, Caitlin. Stay here with me."

"I assume the word *crew* includes me, right?"

"Yes, but I thought we'd sleep in a little longer or order breakfast in bed or..."

"I'm serious, Buck. It's my only chance to head up the mountain and get those scenics I mentioned before."

"I'm paying you good money for this shoot."

"And every dime is going to my father. If I don't get these nature photos this week, my own income for the month of July will be spotty at best. I have a business to think about." She sat up on the edge of the bed and reached for her robe.

"Why do I get the feeling I can't trust you? It rained last night, you know." His old possessive, overprotective tone was evident. Caitlin stood and belted her robe. "Hiking might not be safe," he continued. "I don't like the sound of this, Cat."

"Hey, we agreed I'd make an effort, not a promise. Trust me. I'll choose the safest route and take my dogs. If I start out now, I'll be back by two and then maybe we can think of something pleasant to do together."

"I'll come along as your guide." He sat up on the opposite side of the bed then stood, seemingly oblivious to his glorious naked state.

"No, you won't, Buck. I don't need a guide," Caitlin answered quickly, glancing away. Her need to tell him about his sister felt pressing. If she were going to bring him pain, she wanted it over and done with. But now was not the time. She didn't want the hike to evolve into her confession about Sarah and a discussion of his sister's possible suicide. One issue at a time. "I really need some time alone. I have a sonic blaster with me. If anything happens, I'll set it off."

"If anything happens, you'll set *me* off, O'Malley. And that's a promise." With that threatening comment, his features grew clouded and remote. Silently he picked up his robe and stalked naked through the bedroom door.

All three dogs ignored Buck. They raced through the door and jumped onto the bed. With a sigh, Caitlin lay down on the carpet and began doing an abbreviated version of her daily workout routine. The dogs jumped down to join her.

She interrupted a sit-up to caress both sides of Burrito's face and look the collie in the eye.

"Hey, Beefy Baby, do I look like a woman who just sold out—just a little?"

The dog whined and placed her paw on Caitlin's chest.

"That bad, huh?" Caitlin closed her eyes and pictured herself mincing up the mountain at a snail's pace, risking nothing, all for the love of Buck Rawlings.

"Caitlin's more than an hour late, Chase. She specifically said two o'clock." Buck lifted the binoculars back up to his face and searched the higher elevations for signs of a bright red shirt and a careless attitude. The weather had turned to blue skies and sunshine, but he knew last night's rain had left the upper trails slick and dangerous. He should have followed her or at least taken the usual precaution of asking about her route. "Damn! Where is that woman?"

"Was she looking for anything specific, like eagles or vistas of the lake?" Wearing only a pair of tattered cutoffs and sipping on a beer, Chase sat back in one of the two wood-slatted Adirondack chairs he'd dragged out of storage and placed in the afternoon sun. Country love songs played on the radio perched at his elbow. "Knowing what she was going after would narrow it down a bit, Buck. At least you'd have some idea of where to point those binoculars."

Buck felt put on the spot. He cared deeply about the woman. He should have done everything possible to keep her safe.

He'd matured mightily since the moment more than half a dozen years ago when he'd hauled Cat O'Malley across his knee. She'd risked both of their lives that day, sailboarding on the lake with a storm approaching. He hadn't struck her, of course. He would never strike a woman, but he'd been sorely tempted to leave some kind of lasting imprint on her mind, a warning that might save her from death or injury in the future.

These long years later, he could barely contain his worry. She was only an hour late, but his heart was thudding erratically, beating out her name and leaving him cursing the day he'd met Sean O'Malley and his troublesome daughter.

This morning, she'd said making love had changed nothing. That was fine for her, but in his case, it'd changed everything. He had given too much of his heart. He had more to lose now.

"C'mon Buck. Would you grab a beer, sit down in the sun and relax?"

"I'm not like you, Chase. I can't sit there absorbing sunshine and beer when Caitlin is alone up there facing possible injury." Buck felt his irritation giving way to anger. "I'd like to see a little more concern here."

Chase reached into the cooler and tossed Buck a bottle of beer, then stretched out lazily. "I believe Caitlin O'Malley is more than capable of handling a short hike in the foothills."

Buck sat down on the wood-slatted deck chair beside his brother, took a long swallow of beer then narrowed his gaze at Chase. "We could start searching."

"Give the poor lady some air!"

"You've never seen O'Malley's daughter in action, Chase." Buck nodded across the meadow at the oak in front of the lodge. "The day after the big storm, she climbed the oak to get a group shot of the crew cleaning up storm debris. Then there was the time she climbed on top of those boulders on the lakeshore, and during her last visit she went rock climbing on Shepherd's Rock without a helmet and challenged Sarah to keep up with her. Cat's promised to make an effort to stop taking risks but I don't know. It's such a part of her nature and—"

"Shepherd's Rock?" Chase frowned as he glared up at Buck. "Wasn't that the summer Sarah fell?"

"One and the same, brother."

The younger man sat up straight. He settled his bottle of beer in the grass and steepled his fingers against his chin and swore softly. "You think there's any connection?"

Buck paused, disturbed by the grief etched in his brother's features. Too often he'd forgotten about the impact Sarah's death had had on Chase, the youngest of the three siblings.

"Chase, I used to put most of the blame on Caitlin, but now I think it's somehow more complicated than that. I mean, Mom was impulsive and reckless, and Sarah held her up as a role model. She idolized me, too, and I've always had a rebellious streak. Who can say?"

Chase rubbed his hands together. "So every time Caitlin hauls her pretty little behind up an incline of any magnitude, you're thinking of our sister and tense up inside?"

"*Tense* isn't exactly the word." Buck took another few swallows of beer. He rarely drank and when he did, never in excess. He didn't like to feel the loss of control that liquor brought out in him. But today the cold brew was taking the edge off his worry. "It's hard to let go of the memory, Chase. I witnessed both Mom and Sarah dying violently. So when I look up toward the trail in search of Caitlin, I've got these images that come to mind. I don't know what comes first—getting over the grief or trusting a woman known for her recklessness?"

Frowning, Chase took the binoculars from Buck and searched the hills above the lodge. "If she doesn't show up in a couple more hours, the two of us could round up a small search party, have a look."

Buck leaned back against the wood slats of the deck chair his father had built years ago. He put his boots up on the footrest and pulled his hat down on his forehead. "Thanks for the concern."

"Yeah, sure. Take your T-shirt off and get some sun, Buck."

"I get enough sun. I'm twice as dark as you, leisure boy, and it's early June."

"You always have to be tanner and tougher than me, don't you?"

"Good Lord, Chase, do you go around looking for arguments?"

"Only when I'm around you, Buck, and only lately. We're both changing. Be honest. How badly do you want out of the company?"

Buck ran his thumb along the long-necked bottle, wiping the condensation away with a back and forth motion. "It's not that simple. I like managing the growth and direction—"

"Comanaging," Chase corrected. "But you won't agree to a women's line of clothing or other necessary changes."

"Not until we get a good Christmas season under our belt. I don't have to tell you how much our profits dipped, Chase. Why expand to something so costly and time-consuming until we're ready?"

"All of our competition is moving in that direction. Women and children's outdoor clothing is hot." Chase swore bitterly. "This distrust you have of Caitlin climbing on those trails up there—that and Sarah's death. It all ties in with your feelings about women and the outdoors. You're always bringing up that lame argument about not encouraging women to risk their necks. You're a dinosaur, Buck."

Buck crossed one leg over the other and stared at this boots. These disagreements between himself and Chase usually escalated to a screaming match followed by a week of brooding for Buck, a week of carousing for Chase. Twice they'd come close to striking blows. Lester had intervened in both instances, ordering them to their separate offices as if the two were errant schoolboys.

Lester was swimming down at the lake with other members of the crew, so they were minus their best referee. Once Rawlings's fists started flying, Buck knew the anger and resentment of a dozen years would be packed into each wallop. They were in the middle of a catalog shoot, one of the most important Echo Creek Outfitters had ever produced.

They couldn't afford a week of black moods or black eyes interfering with the schedule or morale.

"I'm not a dinosaur, Chase. I'm simply prudent."

"What do you really want, Buck? Do you want to leave me at the helm and start that wilderness guide service?"

"You'll turn the company into a series of quality-management seminars with incentive programs and quotas, and you'll give a fancy name to every function. You try to sound like someone from Montana, Chase, to blend in, but those East Coast degrees are always showing."

"Would you leave my education out of this? I use my gut when it comes to people, just as much as you do."

"While you were getting your degrees, I worked each of those factory jobs, Chase. The workers remember and respect that."

"Dad wouldn't have assigned me comanager unless he believed I was capable."

"The only reason Dad gave you half of my job was because he blamed *me* for Sarah's death. It was a punishment. You didn't have to pay your dues, Chase, but I've paid mine twice."

"What do you expect of me, then, big brother?" Chase stood up, his hands curled into fists. "How long do I have to pay for your anger and resentment? I've had enough of this. I'm driving into town—"

"Like hell you are." Buck rose slowly, his fingers hooked tautly around the bottle of beer. He'd hoped to work out his differences up here with Chase, away from the stresses of the factory and deadlines.

"Saddle our horses," Buck ordered.

"Horses? What the devil?" Chase took a step closer. "I want this over with, once and for all."

"So do I. But not with fists or with you spending the night in a honky-tonk. Let's ride around the lake, Chase, like old times. Let's talk, not about work but about our lives. We're drifting apart so fast. Coming up here makes me realize how much I miss Sarah and how much I miss the way we used to be.''

"Sorry, Buck. I can't get over my anger that quickly and I'm getting much too old to be ordered around. Like I said, I'll be in town.''

Concealing the tear in her pants and top with an extra shirt tied high up around her waist, Caitlin snaked through a grouping of huckleberry bushes and along late-afternoon shadows on the side of the lodge. Peering into the clearing in front of the log building, she was surprised to find it empty of men. The three dogs accompanying her had long ago loped off to their feeding area, ignorant of her clandestine return to home base.

She took the porch stairs a bit too quickly, jostling the heavy camera bag against her tender body and regretting it when she hit the top step. After concealing her tripod and equipment in the hall closet, she slipped into the kitchen, anxious for a cup of strong coffee.

"Well, there you are," Louie grumbled. "You've got the boss in a lather. Took a handful of men up the mountain lookin' for you, Miss O'Malley. Now I suppose you want some early supper. Well, the kitchen is closed.''

"I can wait for supper. I just wanted some coffee, Louie. Fogcutter's fine. If you don't have any made, I'll make a triple espresso.''

"Your pants are all ripped up, and look here, there's mud all over your clothes. Damn, what'd you do?''

"Please don't mention this to Buck, but I slid down a tree and caught a sliver. But I'm not really hurt.''

"Well, you could have fooled me, ma'am. I'll rustle up some java.'' Louie turned and went to work grinding beans for her coffeemaker. Caitlin smiled to herself, bemused with the man's newfound fascination with gourmet coffee.

Moments later, he handed her a steaming mug topped with extra foam. The wild-haired cook accepted her thank-you in his usual irascible manner. "Just don't tell Buck I had any hand in this," he stated flatly. "He'd have my hide if he knew I was aidin' and abettin'."

"It's our secret, Louie. Did Lester go with Buck?"

"No, he's got a pretty bad sunburn from his swim in the lake. Buck made him stay behind. Didn't think any more time in the sun would do Lester any good."

She walked across the foyer to the Big Room, her only thought that of putting her body down, her feet up and her head back. But rest would have to wait. First, she had to enlist the aid of a trustworthy soul like Lester to help her assess the seriousness of the thin sliver of cedar that ran from just below her belt and across her left buttock.

"Miss O'Malley, you are in a heap of trouble." Lester walked into the room behind her. She turned to face him. His graying eyebrows looking unusually light against his sunburned face. "Buck and some of the men are out there lookin' for you— Good Lord, what happened? Turn around. Look at them pants torn and muddied up."

"Lester, I need your help. Please come into the bathroom with me for a moment."

"Miss O'Malley!" Lester removed the toothpick from the corner of his mouth. "I don't make a habit of—"

"Hush!" Tugging on his shirtsleeve, she commandeered the tailor into the tiled room and shut the door behind them. "Please just take a look at this splinter." She unbuttoned her jeans and allowed him a modest view of the damage.

"Oh, my, you have no right to call this a splinter. You got a log about the size of Delaware stuck in your backside!"

"Lester—"

"Does it hurt bad?"

"It just stings a little bit." She struggled to get a good glimpse of herself in the mirror. "Could you just describe it to me—without mentioning one of the fifty states?"

"It's long and narrow with some pieces of bark off to the side." He gestured with his toothpick. "I can only imagine how far south it goes. It's not what I'd call life-threatenin', mind you, but if you leave it there much longer, it'll start hurtin' pretty bad."

Holding a face mirror, Caitlin angled her body until she had a clear view of the problem. She swallowed hard and pondered her choices. She wasn't enough of a contortionist to extract it herself. There was only one hope. "Lester, you're a tailor. You know all about needles—you probably have quite an assortment."

"Well, now, I do have an extensive assortment, professional quality, of course. I hope you're not thinkin'..."

"You're the only person I trust to pull this thing out."

"No, way, ma'am. I work with needles, but there's a big difference between a yard of denim and a stretch of delicate female flesh."

"I won't make a sound. We could do it in the game room under strong light."

"This is foolish. Doc Morrow's just up the road. I'll call him. It's goin' to take an experienced hand and some intimacy that goes beyond the normal tailor-photographer relationship."

"Doc Morrow retired ten years ago. Besides, he has the biggest mouth and shakiest hand in the county. I trust you, Lester. I don't want Buck to know about my accident."

"I don't like gettin' involved in your trickery. Buck Rawlings is not only my employer, he's a good friend of mine. There's no reason to hide somethin' like this from him, Miss O'Malley."

Caitlin was hesitant. After this morning's discussion about risks, she had every reason to hide her injury, no matter how minor, from Buck. The man was obsessed with safety. Her safety.

She took another look at her reflection in the bathroom mirror. "Hmmm...with a little patience I guess I could pull this out myself."

"That's impossible and highly dangerous, Miss O'Malley." He shook his head and looked down at the tile floor. "The way Buck has his temper up, I wouldn't want him attemptin' to take it out, either. I'll go fetch my sewing kit, Miss O'Malley. Meet me in the gamin' room in five minutes.''

Caitlin stretched out on her stomach on the pool table, feeling the warmth of the rectangle of light above the table on her modestly draped backside. Lester lined his assortment of needles up on the table's edge, humming nervously off-key.

"I got antiseptic, tweezers, cotton balls and gauze, Miss O'Malley—and plenty of whiskey. Buck's finest.''

"Whiskey? I don't need any. I doubt if it'll be that painful, Lester.''

"It's to calm *my* nerves a bit.''

She drew herself up on one arm and looked back at the tailor who held the bottle to his lips and guzzled steadily for a matter of several seconds before pulling it away and gasping.

"Lester! That stuff is potent. Are you all right?''

The man's eyes bulged and his sunburned face turned a frightening shade of crimson. He staggered a few steps away from the pool table as he tried to recap the bottle. Accomplishing that, he placed the fifth of whiskey next to her body, rested both hands on the edge of the table and took several ragged breaths.

"I'm ready now," he announced in a small voice as he selected a needle from the kit at his elbow. "I'll start with a number nine.''

"You'll do fine, Lester. It's just a sliver." Caitlin resettled the bottle near her elbow to keep it out of his reach, then closed her eyes and rested her head once again on the large bath towel she'd put down on the pool table.

"Oh, my stars," he hissed. "I'm feelin' mighty peculiar. I'm gonna step out to the front porch and grab a breath of fresh air.''

Caitlin watched Lester's halting gait as he moved across the room to the double doors.

Long minutes passed. She became increasingly aware of the warmth of lamplight on her exposed skin and felt lulled by the heat. If it hadn't been for this morning's promise, she would have avoided all this sneaking around and simply asked Buck to take out the splinter himself.

After leaving the lodge this morning, she'd begun to think about Buck Rawlings and their rocky relationship. He was basically a good man. Overprotective, brooding and something of a loner, but he had a lusty sense of humor and a romantic streak that delighted her.

It was the little things that had haunted her throughout the day—remembrances of an unforgettable night. His desperado moves on the dance floor had woven a lasting spell. Half a dozen times she'd stopped along the trail today to close her eyes against the memory of his masterful lovemaking.

They'd always been good together. Seven years later, the good simply got better. How could she return to Missoula alone—without her outlaw knight? Caitlin was certain now that she loved him and even more certain that this time it could last forever.

In a stable illuminated by lightning and warmed by passion, they'd passed a boundary, a boundary imposed by Buck. He was the one who'd declared they wouldn't make love until she'd made a decision and agreed to his conditions. Now that the fabric of their lives, rawhide and silk, were bound more closely physically and emotionally, she found the mere thought of making such a decision ridiculous.

Perhaps if she waited long enough, he'd come to recognize her addiction to danger as a form of courage and would withdraw his conditions. If he insisted on his original bargain, there would be nothing but pain. If she said yes, her job, her freedom and her devotion to self would be compromised. If she said no to his condition, she would lose the enigmatic man in black whom she'd never stopped loving.

The trouble was, she herself wasn't certain about how big a risk she'd taken when she'd climbed that cedar this afternoon. Accidents happened to the most careful of people, but Buck's lectures made her overly aware of any physical danger and less willing to tell him about this afternoon's incident on the north trail. It was becoming hard for her to judge.

After her fall, she'd sat for a while in the nearby clearing, cautiously examining her equipment then briefly checking herself for possible injuries. While eating a sandwich she'd packed herself that morning, she'd compared two Polaroid shots of Medicine Bowl Lake. The first had been taken from an alpine meadow with bright splotches of spring color in the foreground. The second photo, taken from her vantage point in the massive cedar, was quite similar.

What she saw in each image and how she reacted emotionally to the different images frightened and perplexed her, and offered a possible clue to her risk-taking behavior. She felt an urge to show Buck the Polaroids and ask for his opinion.

In the game room, footsteps sounded on the tile floor behind her and she sighed with relief. Beyond the windows of the room, the light was growing dim.

"Lester, we'd better hurry. No doubt Buck will be back any moment and I don't want a confrontation."

Caitlin started when she felt a large possessive male hand on her right buttock.

Chapter Eleven

"I can't wait to hear all about today's little adventure, O'Malley."

Buck felt her flinch at his touch. She turned to glance up at him, her eyes wide with surprise. "Buck!"

He tossed his black Stetson onto the green felt.

"I spent three hours beating the bushes, searching for you, and here you are, resting your pretty little butt over the side pocket of my pool table with a bottle of my best whiskey tucked in your arm. I'd say you've got a lot of explaining to do, Cat."

"I didn't ask you to get a posse together and scour the mountain, Rawlings. Why don't you just walk back out that door and—"

"You've got the whole lodge in an uproar. I've got a sunburned tailor passed out in the Big Room, holding a sewing needle and tweezers in a death grip in each hand. Louie's attending to Lester and talking about how O'Malley's daughter fell from a tree and got herself a sizable splinter in her backside."

"If you won't leave, I'll get up and . . . I'll just . . ."

He watched her valiant attempt to rise up on one hip and keep the bed linen discreetly arranged, but the towel beneath her bunched up and the sheet tangled. To add to her dilemma, she'd worn a floral sundress and it was wrapping itself around her waist. In seconds, she'd exposed her entire backside and he caught a glimpse of purple panties and a fairly long splinter that transversed her lower hip and disappeared into the strip of lace.

"If the lodge is an uproar, you're partly to blame, Buck. You overreact to everything."

"I heard you say you'd be back at two o'clock. You even suggested we might do something pleasant together when you returned." Buck crossed his arms across his chest. She was on her side glaring up at him, still struggling to disentangle herself gracefully from the sheet. He rested a hand on her upper thigh to stop her squirming, but the warmth of her soft flesh shot a quiver of desire clean through him.

"I never imagined that doing something pleasant tonight might encompass me picking cedar bark out of your derriere. Why were you so late?"

"Time doesn't mean anything to me, Buck, not when I have a camera in my hand. I thought you realized that. I can only give rough estimates of when I'll return."

"Rough estimates? Sounds like there's another condition I should add."

"No risks and no open-ended assignments? You'd probably like it if I limited myself to something safe and predictable, like photographing kids on ponies. Stuffed ponies."

Buck counted to ten, then on to fifteen for good measure. A part of him was still recovering from the jolt of Louie's news that Caitlin had fallen from a tree. Despite the cook's insistence that the injury was minor, he hadn't believed it until he'd entered this room and seen Caitlin in one piece.

"And another thing. I don't need your help, Rawlings. I'll drive over to Doc Morrow's place right now."

"Like hell you will. Hold still and let me look at this." He moved the rectangular overhead lamp to focus optimum light on the long sliver of cedar in her soft round rump. The air in the room was suddenly heavy. His body reacted with open hunger. The combination of anger and desire disturbed him, but how could he cast one aside for the other?

"Damn, it's a good thing this splinter is off to one side or you wouldn't be able to sit." He tried to keep his voice free of the irritation that burned inside him, but it sounded raspy and strained just the same. Adding to his list of worries was Chase. His brother was no doubt lounging in a tavern somewhere in Twodot and rapidly on his way to getting drunk. He should be rounding up Chase, not pulling a splinter out of Caitlin's backside. Buck felt torn between duty to his family and his need to know Cat O'Malley was in safe hands. His hands. He didn't want any other male at the lodge pulling splinter duty on his woman.

"Your bedside manner is deplorable, Rawlings. I'd rather have Louie in here with his carving fork and tongs."

"I thought I told you to hold still, O'Malley." He finished his inspection then looked over at her face. She eyed him warily over her shoulder and he knew her combative attitude was purely in reaction to his surly tone. If the tables were turned and he were stretched out in the same position of vulnerability, he'd appreciate a more caring, understanding attitude.

Relief and anger. A dozen times since her arrival, he'd warred with conflicting emotions. Nothing was simple when it came to rebuilding a new bond from the ashes of their old relationship. She lay her head back down on top of her arms.

"Caitlin, I'm sorry. Try to imagine how scared I was out there this afternoon, searching the places I thought you'd be drawn to and not knowing where to look." He plucked a twig out of the chestnut cloud that waved down her back. "I felt helpless, Cat. No one else in this world can make me feel so out of control."

"Buck—" She turned and eyed him warily.

"Hush. Let me finish. Like I said," he continued, "I walked into the lodge to find Lester passed out cold and Louie babbling about you falling. My first thought was that Lester had fainted after hearing bad news." He rested his palms on the edge of the table.

Since his birth, generations of strong Rawlings men had taught him the importance of protecting his woman. Perhaps he'd learned the lesson too well and had failed too often. His mother and his sister had died. Buck longed to escape with Caitlin to a sheltered fortress, to keep her safe from all harm forever. Even a splinter was too much, avoidable.

"Buck, I tried to hide this little accident from you so you wouldn't have to experience the kind of reaction you had in the Big Room. I thought it best not to mention the tree, the fall or the splinter."

"And you didn't think I'd notice when we made love tonight?"

She blushed visibly at his words. "After this morning's argument, I wasn't sure where I'd be sleeping tonight. I danced with one of the workmen last night and he said my old room on the third floor had been fully repaired for a few days. I guess you neglected to mention it."

"We're not discussing the status of your room. I'm worried about your fall." He looked down at the array of needles, tweezers, antiseptic, cotton balls and gauze Lester had left on the edge of the pool table. "Are you hurt, bruised, bleeding anywhere else?"

"No." She shook her head too adamantly. "I'm just fine. It doesn't even hurt."

Buck recalled her story of a ten-year-old girl in a haunted castle. The woman liked to keep a strong front, to never admit her need for him.

"You wouldn't lie to me, would you, Caitlin?"

"I might have concealed this little sliver from you, Buck, but I'd never lie to you. Can we get on with this? It's been a long day."

"All right, but you're all tangled up in this flowery stuff. Here, let's get you out of this—" He grasped handfuls of sundress and pulled the garment over her head, letting it flutter to the floor. Quickly she reached back and drew the sheet up over her lower half again.

The sight of her creamy skin instantly reminded Buck of the night, half a dozen years ago, when their game of billiards turned playful and the stakes went up. "That's definitely better," he said softly. "I wouldn't want to drop the needle and get it lost in all that fabric. Just relax while I wash my hands."

"Is the door locked?"

"Yes. No one's going to walk in," he said, turning on the faucet in the kitchenette and washing his hands.

"Tell me, is Lester all right?"

"Louie's getting him some soup and the guys will put him to bed. The man never could hold his liquor, and he's probably the most squeamish person I've met when it comes to medical emergencies." Buck finished washing his hands and grabbed a towel. "You picked the worst possible member of the crew to conspire with this time."

"Poor guy. I had no idea. I owe him a big favor."

"Save your favors for me, Cat O'Malley."

Buck picked up a needle and tweezers and looked down at the enchanting landscape before him. Last night he'd worshiped her body, glorying in her beauty and perfection. He hated to mar a single inch of skin.

"Okay, you might feel a little stab."

She didn't flinch.

He worked for a few minutes in silence, surprised at how easily the splinter lifted and at how little damage was done.

"Can I have a progress report?" she asked.

"This isn't as difficult as I thought it would be. I'm finding the penetration is easier if I use a gentle sliding motion."

She laughed in that fresh and honest manner he'd missed so much. "Sounds like you're talking about last night."

"I won't be able to hold this needle still if I think about last night, O'Malley. Help me get my mind off the subject. Tell me about your accident." He dabbed an antiseptic-soaked cotton ball on the area and heard her sharp intake of breath.

"It's pretty cut-and-dried as accidents go. I climbed. I fell. And I landed."

"Were you up fairly high when you fell? How much equipment were you carrying? What did you land on?"

"What is this? The one-man Echo Creek inquisition squad?"

"No, it's a man from Echo Creek who cares deeply about you, Caitlin."

When she glanced back over her bare shoulder at him, there was a sexy new fire in her eyes. "Hurry," she whispered.

She lifted a naked foot into the air and his attention was drawn to her tanned calf and shapely ankle. When she lifted a second foot and pointed her toes toward the ceiling, the sheet fell away completely, exposing the portion of her body, from her waist to her knees, that had been draped.

"Mind if we just leave that sheet where it fell?" he asked. "I don't want any more of your wriggling. I'm getting to the most tender part now." He studied the way her purple lace panties clung to the delicate curve of her lower buttock, the area he often cupped while holding her.

"As long as you're not distracted, Mr. Rawlings."

"I was distracted the second I walked into this room. I'm sure this whole operation has been far more painful for me than it's been for you, O'Malley. I have another half inch of splinter left to go. I'm going to have to remove your panties." He slipped the lacy strip of fabric over her legs and feet. "I think I'll just hold on to these until later." He stuffed them into his jeans pocket.

"Your constant touch is driving me crazy," she moaned, putting her face down atop her crossed arms on the table. "I feel a little conspicuous here, naked from head to toe and with my back to you, Buck."

"Yeah, I hate it when a loved one turns their back on me." He bent to kiss the curve of her shoulder. "Give me another minute and we'll remedy that situation."

Loved one. Buck was surprised by his own choice of words. The woman was on his mind every waking moment, but he'd avoided definitions and labels when it came to his own emotions. He lowered his free hand to the small of her back and skimmed his fingertips over the enticing rise of her bottom. Tenderness. Possessiveness. Desire. Was it something beyond these feelings that had helped him forgive her? Had he fallen in love with Cat O'Malley all over again?

Loved one. Caitlin felt mesmerized by his admission. His touch seemed to take on a new tenderness. Her breathing quickened and she could only imagine what would happen when he put the needle and tweezers down. The whole process of splinter removal had been maddening, a slow prelude to what she hoped would be a far more intimate possession.

She was shocked at how easily she'd lain naked and trusting before him. The layers of resentment and anger that had accumulated over the years were dissolving.

Looking back over her shoulder, she watched him frown with concentration as he completed his ·delicate task. The rectangle of light from the overhead lamp cast harsh shadows over the planes of his ruggedly handsome features. The effect was softened by the sensual fullness of his mouth and by her embrace of his words—*loved one.* How she longed to touch him with the same forgiving gentleness he afforded her.

Less than a week remained of her assignment at Echo Creek. She wanted to know for certain now if they would stand before the lake together and say farewell to Sarah and to the grief that had stalked their happiness and hope.

Secretly she wished she could extricate the sliver of doubt that kept Buck from trusting her completely.

"I'm done," Buck announced. She watched him put the sewing kit and tweezers on the counter by the sink. He picked up the antiseptic and she hissed through her teeth when he brushed a final application on the sensitive strip of skin. His fingers grasped her shoulder and she turned on her side to face him. "No need for a bandage, but I do believe kissing can make it better."

Heartbeats later, his mouth was on hers, a fire consuming her need, ending her long wait.

Suddenly a fist beat an urgent rhythm on the door of the gaming room.

"Buck! There's been an accident! Open up!" Klyde shouted from the hallway.

"Damn, now what?" Buck pulled away and straightened, seemingly unaware of her naked vulnerability. As he rushed to the double doors in six impossibly long strides, Caitlin sat up, grasped the sheet and brought it up to her breasts. A vortex of cold fear sucked the air from her lungs.

"What happened?" Buck demanded, unlocking the door and wrenching it open.

"Chase hit a tree. We heard the crash and Carlos checked him over thoroughly before we pulled him out of the truck but—"

Buck swore loudly. "How bad is it? Where the hell is he now?"

"Looks like just a head wound but we're not sure. The guys put him on an old door and they're carryin' him up the stairs now, but he's acting irrational, Buck. Doc Morrow's on his way."

Caitlin heard the pounding of Buck's footfalls on the hall carpet. Ignoring the twinge of tenderness on her buttock, she swung her legs over the edge of the pool table and jumped down. She gathered her sundress from the floor with trembling fingers and slipped it over her head. Stepping into her sandals, she scurried after Buck and Klyde, praying aloud that the cloud of tragedy that hung over the Rawlings family had not struck again.

From the entry hall, she could see the men shuffling in the front entrance, their expressions somber as they carried the door holding a half-crazed Chase Rawlings into the kitchen and set it on the table. The dogs ran around excitedly, adding to the confusion. She quickly took the animals in hand and shooshed them outside. A few crew members stepped past her and stood on the front porch, waiting anxiously.

When Caitlin returned to the kitchen, Buck was attempting to hold his brother in a prone position.

"I'm perfectly fine!" Chase roared. "Let me up!"

"Damn, where did all this blood come from?" Buck demanded, tearing the blood-soaked shirt away from his brother's chest. "It has to be more than a simple cut. How soon will the doctor get here?"

"Head wounds bleed like that," Carlos snapped back, clearly taking charge. He was rummaging through the large first-aid kit that was put to frequent use at the lodge. "Chase was drinking. Must have gone out of control on the last turn and hit the maple sapling. Thank God he missed the big oak. We'd be picking up pieces if he'd hit that monster."

In the blazing light of the kitchen, Carlos held a compress to the side of Chase's head and tried to calm the younger Rawlings brother. As Caitlin moved closer, she saw splatters of red on the tile floor and worried that the injury might be quite serious. Chase kept insisting on getting up and Buck kept insisting on holding him still. Wanting to assist, Caitlin put a hand on Chase's shoulder.

"Don't touch me." Chase ground out the words. "If it weren't for you—"

Caitlin pulled her hand away and stepped back.

"Keep quiet, Chase. You don't know what you're saying." Frowning, Buck motioned Caitlin back toward the stove and barked a series of questions at Carlos who answered reassuringly, showing his expertise in emergency first aid and calming agitated patients and relatives alike.

Feeling hurt by Chase's apparent anger and prompted by her old need to keep busy during a time of crisis, she held up two coffeepots and nodded to Louie across the room. The cook gave his approval with a slight movement of his head. Caitlin quickly started measuring coffee grounds. As she set the blue enamel pots on the stove, she saw Lester standing in the doorway of the kitchen, draped in his robe, looking pale and stricken despite his sunburn. Recalling Buck's comment about Lester's squeamishness, she snaked an arm across the tailor's narrow shoulders.

"You want to wait in the Big Room, Lester?" she asked softly. "Doc Morrow will be here any minute. I'll keep you updated."

"No." Lester shook his head. "I couldn't cause you pain by takin' out your sliver, Miss O'Malley, but this is different. Buck and Chase are like sons to me. I've seen them through situations far worse than this."

Caitlin recalled Lester mentioning the week before that he'd been present on both occasions when Buck's mother and sister had died. She watched him skirt the table and settle on the window seat, his hands clasped together, white knuckles evident.

"Doesn't look like there are any broken bones. I think he's just going to need a handful of stitches," Carlos announced after completing his examination. "But we should wait for Doc Morrow to confirm that. Quit fighting us, Chase. You're still bleeding pretty heavy." He handed a fresh compress to Buck and turned back to the younger

Rawlings. "I want you to lay flat until the doctor arrives, buddy."

As Caitlin glanced from man to man in the room, she sensed their relief and realized how much like family this group was. With a flush of warmth and longing, she came to understand how desperately she wanted to belong to the people who were important to Buck.

Buck steepled his hands and rested his fingers against his chin, partly as a means of keeping himself from wrapping them around his foolish brother's throat. He was getting tired of playing the solicitous older brother. While Doc Morrow put seven stitches in Chase's scalp just a fraction of an inch from his temple, Buck ordered all crew members to the gaming room for a mandatory game of poker. He'd reassured Lester and sent the tailor back to bed. Expecting a confrontation, he didn't want longtime family friends and employees to witness a scene between the brothers.

He'd asked Caitlin to stay in the kitchen, believing she might have a calming presence. She'd changed into her tailored Echo Creek Buckhorn Special and slipped a pair of slate-gray trousers over her wounded backside. Buck couldn't forget the scrap of purple lace burning a hole in the pocket of his jeans. He would have preferred to put his brother to bed and concentrate his efforts on smoothing his healing palms over Caitlin's sweetly tempting derriere. But rekindling a romance in a lodge full of misfits called for patience and attention to priorities.

The guilt weighed on him. His father would have said he didn't have his priorities in order, and that would have been the truth. If Buck had put family first today, he would have driven to Twodot, collected his brother and driven him safely home.

Buck helped Chase off the door the crew had set atop the table and sat him in the chair Doc Morrow was holding. Buck picked up the door and set it against the window seat. While the doctor listened to Chase's chest once again and took his blood pressure, Buck grabbed a rack of mugs and sat down at the table. He poured steaming cups of Fogcutter, set one in front of his sullen brother, and another in front of the doctor. Finally he took a sip from his own cup, and leaned back in his chair.

He looked over toward the bank of windows where Caitlin stood staring out at the twilight sky. He'd noticed Chase casting a number of contemptuous glances in Caitlin's direction and pondered their meaning. He'd practically snarled at her when they'd first brought him into the kitchen. Was his brother experiencing sibling rivalry or had there been words between Chase and Caitlin he was unaware of? Could Chase's anger be related to the conversation the brothers had shared on the lawn that afternoon?

Chase had calmed down considerably but still there was an echo of tension resounding through the kitchen.

"Okay, Chase, you should be feeling a little more clear-headed now. You want to tell me what happened?" Buck asked quietly. "You've never had an accident in your life, but the guys say it looks like you drove straight into a tree. It's obvious you had a few beers—"

"Two. I had two beers, Buck, and I had a burger, so it's not like I was drinking on an empty stomach. I wasn't driving drunk. Right, Doc?"

Doc Morrow looked up from his prodding of Chase's ribs and glanced over his half-glasses at Buck. "Well, in my opinion, he's not intoxicated, but alcohol affects everyone differently. I can tell you this. His blood pressure's sky-high for someone so young." The doctor put a hand on Chase's shoulder. "If the accident upset you this much, son, I can give you something to calm you down a bit."

"Nothing can calm me down right now. Look, I was driving mad, crazy mad, Buck, and the closer I got to the lodge, the more angry I got."

Buck was confused and perturbed by Chase's confession. He felt a sense of foreboding. "Hey, I know we said some brutally honest things to each other this afternoon but we argue about the family business all the time. It's no big deal—"

"Don't patronize me, Buck."

"You've never been angry enough to lose control and drive into a tree before. Quit trying to pin the blame on me and take responsibility for—"

"It's not about you or the company." Chase brushed the doctor's hand aside and stood up. He took a few unsteady steps toward the stove, then turned and leaned back against the chrome door handles. "I can't shake what you said about Sarah. It's like a roar in my head—and it just keeps getting louder."

Buck flinched inside. He was just getting used to hearing Sarah's name again, to forming that word on his own lips after seven years, and here was Chase, shouting the name and stirring up a maelstrom of pain.

"I simply said she might have been following Mom's example or my own, Chase. What's so upsetting about that?" Out of the corner of his eye, Buck saw Caitlin move away from the windows and step toward the table.

"Shut up for once in your life, Buck, and listen to me." Chase glanced from Buck to Caitlin. His features hardened. "It's what you said about Caitlin being so reckless, and challenging Sarah on Shepherd's Rock just before Sarah fell. Sarah could never keep up with Caitlin. Never. How can I forget that?"

"Buck, what did you tell him?" Caitlin turned, her voice nearly broken.

Buck exploded out of his chair, ready to defend her from his brother's cruel words. He didn't want a three-way shouting match.

"You *are* drunk and if you're about to make any accusations you'll regret, Chase—I'm warning you, don't do it! We've got a shoot to finish up here and a company to run! You've caused enough of a disturbance for one night."

"You asked me why I drove my damn truck into a tree?" Chase slammed a fist down on top of the table. "I'm just trying to give you an honest answer."

"Well, maybe I don't like your answer. You're way out of line, brother."

"No, Buck." Caitlin curled her fingers around the rung on the back of a chair. "Let him speak his mind. I don't know what Buck told you, Chase, but I can handle whatever you have to say."

"Don't act so sure about that, ma'am." Chase looked down at the floor and took a deep breath. His hands balled into fists at his sides. "I sat in that bar today thinking about all the high jinks you and Sarah pulled years ago. Our sister never got in trouble unless you were with her." He looked up, his features contorted with anger. "How can I *not* feel there's a connection between your challenging Sarah and her death?"

"You want me to open up the other side of your crazy skull?" Never before had Buck felt such intense anger toward his brother. He stepped forward.

"Don't. Please, don't." Caitlin grasped his arm. "Sit down, Buck."

Buck sat down and perched stiffly on the edge of the chair. "You're not being fair, Chase. Caitlin and I have been over this already. I made the mistake of blaming her and now I regret it."

"How can you be objective when you're sleeping with the woman?"

"Hold on a damn minute," Caitlin said tersely. "Whatever you have to say is between you and me, Chase. I don't want to hear your hotheaded comments about anything private that goes on between me and Buck."

"It was relevant." Chase spoke through clenched teeth.

"It was a potshot," Caitlin snapped.

Buck lifted his brows at the haughty way Caitlin stepped up to his brother and traded barbs.

"Now, what burning questions do you have to ask me?" she demanded.

"Why didn't you come to Sarah's funeral, Caitlin?" Chase demanded.

"Young man." Doc Morrow spoke quietly as he stepped toward Chase. "Maybe you need something to calm you down."

"Answer me, Caitlin!" Chase shouted and moved toward the butcher-block island, eluding the doctor's grasp. "If you were so damned innocent, why didn't you come?"

"Buck wouldn't let me go to Sarah's funeral," Caitlin cried out. Tears shimmered in her eyes and her lip quivered, but her voice held a strength that surprised Buck. "Your brother blamed me for everything, Chase. That's why he broke things off between us seven years ago and cut me out of his life."

"I should never have agreed to let you come up here, to let you substitute for your father." Chase pointed a finger at her. "You have no business trying to weasel your way back into my family."

"You've said enough, Chase." Buck took two quick steps toward Chase, grabbed his brother's arms and pushed him up against the stove. "When I talked about Caitlin's recklessness this afternoon, I didn't mean to imply—"

"Wait. The two of you have done enough talking," Caitlin announced coldly. "Buck, Chase, Doc Morrow—I want all three of you to sit down and listen to what I have to say."

Caitlin stared at the two men in black standing beside the antique stove, looking like bookends in tragic tones. Separately, they exuded a brooding darkness and stealth of movement that announced danger to anyone in their path. Together, they created an imposing aura of rebellious energy.

What exactly had Buck said to his brother this afternoon to create such anger and turmoil? When she'd arrived at Echo Creek Lodge over a week ago, she'd been forced to face one accuser. Now the number had doubled. And while Buck's feelings had softened and moved toward forgiveness, Chase's pain was raw and heartrending. His words stabbed her deeply.

The Rawlings brothers both stared at her without blinking, seemingly stunned by her command.

"I asked you to sit down and listen to me," she repeated, gently, indicating the kitchen table with a movement of her hand.

"I have no interest in what you have to say." Chase spaced the words evenly like a sharpshooter squeezing off rounds. Blood had dried on his neck and upper chest, adding to his forbidding presence.

"Just do what the lady says." Buck swore and grabbed his brother by the back loop of his belt and shoved him forcefully into a kitchen chair next to Doc Morrow. Buck then pulled the adjoining chair out with the toe of his boot and slumped into it, his attention focused fully on her.

Where to begin? Caitlin pondered for brief seconds, as dread wrapped icy fingers around her heart. She sat down opposite the three men.

"I tried to tell your family the truth about Sarah soon after her death but none of you would listen. My letters were returned unanswered. So I've kept her secret all these years, unsure whether sharing it with you would lessen your pain... or make it worse."

Doc Morrow bit his lip, took off his glasses and stared down at his hands. Caitlin wondered if he'd been privy to Sarah Rawlings's medical records.

"That last summer I was at Echo Creek I noticed a few things about Sarah that disturbed me. She grew tired more easily and blamed it on a flu bug. I saw prescription bottles in her purse but she brushed off my concern, saying something about allergies. A lot of things would have added up if I'd been paying more attention to Sarah, but that summer, I'm afraid my attention was on Buck."

Now that she'd begun her revelation, Caitlin's only wish was to pack her belongings and leave Echo Creek before the memories of her night of lovemaking with Buck and her hope for a future together were marred by this bitter encounter. But she had to continue, had to get it out once and for all.

"It wasn't until I got back to Missoula that I received two letters from Sarah, a few days apart. In them, she shared her secret with me. While studying for her master's in Seattle, she started having headaches, and lost her sense of smell and..." Caitlin paused and inhaled deeply. "A doctor at the university's hospital diagnosed her with cancer. Sarah had an inoperable brain tumor. Second and third opinions bore that out. There was no chance of survival."

"No." Buck rose slowly to his feet, his features a mask of anguish. "I can't believe this. She would have told me."

Caitlin's throat constricted as she watched Chase's angry glare soften and turn to a look of absolute bewilderment. Wordlessly, the younger man reached up to touch Buck's sleeve. She wondered if Chase was offering comfort or seeking assurance.

"Sarah asked me to keep it secret. She didn't want her family to know because she felt everyone was so athletic and strong, and there wouldn't be much understanding of weakness and imperfection.

"Sarah also said your lives were busy enough. Chase was at Yale. Your dad was engaged. Echo Creek was introducing new products."

"That's outrageous." Buck sank back down into his chair. "We would have understood. I would have taken care of her myself. I would have made time, dammit."

How much did they need to know? Caitlin alone had held these secrets in her heart for so many years, she wanted nothing left of the burden. She wanted all of it, every painful detail, on the table. Buck and Chase could choose what to accept and what to throw away. She'd be done with it and could finally say goodbye to her friend.

"Buck, when Sarah said your life was busy enough, she was referring to me, to my relationship with you. She wrote to me about not wanting to be an invalid interfering with your plans for marriage and a future. I brought the letters...."

Caitlin watched the play of emotions on his face. Anguished shock transformed to grim defeat. No doubt he was thinking of the irony. In the end, Sarah had unwittingly interfered with their plans for the future. Her death had torn their love apart. The very thing Sarah Rawlings was trying to prevent, had taken place and had become far more painful than she would ever have guessed.

Would Caitlin's revelation of the truth about his sister cause Buck to withdraw his love all over again?

"So what did she plan to do?" Chase asked numbly. "Hide the tumor and avoid the truth—what the hell was she thinking?"

"Sarah was desperate. After I got the first letter, I called the lodge. Buck, Lester and Sarah had stayed on after the catalog shoot. I begged Sarah to tell everyone the truth and invited her to come along on assignment with me to eastern Montana later that month. She sounded despondent."

"And you didn't tell me, O'Malley?" Buck leaned across the table. "If she *sounded* despondent, didn't it occur to you she wasn't capable of making lucid decisions regarding her health? Why didn't you do something about it? Why didn't you call—"

"Caitlin *did* do something, Buck," Doc Morrow interrupted. He got up, ambled to the stove and picked up a blue enameled pot. "Miss O'Malley called me and asked me to come over to Echo Creek and check on Sarah. I knew about the tumor because Sarah had knocked on my door one night needing pain medication. I'd been retired three years by then, but how could I not get involved? I spoke with her doctor in Seattle. Things did look hopeless."

The doctor's mouth twisted into a grim line as he poured hot coffee into the four mugs on the table.

"Sarah had no desire to see this thing to its natural conclusion. She was strong and young and beautiful. She wanted everyone to remember her that way." Doc Morrow picked up a mug and leaned back against the stove. "On top of that, your sister was worried about Echo Creek Outfitters. The company was on rocky ground that year and she worried about the medical expenses. Seems the poor girl didn't have health insurance."

"The devil." Chase swore, kicking a table leg with his boot. He turned away from the group to face the windows.

"Dear Lord." Buck brought his hands to his face.

"I stopped to see her every day under the guise of wanting to fish in Medicine Bowl Lake," the doctor continued. "I kept checking her moods, and encouraging her to tell the family the truth. I also tried to give her some relief from the blinding headaches and the vomiting spells."

Caitlin couldn't bear to imagine the pain the two brothers were experiencing but she felt relieved to have Sarah's secret revealed. She had been wise to wait after all. If Doc Morrow hadn't been here tonight, would they have believed her or blamed her further for not telling them of the disease seven years ago? With the doctor's testimony about Caitlin's concern and efforts to intercede, Buck would realize now that she'd done everything possible to help his sister.

"Sarah's privacy be damned, Doc. You should have told me outright."

"It was Sarah's right to request confidentiality," Doc Morrow replied, laying his hand on Buck's shoulder.

Buck brought his hands down from his stricken face, wrapped them around his cup of coffee and stared down into the dark liquid. "So are the two of you suggesting that Sarah's fall from Shepherd's Rock was no accident?"

Caitlin glanced at Doc Morrow whose normally sorrowful brown eyes clouded with added misery.

"I can't assume that, Buck," the doctor said softly, shaking his head. "None of us knows for sure what was go-

ng through her head that morning. The fall could have been
an accident. She'd had some weakness on one side of the
body the day before.''

"I should have been told,'' Buck stated flatly. "I'm go-
ng to spend the rest of my life wondering if she'd planned
o take her life, if her hand slipped out of mine be-
ause...because she deliberately wanted to let go of life. If
had known any of this, I never would have taken her
climbing with me.''

"Your sister was twenty-three years old, Buck. She
wanted to be considered an adult, but with an overprotec-
ive father and brother, that was difficult. Sarah was adamant if not fanatical about her privacy. You've got to
understand that both Caitlin and I were put in difficult po-
sitions.'' The doctor sipped his coffee thoughtfully.
"Looking back on this whole business,'' he said, nodding
oward both Buck and Chase, "if I had to do it over, I
couldn't change anything. I was bound by my oath. Keep-
ng your sister's secret...well, that's one of the most diffi-
ult things I've had to do in my life.''

Caitlin watched as Buck leaned back in his chair and
urned to study his brother, who sat beside him, his body
canted away from the group. With his bloodstained cheek
and neck, and shock of unruly black hair, Chase looked like
the ultimate bad boy, forlorn and unapproachable.

"You weren't at the lodge that summer, Chase.'' Buck
swung his legs around and butted his chair up against
Chase's. With tenderness etched on his features, he put a
hand on his brother's shoulder. "You were studying back
east. There wasn't a damn thing you could have done.''

"Hey, this is all new to me. In a matter of hours, I'm
finding out you blamed Caitlin for Sarah's death—to the
point of breaking off your relationship.'' Chase turned back
to face Buck. "And this business about a brain tumor. I hate
thinking about Sarah being so worried about money and
about coming between you and Caitlin. She was thinking of
everyone and everything but herself.''

Caitlin looked at her half-empty mug, unable to witness the compassionate look in Buck's eyes as he leaned his body closer to Chase's and offered his silent strength.

"Tonight," Chase continued, "when I realized the truck was out of control and heading toward that tree, I felt such utter despair at the thought of dying and leaving loved ones and not accomplishing everything I had to do. Now after hearing about Sarah, I can't bear the thought that she felt so alone and desperate that she would purposely choose to...fall."

"We don't know that, son," the doctor said solemnly. "And it's best that you don't dwell on something no one has the answer to. Just let it be."

"Caitlin." Chase spoke long minutes later. "I'm sorry about tonight. I was angry and frustrated and grasping for answers."

"It's all right, Chase. It's been a long day for all of us. Maybe it's best if we all get some sleep." She felt tension grip her stomach. Buck's visage was still clouded with anger and anguish, his mouth a thin white line. How would her announcement impact their renewed relationship?

While Buck saw Doc Morrow to the door, Caitlin went to the sink and wet a paper towel, then handed it to Chase. "Some of the blood dried on your cheek and neck." She indicated the areas on her own face, throat, and upper chest with her fingertips.

Turning away, she picked up the mugs from the table and put them in the dishwasher, grateful for any mechanical routine that took her mind off Sarah. When she looked back toward the table, Buck Rawlings was standing over Chase talking softly and washing the dried blood from his brother's cheek.

Pondering the mysteries of brotherly love, Caitlin watched them for only a handful of seconds, then slipped out the kitchen door and made her way quickly up the stairs to Buck's bedroom to gather a few essential belongings.

Sarah's room was repaired and ready to be occupied. Tonight it was best that she leave Buck alone with his thoughts.

The man had chased lightning from the sky for her and she longed to linger in his arms, but the burden she'd unleashed tonight now rested on his shoulders. She'd let him adjust to the weight before she asked him to go on.

Chapter Twelve

In the shadows of Chase's room, Buck sat in an heirloom
rocker and watched his brother sleep. After their mother'
death, it had been Buck's duty to tuck in and comfort hi
two younger siblings. Tonight he'd felt a surge of that old
need to chase the monsters from under Chase's bed and re
store order to a motherless child's world. Twenty-four year
had passed and Chase would scoff at the notion of being
"tucked in," so Buck had disguised his motives. Carrying
a glass of whiskey, gripping a cheroot between his teeth and
playing the gruff older sibling, Buck had convinced Chase
he simply wanted a few minutes of brotherly companion
ship.

Odd how most of those monsters had simply changed
shape. The ghosts of grief, resentment and anger had ap
peared again tonight after the painful disclosures by Caitlin
and Doc Morrow.

But the brothers hadn't discussed their family's trage
dies. They'd talked briefly about the events of the day, and

avoided the subject of Caitlin's long-kept secrets. Chase spoke about the more mechanical aspects of his truck accident. Buck mentioned the cedar splinter Caitlin brought home from her photographic excursion. His tale of splinter removal had prompted a few off-color but easily forgivable comments from Chase.

Perhaps, Buck mused, the remarks were forgivable because the subject of tonight's conversation wasn't important. It was the tentative smiles, the eye contact and the reaching out that began a healing of the rift between them.

Chase had finally eased into a fitful sleep, the three resident dogs curled up at the foot of his bed. Buck sat in the rocker, sipped his whiskey and pondered the remains of his family unity. Feeling wistful, he took a small piece of white quartz out of his pocket and stared at it. Sarah's wishing stone looked painfully ordinary, less than magical. He realized no talisman could have saved his sister from her ultimate tragedy.

But what about Caitlin? What magic could he harness to keep her safe from harm? Would she listen at last to his entreaty and stop taking risks?

More important, would she forgive the Rawlings brothers for placing the blame for Sarah's death so unfairly on her shoulders? She'd challenged his sister on Shepherd's Rock. How many times had he and Chase dared Sarah to keep up with them on steep terrains and grade-five rapids? Sarah loved to be challenged. She thrived on the adrenaline of competition and loved nothing better than testing her skills.

The letters. He felt a burning need to read his sister's letters but that could wait. He didn't want the additional pain to interfere with reconciling with Caitlin.

In the muted light of his brother's room, he studied the amber liquid in his glass, so like the color of Cat O'Malley's eyes. Tonight those beautiful eyes had been clouded with pain. The ugly scene in the kitchen when Chase lashed out at Caitlin would haunt Buck forever. In his brother's tirade, he recognized his own narrow-minded judgment and flashed back to the scene at the mortuary over half a dozen years ago. Buck had been far more brutal and had destroyed the love they'd built together.

Or so he had thought. In the time they'd spent together at the lodge, his old feelings for her had been resurrected and strengthened. He loved the woman, with the same intensity he'd heard his grandfather speak of so often when discussing his grandmother. Tonight in the gaming room, Buck had almost said the words aloud. It was time to tell her how he felt.

Buck swallowed the last of the whiskey, set his empty glass aside, snuffed out the cheroot and walked down the hall to his bedroom. He was surprised to find the room dark and the bed linens undisturbed. Had Caitlin assumed he was angry and chose to sleep elsewhere?

He needed to make it up to her tonight, in every way possible. Taking the steps to the third floor two at a time, Buck strode to the door of Sarah's old room and rested his palm against the panels of carved oak. The night of the big storm he'd looked inside for the first time in seven years and the very sight of his sister's mementos had sent him running from himself. Could he walk inside and endure that pain to find comfort with O'Malley's daughter?

Inhaling sharply, he pushed on the door and stepped inside. The pencil drawings of the family, the knickknacks and personal photographs were gone. All painful reminders of Sarah had been removed, replaced by Caitlin's distinctive bouquets of wildflowers and her collection of silk scarves and hats.

Wrapped only in a towel, Caitlin stepped from the bathroom onto the handwoven rug beside the delicate willow bed. Her lustrous chestnut waves were piled atop her head and tied with a blue satin ribbon, but a handful of curls escaped the ribbon's confines and formed a shimmering halo around her flushed features.

The scent of lavender wafted about the room, adding to the mysterious feminine allure that drew him closer.

For years, he'd imagined Cat O'Malley walking through the rooms of their Victorian home, her erect carriage, long graceful neck and high cheekbones mirroring women from another time. She'd never had a contemporary face. Even in her tailored Echo Creek clothing, she was a stunning reminder of an era of elegance and fluid styling.

How could a rancher's son in rawhide hope to win her silken hand, to keep a complicated woman happy in a world of make-believe Victorian nostalgia?

"I didn't expect to see you tonight," she said quietly.

"I sat with Chase for a while."

"How is he?"

"Lucky for him he's got a big truck and a hard head. I hope you don't mind, but I left all three dogs sleeping on his bed."

"Burrito and Fajita will be fine. It's been an incredibly rough day, Buck." She wrapped a hand around one of the willow posts and leaned her hip against it slightly. The way the bottom of the towel hit the tops of her thighs made her shapely legs look impossibly long and sexy. How he craved to feel their silken length wrapped around him, cradling him against her heat.

"After such a rough day, I expected to find you in the master bedroom, Caitlin. What made you come up here?"

"I decided to take a long soak in that old claw tub."

"There's a claw tub in every damn bathroom in this lodge."

She smiled softly. "I know that. But this bathroom is more feminine and private. I wanted to luxuriate." Her hand was on the fold of the towel above her breasts. Buck found himself holding his breath, his eyes focused on her fingers and the gentle swell of her full breasts above the thick terry cloth.

"Maybe I can help you luxuriate, ma'am." He stepped closer, his thumbs hanging loosely through his belt loops.

His groin grew hard and taut at her provocative pose and the precarious positioning of her towel.

She quirked an eyebrow. "My bath is long over."

"I truly doubt that. A lady's bath is never over until she's fully dried, head to foot and back again." Buck ran a fingertip over the rise of one breast. "You have a spot on your shoulder that needs attending to."

"That's hardly my shoulder you're touching."

"Well, I need to borrow this towel—just for a minute—to dry that troublesome spot."

"There's a linen closet full of towels in the bathroom."

"None as special as this towel." With that comment, he tugged at the tuck in the fabric that held the whole business together. To his delight, the terry cloth fell away slowly, lingering temptingly on the crest of one curve, before cascading to the rug.

His aching need was reaffirmed by the sight of her untamed beauty and the eager light in her tawny gold eyes. He bent to kiss the dusky tip of one breast.

Guilt and remorse welled up in him. A few hours earlier, he'd chastised Chase for blaming Caitlin for their sister's death. Touching Caitlin now, Buck felt the old familiar dominoes falling in place and he recognized the pattern. The last domino would fall and he'd be led back to secretly playing the history of that tragic day out in his mind and pointing a finger at Caitlin. He thought he was beyond this.

Buck had to reverse the pattern, stop the momentum. To do that, he had to admit to himself and then to Caitlin that he loved her.

"Cat, let me hold you, must hold you quietly for a moment," he whispered, wrapping his arms around her and embracing her tenderly. He grasped a handful of silky hair and cradled her head tenderly with his palm. Closing his eyes, he sighed and resisted the urge to let his hands glide down her still damp back to the delicious curve of her tight little tush.

For several agonizing seconds, he struggled to sort out his feelings. Had his desire for Caitlin these past ten days been driven by the need to make up for his past cruelty? Would there ever be a time when he could cleanse himself of the need to blame, and the guilt that accompanied it?

"I'm so damned sorry, Caitlin, for what happened tonight, for what happened so long ago." He brought his hand around to caress her face, to look directly into her eyes. "I've put you through so much. Can you forgive me for being so pigheaded and blind and so—"

"Hush." She put her fingers to his lips. "Not another word, about tonight or the past. I've spent the last hour soaking in a hot tub and promising myself I'd forget all that pain, Buck." She grasped the hem of his black T-shirt and peeled it from his body. Splaying her fingers across his chest, she leaned closer and stared up at him. "I want to walk down to the lake with you tomorrow, to stand at the point where you scattered Sarah's ashes, to say goodbye... to all of this, forever. I want to start over without all these complications."

Her hands moved deftly down his midriff to the buckle of his belt.

"So, tonight," she continued, "I don't want your sweet talk or apologies. I want it rough and raw, Buck, without any history getting in the way. Make me feel like I'm in the arms of an outlaw."

Rough? When her fingers moved lower to the button fly of his jeans, Buck was speechless. He'd come to Caitlin wanting to make up for seven years of wrongdoing but she didn't want his gentle caresses or apologies.

His jeans and briefs fell to the floor. He stepped out of the pool of denim at his feet, and before he could lift her onto the bed, she sank to her knees before him. With disbelief, he felt her mouth upon him, her tongue swirling around his arousal. He arched back, his knees nearly giving out, as she experimented, discovering the bone-melting movements that made him tremble uncontrollably.

A sudden hunger consumed him. The power of her words and the sexy ministrations of her mouth combined to feed his desperate fire. When her playful tongue brought him too close to the edge, Buck grasped Caitlin firmly by the arms and drew her back up against his body, relishing the feel of her unclothed body against his naked chest.

"Cat, my grampa made these beds nice and high for a reason." He scooped her up in his arms and tossed her onto the featherbed mattress. He winked at her. "It's the best way to make outlaw love to a woman like you."

Just what did he mean by that? Caitlin felt a thrill as she fell back across the plush white comforter and gazed up at the powerful body of Buck Rawlings, standing at the edge of the bed. From the moment he'd entered the room, he'd been undergoing a metamorphosis from gentle lover to lone wolf. The fiery glow in his gold-flecked eyes caused her to edge up on her elbows, shimmy backward and draw her legs together demurely.

Caitlin had playfully challenged him with her outlaw remark, but there was nothing playful about the way he dragged her back toward him until her buttocks were close to the edge of the bed. Buck eased her legs open, and still standing, bent forward to kiss the tips of her breasts. She felt the hard evidence of his desire dig into flesh of her abdomen and arched her back in response, wanting to join with him then. Now. This minute.

He chuckled irreverently and stroked his thumbs against her open thighs. The frisson of apprehension that skittered up her backbone at his rough touch blossomed, making her feel wild with need.

As he spread the moist satiny petals between her legs with two fingers, she took great shuddering breaths. When she gave him a welcoming clasp, he moaned appreciatively and smiled, his white teeth in sharp contrast to his dark skin. She arched slightly and he thrust his fingers deeper as if to touch her very soul. His thumb found the small nub in her triangle of curls and ignited her heat to a roiling frenzy.

"You want me to help you forget everything, Cat? Is that what you want?" His voice was brazen, bold, as he hastened the wicked movements of his long clever fingers.

As she lay melting on the bed, staring up at his powerful chest and slim hips, the room around them became a whirr of muted white walls and wildflowers. When had these clouds descended to caress her in their dreamy mist?

"Buck—" Caitlin half cried his name as her pleasure crested and she felt the core of her convulse around his fingers.

"I'm going to bury myself so deep in you, you'll forget every mean-spirited thing I ever said to you, lady." He immediately pressed the tip of his arousal to her, pulled up on her legs and sank his entire length into her.

Caitlin gasped at the sensation of total possession.

"Every wretched word," he continued, thrusting with each syllable. "Every scowl. Every time I turned my back and broke a promise."

He plunged into her with swift and forceful thrusts, taking her captive then releasing her on wave after wave of ecstasy until she was sated beyond anything she'd ever imagined possible. Only then did he cry out with his own shuddering climax and lower his body atop hers, kissing her softly, nuzzling her neck with the stubble on his chin.

"I love you, Buck," she whispered, slowly emerging from her luxuriant haze. "More than before."

"No talk of the past," he chided. Gently he moved off her, rolling onto his side and drawing her body firmly into the protective circle of his arms. "We're starting over, Caitlin. Everything is new, fresh, perfect."

Caitlin rested her head against his chest and let the meaning of what he'd said wash over her. Though Buck hadn't declared his love in return, his words were an affirmation of their new beginning, their future together. She thought of the images on her goal collage: marriage, babies, career success, the chance to nurture her dreams. With a pang in her heart, she recalled the pages Buck had torn from magazines: a lone fisherman, one set of footsteps in the snow, a solitary tent...and his lonely Victorian home.

As she nestled in his arms, the meshing of their dreams seemed more possible tonight. Buck had lived in a shroud of grief and unresolved anger for seven years. She had brought him truth where there had been mystery, and laughter where there had been silence and pain. And hopefully, she'd brought him love.

New, fresh, perfect. Could she believe him this time? Against the milky white of the comforter, his ebony hair, shadowed jaw and sun-bronzed skin gave him the look of a haunted, imperfect angel who'd tiptoed into heaven for an illicit nap.

Caitlin stretched contentedly then coiled back into Buck's embrace. She would ask him if they could walk to the lake after completing the catalog shoot and say goodbye to Sarah and put to rest the distrust that had hung between them for seven years. The thought of that walk should have brought a smile to her face. Caitlin couldn't quite understand the fist of apprehension that tightened in her stomach and prevented her from closing her eyes easily.

"Daughter, you should'a told me about Sarah years ago."

Caitlin pressed the phone receiver closer to her ear as she listened to her father's plaintive brogue. At first light, she'd left Buck alone in bed, had coffee with Chase in the kitchen, then locked herself in the library to make the call. It had taken her twenty minutes to explain the whole sordid story.

"Dad, I didn't tell you because I was afraid you'd tell Buck's father."

"It's a sad thing, all this," her father said in a choked voice. "So, has anyone told August Rawlings yet?"

"Chase plans to call his father sometime this morning. I wanted you to know right away, Dad. You're August's closest friend and I thought he might call and need your comfort."

"I'll be waiting. This puts a new light on how I feel about Buck Rawlings."

Caitlin leaned back in the leather chair behind the desk. "Is that a good or bad light?"

"You challenged his sister and that stayed on his mind. I can understand how he came to blame you, Cat. But if he loved you, really loved you all those years ago, he would have worked it out. I never knew why things dried up between the two of you."

"Dad, it's over and done with."

"Hardly. I love Buck like a son, but I can't forgive the man easily for breaking a promise to my only daughter and judging you so harshly."

She stared at the Rawlings' family portrait gallery on the opposite wall. The group shots of Buck, Chase and Sarah no longer clutched at her heart as they had soon after her arrival. Last night's scene in the kitchen had been cathartic. She was letting go of the painful past and filling the empty spaces left behind with dreams of a life with Buck.

Last night he'd insisted on making love a second time. Slowly, adoringly, Buck had paid homage to her body. She'd longed to hear him speak words about love and commitment, and again, had been bitterly disappointed. The promises and declarations of love had come so easily seven years ago. Perhaps after the emotional debris had been swept aside. Buck would talk in more definite terms about his feelings and about their future.

"You're going to have to live with it, Dad. I have the feeling we'll return to Missoula with plans for a future together."

"Ach. So it's like that again?" Her father reacted with surprise at the news of the renewed relationship. "What did Buck promise you this time, daughter?"

"Nothing yet... exactly. He wants to start over. But enough about me, Dad. How are you getting around the duplex on those crutches?"

"Amazingly well. And I have good news about my eyes."

"I heard. I talked to Dr. Leahy when I called the hospital this morning looking for you. He said the specialist in Seattle looked at your test results and is willing to attempt laser surgery next month."

"It looks promisin'. Still, I don't want Buck Rawlings knowing about the problem until we know if the surgery has worked or not. There's no sense alarmin' the man."

"Buck's still your friend, Dad. He has a right to be informed."

"No, I doubt he would sign me up for another year as Echo Creek Outfitters' photographer if he knew. Might take me off the insurance and then I'd be hurtin'."

"Dad, the surgery is going to work." Caitlin hated hearing the note of desperation in her father's voice when he mentioned insurance. She knew how high the premiums were for diabetics seeking private health plans. If only she herself could support him fully. "I still think you should tell Buck."

"No, and if I hear that you've told him, I'll never share another secret with you."

"Stop being so damn stubborn, Sean O'Malley. And keep me informed about the surgery. I want to be there with you when the time comes."

"Actually, Caitlin, if you're not able to make it, Doris has agreed to accompany me to Seattle."

"Doris?"

"She was my nurse at the hospital. Quite a cheerful sort."

There was a joyful lilt in her father's voice that she hadn't heard for years. Caitlin smiled and propped her booted feet on the top of the desk. "I want to hear all about this Doris. Don't leave out a single detail, Dad."

After listening to her father speak in enraptured tones about the red-haired nurse who found him fascinating, Caitlin hung up the phone. Immediately there was a knock on the library door.

When she opened it, Buck stood on the opposite side, his scowling expression enhanced by the shadow of his beard and sleep-rumpled hair. Bare-chested and wearing only a pair of jeans, the top button left hastily undone, he presented an imposing picture of raw sexual energy. She felt some inner sanctum in her lower abdomen grow taut with desire.

"What the hell is going on, O'Malley?" he demanded, holding up a handful of books she quickly recognized. He stepped inside the room and shut the door behind him with the swift kick of a bare foot. "I found these by the bathtub this morning."

How could she have been so careless? Caitlin suddenly felt as though the room was small and airless.

"You must have been reading them while you soaked in the tub last night. Since when did you pick up a sudden interest in—" he glanced at the spines of the books "—*Diseases of the Eye* and *Advances in the Treatment of Retinopathy?*"

"It's pronounced retin-op-*othy.*" She tilted her chin up and faced him squarely.

"I don't care how the damn word is pronounced. I want to know what it is and why you're reading about it."

"Buck, it's private." Caitlin recalled her father's request, still fresh on her mind. "I can't divulge anything for another month or so. After that, I'll be happy to explain everything."

"Another medical secret? Haven't you learned from your first fatal mistake?" He swore loudly. "You're not leaving this room until I find out what the heck's going on." He stepped backward until his body came between her and the library door. "Is there something wrong with you, Caitlin, something that I should know about?"

"Hardly. Look, I have to prepare for today's shoot, Rawlings. We're doing the catalog cover with you and Chase first thing this morning." She pointed to her watch and attempted to walk past him.

When she extended her arm to open the door, Buck dropped the books on the floor and took hold of her wrist, gently but firmly. He led her briskly across the room by her elbow, put his hands around her waist and lifted her up, then set her down on the oak desktop with a soft little plop.

Caitlin sat stunned for a moment staring into the wide expanse of Buck's well-muscled chest. She'd been a pawn between Sarah and the Rawlings family. Was she playing the pawn again, this time in a game between her father and Buck? She resented the difficult position her father had placed her in and knew she had to make a judgment call.

"I've wanted to tell you since I arrived," she started, "but I've been asked to keep this secret until an outcome is determined. I can't tell you, Buck. I just can't."

Buck felt hollow suddenly, as though the tenderness they'd built between them had been sucked clean out of him.

"An outcome? What am I supposed to do until then? Stay in the dark?"

"This news might worry you needlessly."

"Worry me."

"Don't push me to do this, Buck. I know it might seem like I'm making a habit of keeping secrets—"

"It's not just my sister and her letters, Caitlin. Yesterday when you fell from the tree, you had every intention of having Lester pull out that splinter. You were going to hide the whole incident from me."

"It wasn't necessary to upset you, Buck."

"It wasn't *necessary?* Tell me this, O'Malley." He held her by her shoulders and glared directly into her eyes. "In the future, would you ever conceal an illness or an injury from me, especially if you feared I'd restrict your activities if I knew?"

"Of all the arrogant, egotistical—" Caitlin appeared breathless with rage. She spun around, swung her legs over the opposite side of the desk and jumped down. "I'd never allow you to restrict my actions in the first place!"

Buck slipped around the desk and reached for her again. Caitlin moved quickly toward the door and jerked it open.

"You haven't answered my question," he called out.

"Buck, your question is way out of line. Why do I get the feeling you won't make promises about our future until you finish interviewing me and setting conditions? I don't need a protector, Rawlings. I need an equal, a friend."

She stomped down the hallway past the kitchen to the entry, stopping to grab a handful of shot sheets and her red baseball cap from the entry table, before she stepped out onto the front porch.

Buck followed, his fury gathering momentum with each stride. As he passed the kitchen, he whistled loudly and all three dogs scurried from the doorway to race outside.

He searched the clearing in front of the lodge but there was no sign of O'Malley's daughter. Turning, Buck spotted her straddling a porch rail, staring intently at a shot sheet. He was reminded of the night of Chase's birthday party, when Caitlin had jumped from the railing on the side deck. He felt no apprehension now, just a strange need to clear up all the misunderstandings that stood between them. Last night, he'd declared a fresh start for them, and already she'd muddled things with her need to keep secrets and unwillingness to answer his question.

Buck padded to her, feeling oddly boyish in his bare feet. Glancing down, he noticed the button left undone at his waistband. He imagined life with Cat O'Malley might cause him to go barefoot and unbuttoned from time to time.

He straddled the porch rail and faced her. "Put the layouts down, O'Malley."

"I have a job to do."

"I'm not done talking to you."

She looked up at him but the brim of her cap shadowed her eyes. "I won't be able to focus on my work today if we discuss any more personal matters."

He grabbed the shot sheets out of her hand and let them drift to the floor of the porch. "We're going to sit here, Cat, until we finish this conversation."

"It was hardly a conversation. It was Buck Rawlings telling me how things are going to be—according to his way of thinking."

There was a time to talk and a time to listen. He folded his arms across his chest and leaned back against the porch rail. He chose to listen.

"It's unfair, Buck. You don't want me taking risks. You demand to know about every scratch inflicted upon my flesh, and you want me to break promises of confidentiality made to other people."

He only nodded at her words and tried to keep his features emotionless. Caitlin had worn her shimmering hair loose today. Waves tumbled from her shoulders, softening the defiant tilt of her chin. It was difficult not to recall scenes from last night.

"On top of that," she continued, "you hate the idea of my open-ended expeditions where I might be more than two hours late. What about me, Buck?"

"What about you?"

"You want to open a wilderness guide service to take strangers into areas where danger lurks around every corner. Talk about risks." She slapped her hand against her knee. "Talk about treks where you might be one or two *days* late rather than a few hours. Yet I feel no compulsion to set conditions for you, Buck. The thought never crossed my mind. For some foolish reason, I trust you."

Buck frowned and unfolded his arms, letting his hands drop to his thighs. "Caitlin, when are you going to take an objective step backward and realize you're addicted to danger? How can you expect me to return the same trust?"

"Are you bringing up the incident at Shepherd's Rock again? I thought we'd agreed that was long buried."

"An unfortunate choice of words." Buck turned his head and looked beyond the clearing to the sweeping meadow that led down to Medicine Bowl Lake. "I'm not ready to walk to the lake with you, Caitlin, and to say goodbye to

Sarah yet," he murmured. "At the moment, I'm not sure of anything."

"Buck—"

"I was raised to protect the woman I love—physically, emotionally, in every way possible. You want to hobble me in those efforts." Buck looped his leg back over the rail and stood. The feel of the old wooden planks of the porch brought back memories of sitting here observing his numerous uncles, his father and grandfather discussing their womenfolk. He could almost smell the smoke from their cigars and pipes.

Times had changed, of course. Women and men had changed. He studied Caitlin's tailored Echo Creek clothing and the jaunty way she wore her baseball hat. He ached to have her admit she needed his strength and protection, but knew deep in his heart that was a line she might never cross.

Four more days remained before the shoot would end. Perhaps they'd both return to Missoula the same way they'd left it: alone and lonely. He'd prefer to enter the city at her side, to show her the work he'd done on his Victorian, to know once and for all she was his woman.

Buck heard the creak of the front door and glanced up to find Chase waiting expectantly.

"I'm about to call Dad to tell him about—about everything, Buck. I thought you'd want to be in on this conversation."

Buck felt his pulse accelerate in the silent moments that followed. Could he expect the long drought of emotion between himself and his father to come to an end when the truth about Sarah was revealed? Would his father stop blaming Buck and elevate his oldest son back to equal status as a Rawlings offspring?

He shoved the thought aside. Looking out over the clearing in front of the lodge, feeling the weathered planks of the porch beneath his feet, he felt a deep abiding love for the man. His greatest concern now was for August Rawlings's pain. In a space of two decades, the man had lost a wife and daughter. Was it fair to open an old man's wounds in the name of truth?

"Do you really think we should tell him, Chase?" Buck leaned against one of the massive log pillars beside the top step and faced his brother.

"He has a right to know," Chase argued. "And it might heal the rift between you two. I want that, for both of you."

Buck stared at his brother's calm features, then looked down to hide the moisture in his own eyes. There was something new, an aura of maturity, about his younger sibling, that made him surge with pride.

"Dial him," Buck urged gently. "I'll pick up an extension."

Chapter Thirteen

High drama. Caitlin recalled her father's two words of advice about selecting a setting for the cover photo. She'd positioned the Rawlings brothers in the old corral against a dramatic backdrop of blue lake and rocky foothills. The family's four horses had been brought down for the shoot and they added to the distinctly Western flavor.

But the real drama was in the men themselves. Dressed in full-length oilskin drover coats and black Stetsons, Buck and Chase could have stepped right out of the Australian outback or America's early West. Their unshaven jaws and tanned features gave them a sexy earthiness fitting for the rugged apparel. Lone wolf and lone-wolf-in-training.

From the start, she'd wanted her photographs to appeal to Echo Creek Outfitters' female shopper. With this cover photo and the rest of her work, Caitlin believed she'd achieved that goal, whether Buck approved or not.

As she checked light levels, she overheard the men discussing a competitor's shirt design that looked a little too similar to one of their own. Gone was the tension that had so often spiced the brothers' conversations and furrowed their brows. This morning and early this afternoon, there appeared to be a stronger bond between them.

But the rapport between Buck and herself was once again strained. Had they reached their final impasse? Three more days of shooting remained. Could they resolve their differences? She didn't want temporary solutions. She wanted promises both of them could keep . . . for a lifetime.

Lester brought an assortment of props out of the weathered building behind them and motioned her over. "Miss O'Malley, do any of these items appeal to you?"

Branding irons, harnesses, ropes, spurs, a leather hay apron. Caitlin recognized a few of the items that had been hanging on the wall the night she and Buck had made love in the old stable.

Clearing his throat forcefully, Buck picked up a horse whip and glanced in her direction, a wry smile curling the corners of his mouth. It was evident that Buck's memory had been jarred, as well. Had he also recalled her remark about how Western gear reminded her of things sexual and mysterious and earthy?

Caitlin felt a shiver of heat course through her.

"Now here's somethin' that will give us all a laugh," Lester said with a chuckle. The tailor held up the multicolored, gold-fringed Western shirt Buck had threatened to make her wear that same night. She'd refused and chosen to wear nothing at all.

"Remember how we tricked—" Lester was chuckling so hard, he almost swallowed his toothpick "—we tricked poor Joe into thinkin' he had to model this? And the man believed us?"

Members of the crew laughed uproariously. Caitlin watched as Buck took the shirt from Lester's hand, his expression emotionless. He ran a finger along a row of the gold fringe then paused and tossed the gaudy garment back to Lester. Turning toward the horses, he began smoothing his palm down the long sleek neck of his chestnut stallion.

Caitlin stalked back to her camera, recalling how Buck had delighted in the white fringed shirt she'd worn to their picnic at Libby's Pocket. He'd stroked her breast through the long loops of satin. Gold or white fringe. It didn't matter. His movements symbolized his hold on her.

And how little hold she had on him.

Caitlin forced herself to focus on fine-tuning each scene. Buck glanced over the Polaroids before she committed each variation to film, but again and again she felt his gaze on her.

When the cover shot was completed, he eased out of the full-length coat and handed it to Lester. He untied Kodiak's reins from the corral post and hoisted himself up into the saddle. Caitlin approached to ask about the next setup, but Buck took the layout sheets from her and folded them neatly into a square and handed them back to her.

"There's something I want you to do until I return," he said quietly.

"Until you return?"

Leaning down, Buck placed a piece of white quartz in her palm. "Hold on to this for me."

The stone looked oddly familiar. Caitlin closed her fingers over it and stepped closer to the horse and Buck. "I don't understand. We have a full schedule. The kayaking scene takes two—"

"I trust you and Chase to handle it."

"Where are you going, Buck? When will you be back?"

"I need to be alone with my mountain, Cat. This morning, I asked Louie to pack up food and supplies for a short two-day trip. I'll take Farley."

Caitlin felt numbed by his announcement. There was a time when she would have asked to go along with him, but she sensed his need to be alone was soul deep. She was beginning to understand the man, if such a thing was possible.

"Godspeed," she murmured and watched him ride up the path and back to the lodge to begin his journey.

Three days later, Caitlin watched lightning blossom against the latticed window in Buck's bedroom and illuminate the half of the bed where his body should have lain. Beneath the thick comforter, she rose up on one elbow and waited with surprising calm for the accompanying clap of thunder. She urged her frightened dogs closer with soft kissing noises. When thunder rumbled seconds later, the black-and-white collies whimpered and attempted to climb inside the sheets, but Caitlin cajoled them into settling securely between the coverlet and the blankets instead.

Had bad weather always frightened her canine companions so severely? Perhaps she'd been too caught up in her own fright and panic to notice. Tonight, however, she felt no panic.

Caitlin wanted to believe her stormy night of passion with Buck had cured her fear of thunder and lightning and high winds forever. Each time lightning arched, she recalled the surge of his silken shaft inside her, the low thunder of his voice next to her ear, his skilled fingers stirring a tempest in her blood.

A new fear gripped her now. Buck Rawlings was overdue. He should have returned from his ride in the mountains by noon today. Was he deliberately staying away, waiting for her scheduled departure tomorrow, unable to handle a face-to-face confrontation, unwilling to see her crumble at his rejection? The longer he stayed away, the more she played out the same scenario she'd faced seven years ago. Broken dreams.

That afternoon, after the final shot for the catalog was completed, Caitlin lingered by the lake, half expecting Buck to appear out of the shadowy gray mist that descended like a shroud. After an hour of stalling, she climbed the path back to the lodge and congratulated crew members on a job well-done. The men helped Lester pack up the wardrobe and load it onto the trucks.

By suppertime, Buck had not returned. The whole group appeared edgy. Louie walked to the windows repeatedly, scanning the clearing for signs of Buck. Chase stationed himself on the front porch, a lone sentinel whistling Mozart, allowing a remnant of his East Coast polish to slip through the Western facade he clung to.

Alone in Buck's room, Caitlin cleaned and inspected her equipment, and hesitantly packed her cameras away for her next assignment, a two-day jaunt to eastern Montana scheduled for the end of the month.

While organizing her Polaroids atop the bed, she paused to study the scene of Buck modeling the Buckhorn Special in his bedroom. Cinnamon and smoke. Candlelight and silver. She'd set the mood. The man had added the magic. So much magic.

Anticipating the storm and Buck's belated return, she'd left a light burning next to the bed and steeled her heart for any outcome.

A gentle knock sounded on the bedroom door, too gentle to belong to a Rawlings male. Caitlin adjusted the modest nightie she was wearing and invited the visitor to enter.

"Miss O'Malley?" Lester stood in his nightshirt in the doorway holding a tray with two large steaming mugs. "No word yet, but we're sure the storm kept Buck from gettin' back tonight. He's pretty smart about settlin' in and waitin' out the worst."

"It's a little late for a strong dose of caffeine, Lester."

"Now, do I look like a man foolish enough to serve a refined lady coffee in the middle of the night?" Lester crossed the room and set the tray on the bedside table. "I brought you some hot chocolate. Even added them little bitty marshmallows. I thought it might help you to sleep."

"Thanks. You've become a real friend to me." Caitlin accepted one of the mugs and inhaled the rich chocolate aroma.

"I know how you're afraid of storms and all. Didn't want you to feel too alone, Miss O'Malley." Lester plopped down on the empty half of the bed and crossed his bony legs at the ankle. "Whoa, we got critters under these covers," he said with a laugh, lifting up the comforter and peeking inside. "Hey, puppies. Come on out here. Don't be scared."

"Caitlin. Hey, Lester," Carlos called from the open doorway. "I brought you a box of almond cookies my sister sent me. Thought you might be awake with all this thunder."

Caitlin motioned Carlos inside. He placed the cardboard box near the headboard then sat at the end of the bed with his back resting against one of the posts. "Did I ever tell you about the time Buck and Chase almost burned the lodge down?" he asked.

"Hey, no one tells that story unless I'm around to defend myself." Chase sauntered into the room wearing only a black satin robe with a monogrammed *R* on the chest pocket. "I thought of you, ma'am, when I heard the thunder. Brought some CDs of female country-western singers you might like to hear while this storm carries on." He began putting the discs in Buck's carousel. "Oops, there goes that lightning again. You okay, darlin'?"

"I'm okay, Chase," she said after taking another sip of hot chocolate, and arching a brow at the growing number of men who waltzed into Buck's bedroom in their bedclothes, carrying a variety of snacks and beverages, and making themselves comfortable.

"It's starting to feel like a slumber party," she observed after Carlos finished his story about the fiery antics of Buck and Chase.

"Men don't have slumber parties," Louie grumbled from a corner of the bed.

"Well, I see music, food, drink, pajamas and robes—" Caitlin held up a finger for each item mentioned "—and we're sitting on or around one bed. If it looks like a slumber party, why not call it one?"

"Well, now, Miss O'Malley," Lester said in his distinctive drawl, "men have what you might call all-nighters."

Another story about the capers of the Rawlings brothers began, followed by half a dozen more. Caitlin felt her heart twist at these recollections of Echo Creek's original bad boy. She'd placed her bolt of silk next to his bolt of black leather. Was it wishful thinking to believe their patterns could intertwine, could blend?

"Miss O'Malley, I've got a question for you," Klyde said quietly. "Will you be back up here next year, shooting with your father?"

She recalled the doctor's good news about her father's eyes, but hesitated. What if Buck asked her not to return?

"Klyde, if I return, I'll be working as Dad's assistant."

Buck sat up in his sleeping bag and watched as lightning silhouetted a swaying tree branch against the dome of his tent. Was O'Malley's daughter alone on the third floor of the lodge, watching the same storm in terror? Or had his special therapy worked? Was she writhing on the bed remembering their lovemaking that night in the stable, ignoring the tempest outside her window?

One thing was certain. He was in the mountains waiting out a squall, without the woman he loved.

All he'd left her as a symbol of his intent to return to her was a damned pebble. The woman deserved medals for putting up with his moods. The woman deserved a better man.

A torrent of rain slammed against the tent, causing Farley to lift his head and whine. The dog was stretched out beside Buck, chewing on a towel. Buck remembered the night Caitlin had mistaken the Lab for a wolf and smiled.

It had been the first time he'd felt able to offer his strength and one of the many times she'd rejected it.

These two nights and three days alone made him rethink his need to protect her. Had he ever met a stronger, more capable woman? Caitlin had inherited her father's stamina and athleticism. Whatever Sean O'Malley didn't teach her about outdoor survival, she'd learned on her own, including trekking and climbing.

Chase was right. Sarah had always had difficulty keeping up with Caitlin's pace and endurance. Much as Buck hated to admit it, his woman had spunk. If she were a man, the words *fortitude* and *staying power* would come to mind. They came to his mind now despite her gender.

Lighting arced again and Buck felt his groin tighten. Damn, maybe Caitlin had lost her fear, but their little experiment resulted in him having a heck of a physical reaction to thunderstorms. Living in a state known for storms could prove hazardous or physically taxing.

With Cat O'Malley at his side, he might survive the occasional discomfort.

As for her taking risks, he still felt apprehension. Could he really live with a woman addicted to danger? Were his conditions fair?

Buck closed his eyes and felt his body respond to the thunder. If he didn't commit to the woman, he might have to move to another state. One without storms.

The next morning, Caitlin threw a stick far up the rock-strewn shore and watched her collies race to fetch it. Chase and the crew members were finished their packing and promised to begin a search for Buck in the foothills if he didn't return by noon.

She'd talked with August Rawlings by phone this morning, answering his detailed questions about Sarah and assuring him of his daughter's love. Buck's father had expressed guilt and regret over his treatment of his oldest son and vowed to make up for the years lost between them.

The years lost between them. Caitlin could never hope to recover the old dream she'd shared with Buck, but a new vision was coming into focus. Would he be a willing partner or would he disappoint her again?

The sound of horse's hooves on stone made her lurch and turn. Buck rode Kodiak down the trail just above a sheltered inlet, shaded by black cottonwood. Farley broke into a run at the sight of Burrito and Fajita and streaked across the far lakeshore, past her, barking excitedly.

Caitlin walked toward the grouping of cottonwood, toward the only man she knew who could look good with three days' growth of beard.

"O'Malley, you're still here." Buck dismounted and tied his horse's reins to a tree branch. "Come here, Cat." The words were a rush of silken promise. She stepped into his arms and allowed herself to fully enjoy the protective warmth of his embrace.

"Oh, Buck. Are you all right?"

"Just a little hungry, tired and wet. I missed you so damn much, Caitlin. Let me hold you a little longer."

A little? She wanted to hold him forever. "We expected you yesterday."

"Blame it on the wildflowers . . . and my need to be alone and think."

"When you were overdue, Chase talked about organizing a search party. I better tell him you're back."

"Forget about Chase for the moment, Caitlin. There's something more important, something that's far overdue." Buck removed his Stetson. He cupped her cheek in his palm. "I need to tell you how much I love you, how much I want you with me for the rest of my life."

Buck bent his head and captured her mouth with savage intensity. Lost in sensation, she savored the sweet timbre of his voice uttering the words she'd longed to hear.

He broke the kiss and rested his forehead against hers. "Let's go back to the lodge, Cat. Let's make up for lost time."

"No, not quite yet," she said, shaking her head. "I've done a lot of thinking, too, Buck." Reaching into the pocket of her sweater, she pulled out two Polaroids. "I want you to look at these photographs I took."

"Pictures of the lake?" Buck barely glanced at the images. He tried to coax her back into his arms. "Can this wait until after I shower and get a chance to spend some, uh, quality time with you?" His hand slipped down her sweater to her backside. "How's your sliver?"

"This is serious, Buck. I had a flash of insight a few days ago." She laughed when he grabbed her again, and she slapped his hand away. "Look at these. How would you describe these two scenes?"

"Lake, mountains, a field of wildflowers." He slipped around behind her and pulled her back against his chest. His unshaven jaw rasped against her cheek. "Let's see. The one on the left was taken from a slightly higher elevation, but essentially the photos are the same."

"Which do you like better?"

"The one on the right." Buck nodded in that direction, then kissed her cheek.

"Why that one?"

"Because I have to choose one of them so I can hurry you inside to make love to you, Cat O'Malley." He pressed her bottom against his groin in an unmistakable gesture of need. "C'mon. I want to start the rest of our lives."

"Forever can wait one minute longer." Caitlin held the photo in her left hand up higher. "I'm automatically drawn to this image. I took it from that cedar tree the day I fell and got the sliver."

"I really feel a need to inspect the work I did on that sliver."

"Later." She cleared her throat. "I fell, risking my neck o get this picture, Buck. Later that day, I was going through he Polaroids and realized something."

"What's that?"

"I get an adrenaline rush whenever I look at photographs that took a little more hard work and risk to capture." Caitlin tucked the pictures back into the pocket of her sweater. She smoothed her palms over the large male hands that gripped her waist and held her pinioned against him. "In truth, there isn't that much of a difference, but to me there's a *big* difference."

"Your dad's talked about this." Buck nuzzled the hair at her temple with his chin. "Says he gets a rush when he looks at those eagle photos he took in the Rockies or those tricky shots he got from the suspension bridge."

"Exactly. Do you understand now?"

"I think it's more important that *you* understand, Caitlin. Awareness is the first step if you're trying to change yourself. At the moment, I love you the way you are."

"Risks and all?"

"I decided I wasn't going to stomp down out of the mountains demanding conditions, Caitlin. I'll never do that again. C'mon. I've got a tired horse to rub down and you've got a tired man to liven up."

"We were going to say goodbye to Sarah, Buck." Caitlin reached into her jeans pocket for Sarah's piece of quartz. "I don't know if this is the right moment."

Buck instantly sobered, and a soft look swept through his dark outlaw eyes. "It's the perfect moment." Buck released her and stared at the stone in her palm. "Sarah used to wish on this rock. I bet she's missed it all these years. It's time we gave it back to her. But first, let's make a wish together."

Caitlin closed her eyes and wished for all the images on her collage. She felt Buck's fingers brush her palm. Tears rushed to her eyes. A sob tore from her throat as she opened them and watched Buck close his fingers over the stone.

His arm drew back then forward, releasing their grief forever. On the finger of land jetting into the lake, a white heron lifted its head and took flight over a flawless sky.

"Let's go home," Buck whispered as ripples reached the shore at their feet. "C'mon, O'Malley."

* * * * *

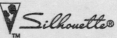

MILLION DOLLAR SWEEPSTAKES (III)

EXTRA BONUS PRIZE DRAWING

SWP-S594

CAN YOU STAND THE HEAT?

Silhouette

SUMMER Sizzlers '94

You're in for a serious heat wave with Silhouette's latest selection of sizzling summer reading. This sensuous collection of three short stories provides the perfect vacation escape! And what better authors to relax with than

**ANNETTE BROADRICK
JACKIE MERRITT
JUSTINE DAVIS**

And that's not all....

With the purchase of *Silhouette Summer Sizzlers '94*, you can send in for a FREE Summer Sizzlers beach bag!

SUMMER JUST GOT HOTTER— WITH SILHOUETTE BOOKS!

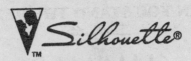

by
Laurie Paige

Maddening men...winsome women...and the untamed land they live in—
all add up to love! Meet them in these books from Silhouette Special Edition
and Silhouette Romance:

WILD IS THE WIND (Silhouette Special Edition #887, May)
Rafe Barrett retreated to his mountain resort to escape his dangerous feelings
for Genny McBride...but when she returned, ready to pick up where they
left off, would Rafe throw caution to the wind?

A ROGUE'S HEART (Silhouette Romance #1013, June)
Returning to his boyhood home brought Gabe Deveraux face-to-face
with ghosts of the past—and directly into the arms of sweet and loving
Whitney Campbell....

A RIVER TO CROSS (Silhouette Special Edition #910, September)
Sheriff Shane Macklin knew there was more to "town outsider"
Tina Henderson than met the eye. He saw a generous and selfless woman
whose true colors held the promise of love....

Don't miss these latest Wild River tales from Silhouette Special Edition
and Silhouette Romance!

IT'S OUR 1000TH SILHOUETTE ROMANCE,
AND WE'RE CELEBRATING!

JOIN US FOR A SPECIAL COLLECTION OF LOVE STORIES
BY AUTHORS YOU'VE LOVED FOR YEARS, AND
NEW FAVORITES YOU'VE JUST DISCOVERED.
JOIN THE CELEBRATION...

April
REGAN'S PRIDE by Diana Palmer
MARRY ME AGAIN by Suzanne Carey

May
THE BEST IS YET TO BE by Tracy Sinclair
CAUTION: BABY AHEAD by Marie Ferrarella

June
THE BACHELOR PRINCE by Debbie Macomber
A ROGUE'S HEART by Laurie Paige

July
IMPROMPTU BRIDE by Annette Broadrick
THE FORGOTTEN HUSBAND by Elizabeth August

SILHOUETTE ROMANCE...VIBRANT, FUN AND EMOTIONALLY
RICH! TAKE ANOTHER LOOK AT US! AND AS PART OF THE
CELEBRATION, READERS CAN RECEIVE A FREE GIFT!

YOU'LL FALL IN LOVE ALL OVER
AGAIN WITH
SILHOUETTE ROMANCE!

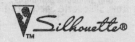

CEL1000

The Jones Gang

Christine Rimmer

Three rapscallion brothers. Their main talent: making trouble. Their only hope: three uncommon women who knew the way to heal a wounded heart!

May 1994—MAN OF THE MOUNTAIN (SE #886)
Jared Jones hadn't had it easy with women. But when he retreated to his isolated mountain cabin, he found Eden Parker, determined to show him a good woman's love!

July 1994—SWEETBRIAR SUMMIT (SE #896)
Patrick Jones didn't think he was husband material—but Regina Black sure did. She had heard about the wild side of the Jones boy, but that wouldn't stop her!

September 1994—A HOME FOR THE HUNTER (SE #908)
Jack Roper came to town looking for the wayward and beautiful Olivia Larabee. He discovered a long-buried secret.... Could his true identity be a Jones boy?

Meet these rascal men—and the women who'll tame them— only from Silhouette Special Edition!

COUNTDOWN
Lindsay McKenna

Sergeant Joe Donnally knew being a marine
meant putting lives on the line—and after a tragic
loss, he vowed never to love again. Yet here was
Annie Yellow Horse, the passionate, determined
woman who challenged him to feel long-dormant
emotions. But Joe had to conquer past demons before
declaring his love....

MEN OF COURAGE

It's a special breed of men who defy death and fight
for right! Salute their bravery while sharing their lives
and loves!

These are courageous men you'll love and tender
stories you'll cherish...available in June, only from
Silhouette Special Edition!